NO EXIT

The young man had last been seen at No Exit, a bar dedicated to the piercing and tattooing scene. Open Fridays only, the place was packed till dawn. The bar screamed hard-edged music, and nothing was too bizarre to shock its nerve-deadened denizens. A place where extremes were relished, where drugs could kill pain. Hustlers hung out there, offering a variety that would satisfy any taste. And now, it was a place where you could pick up death.

It scared Orlando. Because he knew it was only the beginning. . . .

FALSE CONFESSIONS

Steve Johnson

A DOUG ORLANDO MYSTERY

A SIGNET BOOK

SIGNET
Published by the Penguin Group
Penguin Books USA Inc., 375 Hudson Street,
New York, New York 10014, U.S.A.
Penguin Books Ltd, 27 Wrights Lane,
London W8 5TZ, England
Penguin Books Australia Ltd, Ringwood,
Victoria, Australia
Penguin Books Canada Ltd, 10 Alcorn Avenue,
Toronto, Ontario, Canada M4V 3B2
Penguin Books (N.Z.) Ltd, 182–190 Wairau Road,
Auckland 10, New Zealand

Penguin Books Ltd, Registered Offices:
Harmondsworth, Middlesex, England

First published by Signet, an imprint of New American Library,
a division of Penguin Books USA Inc.

First Printing, August, 1993
10 9 8 7 6 5 4 3 2 1

 REGISTERED TRADEMARK—MARCA REGISTRADA

Printed in the United States of America

PUBLISHER'S NOTE
This is a work of fiction. Names, characters, places, and incidents either
are the product of the author's imagination or are used fictitiously, and
any resemblance to actual persons, living or dead, events, or locales is
entirely coincidental.

I wish to thank Rondo Mieczkowski, Kieran Prather, Stuart Timmons, William Moritz, Peter Cashorali, Eric Gordon, and the late Craig Lee for help on this book.

CHAPTER 1

The killer had used a baseball bat.

It lay under the first pew, sticky black tape spiraling like a serpent around its handle. That was good. There would be fingerprints if the murderer hadn't worn gloves. Detective Doug Orlando nodded to himself, then crouched over the black-clad body sprawled facedown at the foot of the altar. Bright light bathed the ruggedly handsome profile. A cruel purple gash marred a head of thick, wavy hair graying at the temples. Only a few times in his ten years at Brooklyn Homicide had the detective met the victim before the murder, and he didn't like the way it felt. The feeling lingered, heavy, in the pit of his stomach. But something else bothered him. Something seemed different.

The priest's collar was missing.

It wasn't on the marble slab floor, with its black and white checkerboard shining in the spotlights directed at the altar. Orlando slipped his hand into the priest's jacket pocket. Empty. Reaching around to the other side, he found the second pocket pinned beneath the lean frame of the corpse. Still, he was able to wrestle two fingers inside. He felt stiff cloth and pulled out the tip of a starched white collar. There was a crackle of plastic deep in the pocket. A wrapper? He couldn't grasp it without disturbing the body. Better wait for the arrival of the crime-scene unit photographer before moving anything.

A dark blur caught his eye and Orlando peered closer. A smear of blood seeping from under the body soiled the marble floor. It couldn't be from the gash at the back of the head, so where did it come from? He read his watch. The forensics team usually took forever to arrive. That wasn't all bad. Their sticky fingers obliterated as many leads as they captured. Orlando needed a little time alone with the corpse. In these precious minutes he often discovered clues that led to the killer.

Next he studied the priest's shoes, spit-shine black with deep scratches grooved in the sides. He knew what that meant. His eyes zeroed in on the carved door at the left of the altar. He remembered the flagstone walk out back.

Orlando touched a pale wrist. Still warm. A sharp flash of memory so jarred the detective that he released the priest's wrist. He recalled his last bitter words to Morant the day before: *You're killing people, you know that? And this is just the beginning.* And he remembered the look of anguish in the priest's hazel eyes—eyes that stared now, seeing nothing.

Orlando observed two beat cops, the first to arrive at the scene, pacing by an artless copy of Michelangelo's *Pietà* in the corner. They knew he wasn't supposed to be here, that this wasn't his case. They'd put up a stink when he showed up, but he'd pulled rank and now they were stewing. They were young, still rookies, but they had learned fast. They knew who Orlando was and they knew how they were supposed to treat him. But that was okay; he was used to it. After two years of the silent treatment, he could take anything. And since his rival, Briggs, had been suspended from the department six months before, things hadn't been so bad.

He rose and surveyed the church. Stained glass, black with night, hovered high above the room, shouldering a dome of tarnished gold. The walls were sterile white, carved with false arches sheltering bas-reliefs of the Annunciation, the Crucifixion, the Resurrection, and the Ascension. Orlando hadn't been to Sunday mass here in over twenty years, though occasional weddings and funerals kept the surroundings familiar. His eyes came to rest on an ornately framed triptych in a shallow niche. In the center painting, St. Sebastian, bound and pierced with arrows, tilted back his head in an enigmatic expression of pain mixed with ecstasy. Mesmerized by the figure as a young boy, Orlando had stared at the painting during incomprehensible Latin masses, trying to solve its mystery. He'd had a child's fascination for the arrows and dripping blood, but it was the saint's skin, so smooth and pale it bordered on translucent, that held him transfixed. The slender curves of Sebastian's androgynous form seemed to speak to him alone, in secret recesses of his soul. Even then he knew his feelings for the painting could be

shared with no one. As he grew older, he slowly
came to understand the nature of his interest,
first with fear, then with gradual acceptance.
But self-acceptance brought rejection of the
Church. Now, seeing the brutalized figure, he
felt only the puncturing wounds of the arrows,
and turned away.

Despite the corpse, the cavernous room
seemed peaceful, silent—a cool escape from the
relentless humidity of New York in August. He
recalled the feeling of Sunday mass so many
years before, the pristine sound of hymns rising
above the congregation. It hadn't been that way
last Sunday, though, not from what Orlando had
heard. There had been screams, shouts, placards
and black arm bands, people throwing themselves in the aisles. And a squad of men in blue
dragging the protesters' limp bodies from the
church.

He looked toward the far corner by the entrance, where the confessional stood absorbed in
shadow. It seemed to breathe, its dark wood
swelling, like a living thing. Just a few days ago,
he had sat inside, touching the varnished seat
smooth with wear—not for any religious rite, but
to feel where the No Exit Killer had sat, the
brutal murderer of two gay men: a serial killer
who had confessed to Morant. A maniac who
would never stop until Orlando stopped him
dead.

Orlando walked to the left of the altar to examine the door, its carved mahogany almost black
with age. The priest's killer had entered here.
Scrutinizing the door, Orlando found no sign of

forced entry. Forensics would check the lock for scratches that might indicate a lock pick and torsion wrench had been used. Or could Morant have let the killer in? The door stood ajar now, and Orlando pushed it open, careful not to leave any prints.

The stuffy August night air assaulted his face. A streetlight down the block dimly illuminated the area. The flash of lights from a squad car he couldn't see threw sickly pulses of amber on brownstones across the street. A grass yard the size of a baseball field, and bluish in the eerie light, was surrounded by a spiked wrought-iron fence. Its height of five feet would be easy for anyone to scale, and spikes or barbed wire had never deterred any criminal in this city. The entire fence would have to be dusted for prints. Orlando's eyes followed a narrow flagstone walkway that led to the rectory and a garage beyond, which had been a carriage house at the turn of the century. A rose garden spilling a thick cloud of perfume surrounded the rectory, casting vague thorny shadows against the building. Night made the red roses black.

He followed the walkway to the rectory. It was in the same Gothic style as the church, but smaller and lacking the ominous gargoyle rain spouts of the larger building, monsters that had visited his dreams as a child. He pressed the door open and stepped inside, entering a comfortable yet impersonal living room, with large couches, a thick rug, and a bookcase covering the only wall that wasn't plastered with religious pictures.

A woman stood in the arched doorway to the hall. Middle-aged, wary, shy, she had the plain hair and dress of a housekeeper. She dropped her eyes when she spoke and they became pools of shadow. *"El padre esta en la biblioteca."* She stepped into the room and he could see her eyes, brown and haunted eyes that knew worry and fear. She pointed a shaky finger to a door down the hall. "In the library." As Orlando passed her, she stared at the carpet. He found the door and stepped inside.

Thick mist hung in the air, so the library had the oppressive atmosphere of a hothouse. Dew clung to a partially curtained window overlooking the silver-blue playing field. Orlando spied a humidifier pulsating in one corner. A cat, spotted gray and white, rubbed aggressively against bookshelves lining the walls. Its tail twitched like a windshield wiper gone spastic. The room smelled of old books, alcohol, and sickness.

Behind an ornate mahogany desk scattered with paper, an old man leaned back in a big leather chair. He had found the body, made the call. His watery blue eyes were recessed under thick, hairy brows that contrasted with the few white hairs that stuck to his pale scalp. He looked smaller than he should be, shrunken, as if age and illness were eating him away from the inside. Only his big ears and formidable nose had resisted the ravages of disease, hanging off him like features in search of a new face. His nose and cheeks were red—from tears? Prongs protruded from his nostrils, joining a clear plastic tube that twisted around his ears and attached to a miniature oxygen tank that rested on the desk. He sucked air like a man drowning.

Orlando stripped off his jacket, rummaged in his pocket, and bared his badge. Dark spots were already spreading under his arms. "Detective Orlando, Homicide."

The old man offered a firm, moist hand, and a stronger shake than Orlando would have thought. And when he spoke, his voice was deep and authoritative—not a shred of the plaintive, passive tone of some terminally ill. Only a slight wheeze betrayed his illness. "I'm Father Shea, the pastor of St. Agatha," he said. "Sorry for any discomfort; emphysema has made me a man difficult to be around." He gave a wistful smile that showed crooked teeth. "You can't imagine how swiftly visitors drop off when the humidity rises. As if the weather outside isn't bad enough." His hand indicated a leather chair. "Please, have a seat."

Orlando took it, draping his jacket over the back. He sank in cushioned leather damp with mist. Back when Orlando was a kid, St. Agatha had had another pastor, a jovial, obese man the boys called Friar Tuck behind his back.

The father pushed himself up from the desk with effort and attached the oxygen tank to the belt cinching his loose black trousers. He'd lost weight lately. "At least I can offer you something to cool you down. Seltzer?" At a rosewood cabinet in the wall he revealed a bar and a small fridge. The cat came over and rubbed his ankles, making a clucking sound. Shea twisted a cap, and seltzer sizzled over ice. As he brought the glass to Orlando, the detective half rose.

"No, no, I am quite ambulatory. My doctors say I should get what exercise I can." He watched Orlando take the glass. "You know, that does look good. I think I'll have some myself." Close up, Orlando could see the splotchy redness on his nose and cheeks were not from crying. Father Shea was a regular communicant at the liquor cabinet.

Shea went back to the bar, hid a bottle in front of him, and poured himself something stronger than seltzer. Straight. Orlando looked away. He didn't resent the priest liking his liquor. He knew the feeling. He'd fought that urge not long ago and beaten it. The question was, would more booze open him up or close him down?

"There!" Shea exclaimed with seeming relief, taking his glass back to the desk. He set the drink down, untied the oxygen tank, and laid it on the scattered papers. "You'd think children would be afraid of all this, but it has endeared me to them. They are so curious. They think it makes me look like a bit of a spaceman." A gentle smile parted his anemic lips.

Orlando sipped. Effervescence tickled his straight, slightly upturned nose, and played in his aggressive mustache. "Can you tell me about tonight?"

The smile died, a pained expression taking its place. Shea sunk into his chair and looked like an invalid again. "The last time I saw him"—he paused and let out a tired sigh—"alive, that is, was here in this room. We spent the evening together."

"Doing what?"

Surprise widened the blue eyes, as if the question was unexpected or absurd. "Why, we watched a little television, and discussed an upcoming parish event, Detective Orlando."

"Anything else?"

Shea blinked. "I'm not sure what you're getting at."

"He didn't come to you for advice ... about the murders of those young men?"

Shea's mouth sagged and he picked up his glass. He drank as a miser fingers money: slowly, methodically, as if counting each drop with morbid satisfaction. "Now I know why your name seemed familiar." His voice hardened and carried an accusatory edge. "You're the one investigating those terrible murders."

Orlando didn't have to be told the murders were terrible. He saw them every time he closed his eyes: needles, hundreds of them. And the punctured bodies of young gay men. They haunted his sleep, what sleep he got. "Two men are already dead. And it's not going to stop. Morant was my only lead. Whoever committed these murders confessed to Father Morant. Did you two talk about it?"

"I can't answer that. I do know you brought Father Morant a lot of anguish. This wasn't his fault."

"I have a job to do," Orlando said stiffly.

"So did he, so did he. What did he tell you?"

"That he didn't make his vows to the N.Y.P.D."

Shea chuckled sadly. "I think that puts it succinctly. Detective Orlando, the confessional would be meaningless if people had to worry their priest would run off and tell on them. What people say in the confessional is between them and God. All a priest can do is suggest the sinner take responsibility for his actions. Suggesting they turn themselves in, yes. Squealing on them, no. Break the seal of the confessional, and the Church will fall. As difficult as it was, Father Morant did the right thing."

"A lot of people would beg to differ."

Shea laughed bitterly. "The protesters, you mean." He drained his glass and looked longingly at the cabinet, but remained seated. "These people, they call themselves, uh"—he was uncomfortable with the name and said it as if in quotations—"*Queer Nation.*" His nostrils flared in anger and Orlando thought for a moment the prongs were going to lose their grip. "They disrupted Sunday mass, shouting, screaming like animals. Calling us murderers. Throwing themselves on the floor. They came up to me during communion and hissed, 'I don't take communion from murderers.' " His fist came down on the desk. The watery eyes burned and his face went red from more than booze. "They defiled the host!"

"I missed it," Orlando said blandly. He finished his drink. "They never specifically mentioned the issue of the confessional and the serial killer, did they?"

"No, they seem to hate us on more general grounds. All their problems in life seem to stem directly from the Church. They didn't dare specifically protest against Father Morant's refusal to discuss what he had heard in confession because they have absolutely no proof the killer ever came to him in the first place. All they have is rumors, and I don't think the public would take kindly to them demonstrating on such flimsy cause. But let's face it, they would have taken their protest to Fifth Avenue if they hadn't particularly been out to torment Father Morant."

The pastor's assessment wasn't precisely so. The informant who'd tipped Orlando off had also alerted the radical group, and he'd known too many details of the murders to be telling anything but the truth. And Orlando had seen Morant's distressed eyes and knew the informant's claim was right on target. Morant could have identified the killer.

"Let's get back to this evening." Orlando rose, approached the desk, and took Shea's glass away. The priest clung to it like a life raft. "I'll freshen that for you." At he bar he filled the glass with vodka and his own with seltzer. He handed the glass to Shea, who sniffed at it, and looked up with suspicious, then grateful eyes.

"Yes," he said as he sipped. "I think this will soothe me." Orlando grunted. They understood each other.

Shea had recovered from his tirade. His hand was no longer a fist and his eyes went apologetic. "I'm afraid Father Morant couldn't help you very much."

Orlando shrugged and returned to his seat. "He could have made a greater effort. Two men are already dead. Now three, counting Morant."

Shea winced. "Yes. It's three now." He was sipping again. It didn't seem to affect him. He'd had lots of practice.

"So you watched TV and talked. What then?"

"He left me about eleven. To go to bed. His bedroom is next door down the hall."

The cat jumped into Shea's lap and let out a deep-throated meow. "Poor Edgar." Shea stroked the cat and it thrust its back end in the air. "I'm afraid we were persuaded it was a 'he' when we agreed to take it, and now we find our Edgar is in heat." He attempted a fragile smile, but the bloodless lips couldn't do the trick. "We're keeping her inside, but she fights us all the way."

"Sexuality is hard to control. You say he went to bed about eleven."

"Uh, yes. And then I may have dozed for a while. I seem to live in a halfway world between sleep and consciousness. I think I was jarred awake by a noise. I can't say what. Outside. And then nothing. I waited for a moment, but nobody in the rectory stirred. Then I remembered fathers Fernandez and Bronson were away. That left just me, Father Morant and our housekeeper, Margarita. I went to Father Morant's bedroom and tapped on his door. But when I looked in, he was gone. Then I did become concerned. I went out in the yard, but everything was peaceful. But when I checked the door to the church, it was unlocked. I made a mental note to chastise Juan, our custodian, in the morning for being so careless, then I recalled the protests. I stepped inside the church, and I remember feeling a sudden fear. The lights were off, but I couldn't help feeling I was not alone." He gave a sad smile. "When I switched on the lights, I found I was not wrong."

"And you didn't see anyone?"

Father Shea shook his head. He latched his face on the glass like an opener on a bottle cap, then mused, almost to himself, "What kind of a person would kill a priest in a church?"

Orlando glanced at his watch. Whoever was assigned to the case would be here soon. He'd gotten what he needed, now he wanted first crack at Morant's bedroom. He downed the seltzer, pushed up, and took his jacket. Strolling over to the bar, he set the glass down. "Thanks for the drink." At the door, he turned. "If it makes you feel any better, Morant wasn't killed in the church. Mind if I take a look around?" The cat curled around his legs, yowled. Her purr throbbed against his pants leg, and she looked up beguilingly.

Shea stared. "Feel free. But what do you mean? He was lying at the altar when I found him."

"His shoes. Big, deep scratches. Somebody dumped the body in the church for effect. After dragging it over the flagstone path that leads from the rectory to the church." He placed his hands on the doorknob. "He died elsewhere."

"Where are you going?"

"To find out where."

The cat followed him down the hall to the next room. Orlando flipped a switch, and lamps on both sides of a double bed cast soft light. The bed was made, covered with a flowered brocade spread. The cat jumped up, crouching twitchy-tailed by a fat pillow. An oak dresser with a mirror dominated the wall with a closet. He tossed his jacket on a stuffed chair angled in a corner. Religious and inspirational titles filled a small bookcase by the chair. Orlando's nose wrinkled. The room smelled faintly of air freshener—air freshener covering up the odor of burnt paper. He searched for the wastebasket, finding it beside the dresser. Ashes, black and fragile, curled inside. He picked up a leaf of ash, and read on an unburned fragment of lined white paper, ". . . you're crazy if you think . . ." and on another, ". . . I will always lo—" And that was all. The rest was dust.

Orlando peered closer. The bottom of the metal basket was black from repeated scorching. This was not the first time Morant had burned letters here. He set the basket aside.

On top of the bureau, next to a Bible, a narrow volume of Tennyson's *In Memoriam* lay open, facedown. Underlined in pencil were the lines, "There lives more faith in honest doubt, Believe me, than in half the creeds." He leafed through the book, but nothing else was underlined. An old news clipping and a slip of lined paper fluttered out onto the bureau. Orlando scanned the yellowed article.

WOMAN KILLED
WITH BASEBALL BAT
Police Search for Husband
Susan Krouse, a Brooklyn housewife, was

found yesterday bludgeoned to death in her Fort Greene home. Social workers from the Holy Family House, a home for battered women, discovered the body after Krouse failed to return their calls. Police spokesmen say a baseball bat was used to crush the victim's skull. Her six-month-old baby was found unharmed but suffering from dehydration. Police seek to question the victim's husband, Roger Krouse, who has been missing from work since Tuesday.

Next Orlando read the letter.

Michael:
Do you understand now what you have done? How many more women are going to have to die?

Serra

The letter had no date. Orlando crouched and examined the remains in the wastebasket again. The paper was different. So was the handwriting.

He went through every drawer. Socks, underwear, folded white T-shirts, all crisp and new. He was looking for a diary or a journal. Any record of Morant's relation with the No Exit Killer. Orlando placed his hands on an album in a bottom drawer. Easing into the stuffed chair in the corner, he flipped stiff black pages of photographs. Orlando was never comfortable going through the belongings of murder victims; it was such a violation of privacy. He always asked himself if the victim had known, would he have left these things for strangers to judge his life by? He recognized Morant in many of the pictures: younger, grinning, handsome. Others were mostly group shots of smiling faces. The detective supposed they were members of Morant's flock, but didn't recognize any of them from the neighborhood. He wondered if the priest had been recently transferred to St. Agatha. A page of newsprint was folded in the back. Orlando took it out and spread it on his knee. It was a full-page ad from the *New York Times*.

THERE IS DIVERSITY OF OPINION AMONG CONSCIENTIOUS CATHOLICS ON THE SUBJECT OF ABORTION

He studied the ad. It was an open letter addressed to the pope, saying there was room for dialogue in the Church about abortion. Then a long list of signers. Orlando ran his finger down the list. Morant was there. So was a Serra: Sister Serra Pritchard, O.S.B. He pulled out a pen and pad from his jacket and scribbled notes, then put the album back in the drawer.

He rolled open the double door of the closet. Dark suits, casual wear. Shoes lined the floor of the closet. Nothing that interested him. Next he squatted and peered under the bed. Nothing but clean. Margarita certainly did her job. He examined the carpet, running his fingers through its pile. No blood stains. No dampness to indicate stains had been scrubbed away.

"What you do?" Margarita stood in the doorway.

"I'm looking for the murder scene." Orlando glanced back at her, then went on examining the carpet.

"He don't die here. He die in church."

"No, he didn't." But Morant hadn't died here either. Orlando remembered the smear of blood seeping from under the body. There had to be blood somewhere.

"Were you awakened by a noise tonight?"

She shook her head. "I hear nothing. Father Shea, he wake me, say Father Morant die in church."

"I'd like you to wait at the front door of the rectory for the arrival of the detective assigned to this case. Please don't touch anything." He looked up. "You don't have to mention that I'm here."

She eyed him doubtfully for a moment, then disappeared. Orlando quickly searched the rest of the house. No blood spill anywhere. Where had the murder taken place? As he passed the library, he saw Shea through the half-open doorway. His head lay in his arms, on the desk. At first Orlando thought he'd passed out, then saw the pastor's whole body convulse, and knew this time the red blotches on the priest's face would come from tears.

*   *   *

The crime-scene unit photographer had arrived.

Lights exploded at the altar. The body hadn't been moved yet. Orlando went inside the church and found Brightman, the medical examiner, standing by with his black leather case, waiting for the photographer to finish. He looked like he'd been awakened from a heavy sleep. Orlando gave him a nod, but Brightman didn't nod back. Instead he tilted his head toward the main doors of the church. "You better take a look outside." His groggy eyes said the advice was worth Orlando's while. Orlando strode up the aisle, wondering what the hell was going on. After what he'd been through in the last two years, nothing would surprise him. He passed wooden pews with red vinyl knee pads, remembered kneeling on them as a child and the ache of discomfort when the padding gave way to the hard wood underneath.

He stepped into the night heat. A glassed-in sign announced masses in English and Spanish. Confessions, weddings, bingo. All bilingual. The church was only three blocks from where Orlando lived, but a different culture inhabited this side of State Street, the demarcation line where Spanish voices became dominant. Squad cars parked at angles in front of the double doors of the church, their light bars strobing yellow, white, orange. A dark figure hovered across the street in tree shadows by Orlando's red Chevy. Crossing the street, Orlando placed his right hand in his jacket. It settled on a holstered

Smith & Wesson. Then he recognized who it was and slowed his gait, but his hand remained on the handle of the gun.

"Get away from the car, Briggs."

The big man stepped from under a tree and into the glow of a streetlight. He was close to fifty, with short, wavy hair flecked with white. Broad shoulders cast a wide shadow and his face was a scowl. "Orlando, you don't belong here. This is my case, and we don't work together no more, pal. You can't even solve your own cases, and here you are butting into mine."

"I need to solve your case before I can solve mine." Orlando glanced over his car. The new paint job on the old war horse looked okay. "I saw the squad cars on my way home. Figured I'd better check it out. Don't say there couldn't be a connection."

Briggs grunted. "I hear you haven't been doing so good. Pretty *prickly* case you got, huh?"

Orlando had heard the joke before. He didn't need it.

"Aw, don't go humorless on me," Briggs said. "And don't take your case so hard. Nobody really cares about people like that. I certainly didn't mean to *needle* you."

Orlando had learned to ignore the remarks around the station house. "I'm surprised to see you here," he said calmly. "I thought they caged you, Briggs."

A nerve twitched in Briggs's jaw and his thick black eyebrows grew together. "Fuck your mother," he barked. "And give her AIDS instead of other people's kids. My suspension's over. Six months. And I owe you and that queen Herb Chiligny for that. I owe you good."

Briggs hated Orlando for testifying against him at a grand jury probe two years before. When the grand jury failed to indict Briggs for shooting a black youth in the back, Orlando had become a pariah on the force. A turncoat—the man who had broken the code of silence. To annoy Orlando, Lieutenant Reilly, who wouldn't rest until he was booted from the department, had teamed him with Briggs on a case six months earlier. It ended with Briggs killing another boy in an alley. Orlando gave the story to Herb Chiligny, an iconoclastic journalist who wrote for the *Village World* and knew how to turn a controversy into an uproar. "Six months," Orlando mused. "Not bad for shooting a boy in the back and falsifying a police report."

"The six months was for the report." Briggs gave a brittle smile, showing big teeth. "Killing the punk, that was a freebie."

Orlando felt his fist knot, and he knew it was time to leave. He had held the boy in his arms, heard his last breath. He unlocked the Chevy door and slipped inside.

"See you got a new paint job."

"I should have sent you the bill." Briggs had scrawled "FAGGOT" on the Chevy door during that case.

Briggs gripped the open door. "You'll be hearing from me soon, friend. A message." He leaned closer. His voice was a whisper. "You see, it's all planned. You're on your way out, pal." He grinned and his wide teeth and thick lips looked hellish in the pulsing light of the squad cars. "But first I'm going to make you bleed."

CHAPTER 2

Orlando's neighborhood, solid working-class Italian since he was a kid, was rapidly being invaded by yuppies. BMWs now parked in the spaces where burly men had gathered on Saturday afternoons, shooting the breeze while tinkering with noisy Fords that spewed black smoke and leaked oil on the pavement. Expensive pastel lawn furniture supplanted front-yard shrines to the Virgin. Hunched old women in flower-print dresses waddling home with grocery carts trailing behind, once a mainstay on the block, now composed an endangered species. If businesses in the area were any indication, colonization seemed nearly complete. The Mr. Video on Smith Street, which had displayed gruesome straight-to-video splatter flicks in its windows for Italian teen audiences, now catered to smartly dressed women who appreciated gentler fare. Even the fruit stand on Court Street had gone with the flow, offering strange produce whose names old Italians couldn't pronounce and didn't know what to do with. Still, holdouts remained in Carroll Gardens. The Mantalini Funeral Home on the corner, where fat old men lounged in folding chairs on the sidewalk, puffing on cigars, staring with hostility at strangers, kept up the venerable neighborhood tradition of dour suspicion of anyone different.

Orlando drove past his mother's brownstone; its shiny fire-engine red front with mortar painted white horrified the new inhabitants on the block, but it hadn't seemed so bad in the old days. Marie Orlando owned several buildings on the street, including the landmark the detective lived in, all bought cheaply many years ago, and a windfall after real estate values skyrocketed. Even so, she still lived like a middle-class Italian widow. Orlando edged his Chevy into a parking space between two obnoxiously curved cars he couldn't afford. A sign of the times.

Stewart was lying on the living room couch, feet propped on an armrest, watching television without any lights on, when Orlando stepped into the front hall. Stewart was an English professor at NYU, and the university had just published his book of literary criticism. He'd been reminding Orlando all week about the dinner party tomorrow night celebrating its publication.

Reflection from the TV screen played on Stewart's glasses and threw a swirling kaleidoscope of light on his finely chiseled face and short blond hair. His muscular body was naked and uncovered, except for a glass of iced tea balanced between his navel and a plume of sandy pubic hair. The air conditioner muttering in the window did little to cut the humidity hovering in the living room. On the TV, a throaty female voice that sounded anything but sensual urged listeners to call a 976 party line for a great time.

"You're missing *Cobra Woman,* starring Maria Montez, Jon Hall, and Sabu, arguably the greatest bad film of all time," Stewart called, his blue eyes mesmerized by the screen. "Get naked and come over here quick. It's almost over. After this commercial the Good Maria Montez is going to hold up the Cobra Jewel by the window and her evil twin, the Bad Maria Montez, is going to say, 'Gif me dat Cobra Zzhewel, I vant dat Cobra Zzhewel.' Then she's going to make a grab for it and plunge out the window to the joy of her brutally oppressed subjects."

Orlando's clothes became a jumbled lump on the easy chair, his wilted jacket on top, and he deposited his holster and pistol on the lamp table. He stood there, raking his fingers through his thinning hair, shaking his head fondly at his lover. He had put up with Stewart's esoteric taste in film for twelve years. Dragged to midnight showings of *Glen or Glenda?,* all the while wondering why everyone in the audience was laughing. Forced to watch grainily filmed drag queens eat poodle shit. Even on their trip to Paris, Stewart had insisted on a visit to the Cinemathéque, where they had viewed the musical remake of *Lost Horizon* at a Sally Kellerman retrospective. Orlando definitely would have preferred sightseeing.

"And you complain about the dubious taste of your students," Orlando reproved.

"That's different," Stewart said. "They were raised on reruns of the *Brady Bunch,* a daily diet of which is enough to stifle anyone morally and intellectually. The guilty pleasures I indulge in are rare enough gems on the cinematic landscape that only a few brain cells are destroyed in their enjoyment."

Orlando took the iced tea from Stewart's abdomen and sipped, ice cubes chinking against the sweaty glass. Poindexter, their dog, struggled up from his cushioned basket in the corner and sauntered over to greet Orlando, giving a few perfunctory laps toward his master's groin with his lazy basset tongue.

"Go away, you pervert," Orlando said, gently pushing Poindexter to the side, lifting Stewart's feet from the armrest and plopping on the opposite side of the couch.

"Yes, Poindexter," Stewart said. "I'm the only pervert who gets to lick his balls."

"He's getting worse and worse. I don't know what you do to him during the day." Orlando took up one of Stewart's feet and began massaging, pressing his thumbs deeply into the sole. For years now, they had fallen into the habit of massaging each other's feet while watching the tube.

"Please don't abuse that dog," Stewart said, caressing Orlando's foot. "You know full well I believe the family pet is always the barometer of the health of a gay relationship. Remember your Feeni story."

Orlando groaned. At fourteen, he had met his first gay couple, two old queens on his paper route who would call him in for Coke on hot summer days. They communicated through their dog, Feeni, an ornery corgi whom they lavished with love. "Feeni missed you," one would announce when the other arrived home late. "Feeni is depressed today," the other would declare when in a glum mood. When they had got Poindexter from the pound years ago, Orlando had made Stewart swear the dog would never be more than a dog to them. Sometimes it was hard to keep that promise.

The movie began again after feature-length commercials for the lonely and injured, and the Good Maria Montez was restored to her rightful place as ruler of Cobra Island. It was late when Orlando and Stewart finally slapped the TV off button and hit the sack. Orlando wrapped his arms around Stewart's waist, pulled him close under the cool sheet, felt firm buns rub his groin.

"I've got some bad news," he said in the darkness. He had put off talking about it as long as he could. The few hours he had with Stewart each night were the only time he could escape the difficulties of his job, and he resisted allowing the miseries of the day to invade their home life. Orlando wouldn't mention Briggs's return; he wanted Stewart to get some sleep tonight. He thought he was doing Stewart a favor, but his lover often accused him of not communicating. "Father Morant was murdered tonight."

Stewart turned, propped his head in his palm, his elbow in his pillow. "You mean the guy the No Exit Killer supposedly confessed to? Geez, what does that do to your case?"

"It means I have no leads whatsoever now. At least when Morant was alive there was a chance that psycho would come back for another confession. Now there's nothing to do but wait. And the No Exit Killer is going to strike again tomorrow night. I know it." Orlando felt a hand in the curls of his chest hair.

"Let me help, Doug. Whatever I can do. You know as well as me that I don't have anything to do this summer." The edge of irritation that Stewart often showed toward Orlando's job was absent; he just wanted to get Orlando through this tough case in one piece.

Stewart had taken off summer session at NYU so he and Orlando could travel. They'd had the tickets to the Bahamas in their hands. Then the No Exit Killer struck, and Orlando knew any other cop assigned the case wouldn't feel his obsessive drive to snare this psycho. Gay victims, especially underground-culture gays, won little sympathy from the police department. It was the passion to solve a crime, the unerring commitment by the investigating detective to strive beyond mere job duty, that broke tough cases. Lack of compassion for the victim sent cases on the fast track to the graveyard file, where unsolved killings languished while new murders took precedence in the detective's workload. Orlando vowed this case wasn't going that route, not as long as he was on the force.

Stewart didn't like Orlando being a cop, not in the last two years at least, when harassment over Orlando's testimony against Briggs had made life ugly at the station house. At first Stewart had been angry because of the cancellation of their plans, but Orlando explained the impor-

tance of his staying with the case. When Stewart
learned the terrible modus operandi of the killings, he supported Orlando's decision to delay
their vacation. Orlando resisted Stewart's offers
of assistance, however, despite the lack of manpower aiding him on the case. Police work could
be deadly anyway, and now that Briggs was
back, anyone Orlando loved would be fair game.
Briggs had been even more off-kilter tonight
then usual, and Orlando knew how dangerous a
cop ready to explode could be.

He came up with a relatively safe way Stewart
could aid him, and, against his better judgment,
he said, "I need someone to take pictures of everyone coming and going tomorrow night at No
Exit." He tried to make it sound dull. "You'd be
stuck all night crouched in the car."

"If it will help, I'm willing."

Orlando reached around Stewart's narrow
waist and drew him close; there were times when
Stewart made him feel so good. "Now," he whispered in Stewart's ear, "if you just said that to
all my requests, I'd be one happy man."

Stewart fell asleep in his arms in a couple of
minutes, his breathing slow and shallow; it was
something Orlando had always envied, that ability to shut one's day off and drift into peaceful
slumber. Untroubled sleep was a gift Orlando
hadn't received in years. Inevitably, the day's
roller-coaster ride would heave and buckle through
his mind, and only exhaustion finally brought a
rest from consciousness. Tonight proved no dif-

ferent, and he found himself reliving his current case again.

After ten years in the muck of Brooklyn Homicide, Orlando had thought he'd seen everything. Husbands bludgeoning wives, soured drug deals erupting in murder, even kids knifing their parents. Just last month he'd been saddled with a case that hit a new low: a two-year-old girl bled to death after being raped with a curling iron by her own teenage father. Only the vision of a new horror could diminish the last in his mind's eye. He got them all, and Lieutenant Reilly made sure he got the ugliest. The only good thing Orlando could come up with to rationalize all the misery he waded through daily was that the victims were out of their pain and sometimes he caught the killer.

But the No Exit murders were different. He had sensed it the moment he arrived at the first murder scene. Obviously not a murder of passion or revenge against wrongs done, it was more diabolical, insidious.

Intelligence and planning lay behind it, and something more disturbing. Orlando perceived that this deranged mind clicked in a way he couldn't fathom, constructed the building blocks of murder in a manner that defied ordinary logic. Most murders were boring family affairs, committed over a cold dinner or bad reception during the World Series, and the perpetrator usually held the smoking gun. But the No Exit murders had meaning, a brutal message encoded into shocking images, a twisted anagram that Orlando had to unsnarl to stop the carnage. The bodies represented not just the detritus of an act of violence, but a symbol to be viewed: a monument to a tortured psychopathic mind.

The killings seemed random, the only connection the location of the pickup and the m.o. of the crime. Links between serial killers and their prey are often by chance—wrong-place, wrong-time scenarios—rather than by acquaintance. So the solution to the crime lurked in the killer's mind. The *why* of the m.o. could lead to finding the monster.

Every time Orlando closed his eyes he relived the scene of the first murder. The sickening smell of chloroform hanging like death in the air. The naked body of a young man flung on the floor. Pale skin, cropped hair. A black skull grimaced on a thin forearm. A red and blue cobra hissed from a bicep, ready to strike. His ears sported gold rings, as did his nipples, and the head of his penis. And the rest of his body was pierced with death-giving needles, needles everywhere. A human pin cushion. Punishing, puncturing, brutal.

Orlando easily put the picture together. The perpetrator had picked up the young man, gone home with him, and knocked him out with a rag doused in chloroform. The medical examiner discovered Ketamine in the victim's system, a drug that made you semiconscious, hallucinatory, unable to make voluntary muscle movements. The monster had injected the drug while the young man lay unconscious from the chloroform. Then the killer methodically bored two-inch needles into the naked victim's backside, head to foot. When he flipped the helpless victim over, slow death began. The needles worked their way deeper into the flesh, piercing the vital organs. Needles forced in the face and the front of the body were just for decoration, an afterthought to aesthetically please a sick mind. Also, as if to add a barbaric flourish, the killer stuck a needle up the victim's anus.

Forensics traced the needles to a company that serviced three-quarters of the country. Calls to local outlets produced gruff and harried replies from clerks insisting no customers had bought greater quantities than usual. The Ketamine should have been easier to trace, but there had been no reports of the drug being stolen. A lot that mattered. Plenty of corners in New York acted as de facto pharmacies, different from legitimate practices only in the absence of a license, and stranger drugs found their way to the street every day.

The young man had last been seen at No Exit, a bar dedicated to the piercing and tattooing scene. Open Fridays only, the place packed them in until dawn. The bar screamed hard-edged music, and nothing was too bizarre to shock its nerved-deadened denizens. A place where extremes flourished, where drugs could kill pain. Boy hustlers hung out there, offering a variety that would satisfy any taste. And now, within those walls, you could pick up death.

Archy Stigler, the police psychiatrist Orlando had consulted, offered no help. The shrink had developed a test in the sixties to screen out gay applicants from the force with questions like

"Do you ever fantasize about changing your sex?" and "Have you ever been interested in becoming an interior decorator?" Orlando hadn't expected much from him and he'd gotten nothing. A laconic "latent homosexuality" constituted his usual diagnosis for any psychopathic behavior. Stigler dismissed the first killing as a one-time thing, an S&M adventure gone bad. A consensual act between degenerates that deteriorated into what they both really wanted. And Orlando got a tired anecdote on homosexuals, light bulbs, and emergency rooms from the doctor's days as a resident. Behind Orlando's back Stigler had informed Reilly that a task force—only mandatory when serial killer cases arose—would not be necessary.

Then it happened again, last week, like clockwork. A Friday night murder, same m.o., and like the one the week before, the second victim had also been at No Exit the night of his death. And it scared Orlando.

Because he knew it was only the beginning.

Tomorrow night it would happen again, and he didn't have a clue how to stop it. The confession to Father Morant had been his only lead. An anonymous phone tip had sent him to the priest. Homicide detectives took anonymous tips with a grain of salt, but this one had been different. The tipster had known enough about the specifics of the murders to get past the secretaries and to Orlando. The newspapers had reported only that the murders had taken place; the department had withheld mention of the m.o. of the murders or that No Exit was the assumed contact point between the killer and the victims. The voice on the phone, male, muffled, perhaps electronically distorted, knew the facts of the case. Orlando had jolted up in his seat as the man recounted the ugly details of the murder scene. He insisted he wasn't the killer and didn't know the maniac's identity; but he knew who did. The murderer had confessed to a priest, one Father Michael Morant of St. Agatha in Brooklyn. And Father Morant had told the tipster he knew the killer's name. When Orlando confronted the priest, Morant never admitted he had given confession to the killer; it was against his role as a priest to even discuss it. But Orlando could see it in the troubled hazel eyes. The guilt, the fear, the torment. And the anguish in that handsome face when Orlando blamed the priest for what was to come.

Stewart mumbled in his sleep, shifted, and moved to the other side of the bed. Hugging a pillow as a replacement, Orlando lay comfortably, but he didn't sleep. He listened to the tick of the clock on the bureau for a long time.

CHAPTER 3

The station house was abuzz early Friday morning. Orlando passed the secretarial center—word processor keyboards chattering, printers grinding out pages—and unlocked his office door. The janitor had given up scrubbing and finally painted over the hastily scrawled words "AIDS DEN" on the door. But the splotch of new paint was there to remind him he wouldn't soon be voted officer of the month.

As Orlando settled in the whining swivel chair at his metal desk, he looked up to find Mrs. Burdict peering in the doorway. She wore big glasses that set low on her nose, with thick lenses that made her look inquisitive even when she wasn't. Her hair was big, too, and dyed a red she could never have had naturally in younger years, a red that would protect her crossing a dark street at night. She and Orlando had a history together. She'd been his secretary for over ten years, and he was her favorite of all the homicide detectives she'd worked with in forty years of police department service. A morning tabloid was snuggled in her armpit.

"Coffee this morning, Detective Orlando?" She toyed with something in her stiff hands.

"Thanks, but I can pick up some myself later, Mrs. Burdict. I could use some help, though, if you have a minute."

She stepped into the office, looked down at the object in her hands. "I have something for you. I made it myself." She set a transparent plastic paperweight down on the blotter. A shiny coin was angled brightly in the center. "It's a paperweight," she explained.

"Isn't that something?" Orlando injected the same enthusiasm in his voice he reserved for the turquoise cardigans his mother gave him for Christmas, year after year.

"Oh, I know it isn't very imaginative," Mrs. Burdict conceded. She rubbed her gnarled hands. They looked worse than just months ago. "But I long to do something creative again. Knitting is out. I used to do such beautiful things. Thank God I was able to make an afghan for each of my grandchildren before this arthritis got too bad."

"I love it," Orlando said, and he meant it. Suddenly the stupid little thing had taken on a poignancy of its own. "I could use it around here."

Mrs. Burdict shrugged. "I guess paperweights are my future. I just wish I could make one with *meaning*. I feel so useless." She glanced back with despair at the secretarial center outside the office. The younger women resented Mrs. Burdict. They got stuck with the typing she was supposed to do. As far as Orlando was concerned, she more than made up for her deficiencies with experience and careful research skills.

"Don't listen to them. You're like a partner to me in my cases. You know I couldn't do it with-

out you." He placed the paperweight firmly on
a stack of documents at the corner of his desk.
"There." Orlando leaned back in his chair. "I
want you to get me everything you can on a
Susan Krouse." He spelled it. "A murder victim." He remembered the yellowing newsprint.
"You're going to have to dig back a ways. Years,
probably. Also find out if we have anything on
Serra Pritchard. S-e-r-r-a. She's a nun."

"I'll get it done right away."

Orlando drummed a pencil on the desk. "I also
need some discretion from you. Can you get me
a copy of Briggs's report on the murder of Father
Michael Morant last night? And without him or
the secretaries knowing. Also bring me the forensics file on the Morant case."

"No problem. Whisper 'coffee break' and these
young gals storm down to the lounge like a herd
of buffalo. I'll get it for you." Mrs. Burdict
turned, but she didn't leave. She pursed her lips,
lingered by the door.

"Is there anything else?"

"You're not going to like this," she warned.
She grimaced and walked to his desk, placing
the folded tabloid in front of him. He flipped it
open, stared, and felt anger rise like heat. Kicking back in his chair, he examined his desk
drawer. The little round keyhole at the center
held fresh scratches. Someone had taken a knife
to it. Orlando fumbled in his pockets, took out
his keys, and slid open the drawer. Photographs
lay inside. The photographs that gave him night-
mares. All but the one that was plastered on the
front page of the tabloid.

Mrs. Burdict was right. Orlando didn't like it. He didn't like it at all.

"Can't you see I'm busy?" Lieutenant Reilly let out a grunt, shoved the barbell into the air, and gritted his teeth. His nostrils flared and the road map of veins covering his nose became engorged. Knuckles white, he wrestled the weight above his head, where it hung unsteadily for a moment, then plunged back to the floor. The dull thud on the carpet seemed to satisfy the lieutenant, who stared at the barbell like a complacent toddler peering into a toilet at a job well done. "A closed door," he panted, "usually means you're not supposed to enter." He breathed heavily, hunched over, his hands pressed against his knees.

Orlando shut the door behind him. "That's what I mean to talk with you about."

The office of the watch lieutenant had seen a rebirth of sorts in the last few months, thanks to Reilly's wife. She had left him after forty-one years of marriage, and the blow to his esteem had made him a nice guy. Self-doubt made him deferential. Sadness engendered empathy. For about two weeks. Then resentment and the desire to remake his life had set in. The Venetian blinds yellow with smoke had been replaced by cool blue Levelors. The old squeaking swivel chair was now new, and extra padded. The carpet had gone Berber and the sickly plant straining for sunlight by the door had become a plush palm. Only the industrial metal desk and files remained the same—and the heap of papers on the desk, which Orlando suspected the lieutenant shuffled but never did anything with.

Orlando settled into a new director's chair, black leather slung over stainless steel. He found a spot of desk among the papers, set his styrofoam coffee cup down, and put his briefcase on the floor. "I think it's time we had another chat about the No Exit murders. And the leak."

Reilly wiped an army of sweat beads off his brow with his sleeve. For a moment he appeared thoughtful, as if his devotion to police work might break through hostility to Orlando and antipathy toward gay murder victims. Then his face hardened again. "Awright, I can give you five minutes." He gripped his hips with beefy hands, his fat stomach peeking under the sweatshirt, lint crouching in the crease of his belly button.

"Better take a seat, Reilly. You don't look so good."

"That's not what the scales say." Reilly sauntered over to a portable refrigerator in the corner. He had ordered the janitor to cart off his coffee maker, and this had appeared in its place. He poured non-fat milk into a blender, flipped the lid off a Tupperware container, and spooned powder in. "I've lost fifteen pounds in three weeks." He looked Orlando over. "Wouldn't hurt you to try this." The blender screamed, then calmed down. He filled a big glass to the brim.

Reilly went around the desk and sunk into thick cushions. Taking a gulp, he fought the puckering of his lips. "Doesn't taste all that bad either. One of these for breakfast, one for lunch, then you can eat a regular dinner." His hand lovingly stroked his protruding stomach, like a mother-to-be caressing her unborn.

"Thanks for the diet tips." Orlando took a swig of coffee, felt it go smoothly down his throat. The janitor had installed Reilly's coffee maker in the lounge, and for the first time in years the brew was guaranteed to be good. The detective mentally thanked Reilly's wife.

Rummaging through his briefcase, Orlando found what he wanted and slapped the morning tabloid on the desk. "I guess you've seen this."

"I seen it."

The front page displayed a grainy color blow-up of the second No Exit victim's face, jaw sagging, eyes blank, needles puncturing the pallid skin. It was a crime-scene unit photograph. "Somebody leaked that picture to the press. After tinkering with the lock on my office door and knifing my desk. I want you to find who did this and bust his butt."

Reilly smirked. "I'll leave that proclivity to you." He took a satisfied swig of his drink, leaving a white film mustache on his thick upper lip. Then he sobered. "To be frank, I don't like this any better than you. We don't need the bad press and we don't need the pressure. I assumed it was you that pulled this stunt, to get your task force."

Hardly. The photograph would cause an uproar and increased public pressure to find the killer, but all Orlando could think of was the devastation inflicted on the victim's family, who'd already suffered such loss.

"You can start with your pal Briggs. I see they let him out of his cage. You can tell him he made a big mistake. Now that the general public is aware of what's going on, they're going to demand a task force. I'm going to get the men I need, or you're going to look very bad."

"Tell me about it." A pink tongue ran along Reilly's upper lip, erasing the mustache. "The switchboard has been lighting up with angry gentlemen with falsetto voices." A resigned sigh. "I'll see what men I can spare."

"Good. I want them at No Exit tonight, about midnight. Looking inconspicuous." Orlando folded the tabloid over, hiding the cover, then slipped it into the briefcase. He didn't need to see it now. The visits in his dreams were enough to prod him on. "This murder last night troubles me. The priest—Father Morant. His murder coinciding with the No Exit killings is too disturbing to ignore. And I don't like it that Briggs was assigned to the case."

Reilly shrugged. "He's a good cop. You think we have one killer?"

There was a hint of a smile on his lips and Orlando didn't like it. He took a long sip of coffee and wondered what was up. "Totally different m.o. A middle-aged priest killed at his church with a baseball bat. Young gay men with a penchant for tattoos and piercing picked up at a sleaze bar, then drugged and harpooned with needles. There's obviously a connection, but I don't think we have the same killer."

Reilly finished his concoction with a slurp, wiped his mouth, and pushed back from the desk. His suit dangled from a wooden hanger curled around the handle of his metal file's top drawer. Reilly threw a warning glance as he toweled himself off and changed. Orlando knew the rules; he looked away to assure the lieutenant he wasn't interested in his rotund body. The things gay men did to keep the peace.

"But you see a connection. Maybe the No Exit Killer saw Morant as a threat and decided to do away with him any way he could. Perhaps he regretted confessing to him." He glanced at Orlando and his blue eyes glinted under snowdrift eyebrows. Now Reilly was playing with him, clearly perpetrating a ruse, with Orlando as the dupe. What in hell could the lieutenant be up to? Reilly regarded himself in a mirror on the wall, flipped up his shirt collar, and wrapped his tie around his neck. How many times in the last two years had Orlando wished he was the one tightening that knot?

Orlando grunted. "Anything's possible." He was waiting for the ax to fall. Reilly could never contain his little tricks long.

After flapping on his suit jacket, Reilly returned to his seat. "Maybe you ought to check down in the holding area. We have a suspect in the Morant murder that might interest you. Someone who threatened his life. A friend of yours." Reilly looked like he'd just won the America's Cup. "Herb Chiligny."

Chiligny would be a trophy for many cops. He'd been a thorn in the side of the N.Y.P.D. for years with his incisive exposés of police corruption for the *Village World*. After the grief he'd showered over Briggs and Reilly, they'd love to see him behind bars. Orlando sat up in his chair. "You gotta be kidding. Herb Chiligny is a respected journalist. He wouldn't hurt a fly." He didn't mean it to come out a growl.

The white canopy eyebrows rose. "Oh, no? What about his arrest record? Two decades long and running. I don't take habitual criminal behavior lightly."

Orlando made a throwaway gesture. "You're talking civil disobedience raps. Sit-ins at lunch counters. You're going to have a hard time making this one stick."

"He threatened to kill Morant. His fingerprints are on the murder weapon, and he has no alibi for the night of the murder." Reilly told him the details, chuckling sourly. "This'll stick, like gum to a shoe."

"You've got the wrong guy." Orlando stood, dunked the coffee cup in a waste basket, and gripped his briefcase. He wanted to get out before he got mad.

"I dunno. The gays are becoming increasingly militant and violent. You see it on the news all the time. Back in the old days they'd just do each other in. Now they're after heterosexuals. Look how they invaded Morant's church like a bunch of wild banshees." Reilly leaned back in his chair and clamped his hands at the back of his head. "I guess it had to end in murdering straights sometime."

"Yeah," Orlando said dryly. "Think of all the times we grab our baseball bats on a Friday night, cruise over to Jersey, and bash some hapless heterosexuals."

"Spare me your paranoia." He leaned forward, elbows on the desk. "You learn anything new about the No Exit murders?"

Orlando turned at the door. His eyes were bleak. "All I know is that it's going to happen again," he said gravely. "Tonight."

Reilly wasn't looking at him anymore. He was playing with the papers on his desk. But Orlando could hear the grin in his voice. "When you see your friend in the holding cell, you might ask him if he has a fetish for needles."

Orlando didn't answer. He figured slamming the door made his point.

Orlando heard the ruckus from upstairs. Shrieks. The thud of falling bodies. Cries of police brutality. And a shouted chant above the din: "We're here! We're queer! And we'll get the last laugh!" Secretaries stopped typing and strained their necks to see where the noise was coming from. Mrs. Burdict stood clasping a folder to her breast, mouth agape. Uniforms stormed past, their faces like steel, nightsticks gripped in their fists. Orlando followed them down the main staircase.

Bodies lay strewn on the floor like the aftermath of a terrorist attack, but these bodies were very much alive. They held placards dripping with blood red lettering: "ARREST THE NO EXIT KILLER, NOT HERB CHILIGNY and FREE HERB CHILIGNY, POLITICAL PRISONER OF THE N.Y.P.D." The desk sergeant stood perplexed behind his desk, scratching his locks of white hair. A throng of cops surrounded him. News people were already there; clearly they'd been alerted beforehand. The protesters had media savvy—they could get their message across to a wide audience, safe from police violence that accompanied protests where cameras weren't running. Flashbulbs burst in shocks of light for the daily papers. Video cameras whirred for the evening news. A familiar blond newscaster kneeled and stuck a microphone in the face of one of the protesters, whom she seemed to know from previous demonstrations. She called him Anthony, and he was clearly their unofficial spokesperson.

He looked like a deranged Jesus, sprawled there on the floor. Stringy dark hair, a shaggy beard, thin. He wore a battered biker's jacket that was bumper-stickered with "FAGGOT" on the back, a handbag slung over his shoulder. Handcuffs dangled from the jacket epaulets. His gloves were black net and so were his stockings, which reached up his shapely thighs to cut-off Levi's. Stiletto high heels went well with the stockings. Anthony brandished a gloved finger at the camera, and had the voice of a seasoned speaker. "The New York Police Department is more concerned with arresting its critics on trumped-up charges than in going after the brutal serial killer stalking gay men in this city." He thrust the picture from the morning tabloid at the camera. "Take a long look at this. This is what's happening to gay men in this city. What is the police department doing about it?"

The desk sergeant stood on his chair, raised

his arms, and boomed, "Listen up! I want you to take your protest outside. Take it outside, *now*, or we're going to have to arrest you."

"Before we decide," Anthony shouted back, "do we get to choose who is going to frisk us? I want cutie-boy there. The one with the short red hair and the cute buns." A redheaded rookie's complexion turned the color of his hair. The desk sergeant waved his hands in disgust and got off his chair.

Briggs approached the crowd of cops around the desk sergeant. They conferred in quiet tones, glancing occasionally at the protesters. They were waiting for something. Orders from above? No. A rookie scurried down the staircase past Orlando with a box in his hands. Latex gloves. The box was passed around. They pulled the gloves on with the solemnity of surgeons in an operating room, then moved in on the protesters. Cautiously. Their stiff faces said nothing, but Orlando could smell their fear. Fear of being bitten. Fear of blood. The news media pulled back to capture the scene, still photographers blitzing the room with light.

Anthony looked aghast as the police advanced, nightsticks ready. His mouth dropped open in horror. Eyebrows raised, his brown eyes registered shock. He shrieked, "*Darlings*, your gloves don't match your shoes!"

Cackles erupted from the other protesters. They pounded their fists on the floor, chanting, "Your gloves don't match your shoes! Your gloves don't match your shoes!"

A lean-faced woman with a dutch-boy cut and

pointed glasses set with rhinestones screamed,
"Dear God, they're killing me!" at the camera as
a rookie twisted her arm and led her to the front
door. Some flailed their limbs as they were
dragged, others went dead limp.

Briggs dived for Anthony, grasped him in a
head lock, and yanked him toward the front
door. Anthony kicked his legs all the way. Jane
Russell would have envied those gams. "Officer
Pricks," Anthony shouted, more to the cameras
than Briggs, "tell the reporters you arrested the
wrong man. A man with an alibi." Briggs tightened his grip, and Anthony wasn't talking anymore. His face turned blush red and he gasped
for breath. Orlando had seen that look before, in
the old days when no holds were barred, moments before the sickening sound of an esopha-
gus being crushed.

Orlando strode across the linoleum floor, thread-
ing around prone bodies, and put a firm hand on
Briggs's shoulder. His eyes warned. "Watch it."

Briggs stared up at him stupidly, his face col-
ored with rage, then looked over at the TV cameras. He slowly freed his grip. "Yeah. Right," he
said vaguely. He probably hadn't even known
what he was doing, and that made him all the
scarier. Anthony heaved, curled in a ball, his
hands grasping his throat. He wasn't kicking
anymore.

"Get yourself under control," Orlando spat at
Briggs. "Go take a fucking shower." He turned
to Anthony. "Let's move outside." He helped
Anthony up and walked him to the sidewalk.
The shaggy protester gave Orlando a curt nod of

appreciation as he rubbed his neck. He found some sensible shoes in his handbag and exchanged them with the high heels—evidently the camp effect had been for the media. In a moment someone had given Anthony a bullhorn, and he was hoarsely shouting to the others, forming them in a circle.

Orlando stood by, observing the uniformed officers' conduct. He didn't want any more brutality. When the last protester had joined the circle on the sidewalk, he went inside to see Herb Chiligny.

CHAPTER 4

His spiky hair had gone droopy, but his brown eyes hadn't lost their sparkle. Herb Chiligny rose uncertainly from the narrow bed in his cell and hobbled to the bars. His oversized chartreuse jacket and baggy slacks, etched with wrinkles, hung casually on his slight frame. Even when he looked a mess—and he did right now—he radiated style.

"A visitor at last," he said. His lips pouted. "But I was expecting Perry Mason." Despite the devilish tone of his voice, he looked very small gripping the iron bars.

Orlando grunted. "You've got plenty of visitors, but I don't think there's a lawyer in the bunch. Your Queer Nationals are out front protesting on your behalf."

Chiligny fluffed his hair with his slender hands. "My public? I must prepare to meet them. Even Susan Hayward didn't look this good when she walked her last mile."

"This isn't funny."

Chiligny grasped the bars again. He had to or he'd be flat on his back. Diabetes was working him over, and he had a hard time rolling with the punches. Briggs must have taken his cane away when he booked him. The journalist's voice went hard. "I think it's hilarious."

Turning, Orlando threw a signal to an officer down the corridor who lounged behind a tall desk. The officer nodded, fed a key into a panel implanted in the wall, and pressed a button. The cell door shuddered, hummed open.

"Why don't we sit and talk?" Orlando set a steadying hand on Chiligny's spine as they walked to the bed. The smell of Pine-sol lingered in the cell. In the corner a sink stained with mineral deposits dripped a steady beat. Chinese water torture for hot summer nights, and completely legal. The door hummed closed behind them. As Chiligny settled on the wafer-thin mattress, he patted a spot beside him. Orlando took it. The mattress creaked under his weight, and the metal springs beneath jutted up punishingly.

"Why, Detective Orlando! And here I despaired over ever luring you into my lovely boudoir! And to think I never believed Sister Ignatius when she said every cloud has a silver lining."

The detective found it hard to separate his feelings of annoyance from fondness for the columnist's flip ways, and he muttered what was becoming a cliché between them: "Cut the bullshit, Chiligny."

Chiligny sighed, looking contrite, though only mildly so. But he was serious now. "You know why I'm here."

"Reilly told me the basics. You threatened Father Morant. I believe you said, uh," Orlando cleared his throat, "that you were going to fuck his face with a baseball bat."

"*Moi?*" His eyes shone humorous for a moment, then went dull. He stared at his feet, picked a speck of lint off his slacks, and watched it flutter to the floor. "Yeah, I guess it looks pretty bad. But that's not why I'm here and you know it. Don't you find it even remotely suspicious that the leading journalist critical of police department policies gets arrested for murder?" He twirled a pointed finger coyly into his cheek. "Gee willikers, now there couldn't be a conspiracy to shut him up, could there? And don't you find it just, well, just a teensy bit peculiar that the very officer who arrested me was suspended for six months and very nearly lost his job because of an article I wrote about him? An article exposing Briggs's falsification of a police report concerning the shooting of an unarmed boy he plugged full of holes, *in the back*?"

The unlikely coincidence had not been lost on Orlando. "Still, you did threaten the murder victim with a baseball bat, and that's how he was murdered. And saying you were home alone the night of the murder does not make for a solid alibi."

Orlando watched Chiligny gnaw his lip in silence and stare into the distance, the only sound an occasional muffled chant from the protesters outside and the rhythmic lament from the faucet. The cell walls were green, painted that hue after a psychological study showed the color soothed aggressive minds. Orlando didn't know, it just made Chiligny look a sickly gray.

"Suppose you tell me what you know about Morant."

Chiligny laughed icily. "Well, I guess you could say he was a self-loathing closet case who let gay men die rather than stand up to the barbaric policies of the Church."

"Who says he was gay?"

Rolling his eyeballs, Chiligny touched Orlando's knee. "What an innocent lamb you are, my dear. According to their own statistics, up to sixty percent of the Catholic Church's priests are gay. And if they admit to sixty percent, I say ninety-nine percent. It's a simple matter of probabilities."

Footsteps echoed in the corridor, and a young Latino man, wrists cuffed behind his back, was escorted past the cell. He glanced in at Chiligny and jeered. His peach-fuzz mustache and complexion tortured with blemishes said he was only in his teens. Chiligny's small hand clutched his collar. His voice went throaty, theatrical. "Detective Orlando, you've got to spring me from this joint! I can see that thug wants me to be his bitch!"

"I've got a feeling you can fend for yourself." The gate to the next cell hummed open, slammed shut. "Tell me your connection with this mess from the beginning."

Chiligny fingered the coarse wool blanket on the bed thoughtfully. "Well, it began with a book called Leviticus, a very bad book, a book taken out of context to justify annihilating gay men. Fast forward a couple thousand years. A boy is raised to hate faggots by the Catholic Church, and as he grows to manhood, he thinks, wow, wouldn't it be fun to turn gay men into pin cushions? Wouldn't it make Sister Ignatius proud?"

"Fast forward to your involvement."

Sighing, Chiligny crossed his arms. "We learned the serial killer had confessed to Morant the same time you did. We have our informants."

"I've got to know who that informant was. He could be an important key to this. You got any ideas?" Orlando shifted his position and the mattress groaned.

The doe eyes blinked. "Probably one of the few closet cases in that church with a conscience. But I truly don't know who it was. Information like that, it just ... *appears* in the community. Don't ask me how it gets there. If it's important, we hear about it."

Orlando knew when he was being lied to, but he didn't say anything. Who was Chiligny trying to protect?

"Anyway, when we learned that cannibal-in-a-dress knew who the killer was and wouldn't tell the police"—Chiligny let out a sound that was part snort, part laugh—"well, it made us rather disenchanted with Church policies."

"Disenchanted enough to kill? You could be in jail for something one of your pals did."

Chiligny looked directly at him. "Disenchanted enough to protest. We had an action against the Church, during mass last Sunday. That was it." He paused. "Well, the next day we *did* visit Morant while he was coaching the good Catholic boys at baseball. It could be said that things got rather heated. I may have grabbed a baseball bat and said something picturesque like, 'Tell us who the No Exit Killer is or I'll fuck your face with this.' "

"Maybe, nothing. Your prints are on that bat."

"It just goes to show you," Chiligny said with raised shoulders. "The bat I grabbed was used to frame me. Think about it. You know my health situation. You really think I could have swung that bat hard enough to kill Morant? Yeah, sure, I just limped up to the guy and whacked him on the head while he stood there grinning."

"He *was* hit from behind." Orlando rose, stretching his legs. He couldn't take the mattress anymore. He stared out the sliver of a window. Queer Nationals were circling the sidewalk with placards. "Who saw the incident between you and Morant?"

"Well, other than the protesters, just the kids on the baseball team."

Orlando saw Anthony raise a bullhorn to his face and shout a muffled chant.

"I met your friend Anthony," Orlando said.

Chiligny turned, raised his eyebrow. "Friend? I don't think so. If Anthony is out there, he's there for himself, not me. Anything to snatch the limelight. We were lovers once, off and on, starting back when dinosaurs ruled the Earth, before the plague, before the disco frenzy, before gay was good. Back when it dawned on scared kids that the long hair and beads and paisleys of the sixties might mean a crack in the status quo that could transform their lives. Back when kids ran away to the Village because that's the only place where homosexuals were."

Orlando cracked a smile. "You're making me feel ancient."

"You're not the only one. Anthony and I had a relationship that lasted a few centuries, or at least it felt like it. We were in radical politics then. I wrote for a gay rag, a newsletter really, that we handed out free in the bars. 'Smash the Church, smash the State, smash the Patriarchal Family,' we'd chant."

"Herb, I don't think you've changed much."

"Oh, I have. But if you stick around long enough, and God knows I have, it all comes around again. And again. I can barely wait for the next go-round when I'm sixty."

"What happened with you and Anthony?"

"We got into a screaming match during a political meeting over his egotism and ended up throwing chairs at each other. We took our politics very seriously. The next day he was on a plane to San Francisco, where he experienced an alcoholic binge that lasted more than half a decade before returning here a few months back. He hasn't changed. The alcohol bloated his ego as well as his face, and he's as controlling and horrible as ever. Why are you so interested?"

Orlando twisted the knobs on the sink, hoping a firm hand would stop the dribbling faucet. No such luck. "Because whoever framed you knew about your argument with Morant. That means your Queer Nationals or the boys on the baseball team. And I got a feeling the boys had nothing against the father."

"Don't be too sure. Maybe Morant should have been renamed Father Boylove, considering what

I've been reading about priests in the paper. And you're crazy if you think Anthony—" Chiligny broke off, and fell into deep thought. Then, quietly, "No, no, I don't believe he could do that to me." But he wasn't even convincing himself, and he stared at the detective.

Orlando paced the dull tile floor, heels clacking. The faint echo following his feet showed just how small the room was. "Are you going to be able to make bail?"

Chiligny nodded. "I see the judge later today. If he won't let me out on my own recognizance, then the paper will scrounge up the money."

"Anything I can bring to make you more comfortable?"

Chiligny's tough core returned, the activism that drove him. "You can start be telling that pig Reilly I need my insulin. And if I don't get it before lunch, I'm filing a ten-million-dollar suit against the P.D. in general and his fat ass in particular."

"I'll get it done. When he arrested you, did Briggs—"

Chiligny waved a dismissing hand. "You have to remember, this isn't my first arrest. I'm an old hand at getting roughed up by the boys in blue. I've been dragged off to paddy wagons from protest rallies more often than I can count. Briggs, he's really a powder puff."

Not the Briggs I know, Orlando thought. But he appreciated Chiligny's strong facade. He waved the guard down the hall to open the door. The teen in the next cell coughed, cleared his throat loudly, and spat phlegm into the corridor.

Chiligny glanced over his shoulder at the slit
window fortified with a single bar, as if searching for a means of escape, then back at Orlando.
He limped over and clutched Orlando's sleeve.
Tightly. "Just get me out of this mess," he said.

He didn't recognize her at first.

Flecks of crimson hung in her black hair like
particles from a deadly fallout. A wide smear of
blood blemished her chest like a stroke from an
abstract painter's brush. Blood dripped from
gloved hands. Goggles speckled red hid her pale
blue eyes, and a mask covered her nose and
mouth.

"Yes, it's me," Ronnie Bell said with a muffled
sigh. "I'm just about done here. Just hold a sec
while I put his head back together and I'll be
right with you."

Orlando looked away from the body on the
steel tray and let the medical examiner return
to its proper place what she had just sawed
apart. It didn't look like Morant anymore. The
body reminded him of the incompletely formed
pods in the old *Body Snatchers* movie. There was
something strangely empty in his face, as if it
had never known pain or wisdom. His wrinkles
had vanished with his life, a vague puffiness taking their place. He looked like someone who'd
spent the night in a refrigerator. Orlando was
glad he hadn't arrived earlier. The buzz saw in
the autopsy room made the most dreaded sound
in existence. The acrid stench of formaldehyde
was bad enough, sending less intrepid detectives
scurrying from the room.

Ronnie snapped off her rubber gloves and stepped on a pedal at the base of a garbage can. The top jumped open, revealing a bright red plastic bag inside. Red for contaminated. She dropped in the gloves, turned to a pretty blond assistant with shapely legs and a tape recorder, and dismissed her with a nod and a "See you at lunch" that sounded more than just friendly. The woman returned a knowing smile, showed predatory teeth like a little animal, washed up and slipped out the door.

"Ronnie," Orlando said sternly, "did I just observe a lesbian flirtation?"

"No," Ronnie said indignantly from under the mask. "You know full well I'm married." Ronnie and Sally had been lovers for eighteen years and had a seven-year-old daughter. She pulled off the goggles and her eyes went sly. "But I'm not blind." She let out a deep satisfied breath. "All I can say is"—she sang it with a French accent like Maurice Chevalier—"*thank heaven for little girls.* They're coming up through the ranks like wildflowers now. All our struggles for women's rights are finally paying off."

Orlando winked. "And what dividends."

"And what distractions. It was so much easier in the old days when we could hate sexist men who fondled our rears and made ugly cracks. Now I have to watch who I touch and what I say. Equality does have its down side. And I hate all these young women expecting me to be their mother-lover. They make me feel old."

"Join the club." Orlando had never seen Ronnie as a lesbian heartthrob. She usually wore a

boyish haircut, thick aviator-style glasses that
magnified her eyes, boots, faded Levi's, and baggy
T-shirts. She had even said she dressed that way
to rebel against the fashion industry's narrow
definition of female beauty and to squelch sexual
harassment at work. As she shed her mask and
disposable lab coat, Orlando started.

"Ronnie!" he exclaimed. "You've really
changed." Now he understood her sudden popularity. He'd noticed her hair color switch from
sandy brown to shiny black, and that the style
was different too. Curly, all moussed up. It gave
her an impish look. Also, the thick glasses had
disappeared—contacts?—and she'd worked on
her eyelashes. Gold hoops circled her ears. Her
lips mimicked the color of blood. A black V-necked
pantsuit showed what curves her boyish body
had. "You look great."

"I don't want to talk about it," she said gruffly.
"Just blame the tyranny of the lipstick lesbians."

Orlando didn't push. He knew Ronnie would
tell the story in her own good time. He had
known and respected her for years, always re-
lieved when she was assigned to his cases. Her
brilliant mind and penchant for detail had
helped solve many crimes. In the last few months,
since Orlando had tracked down those responsible for the bombing of an abortion clinic run by
Ronnie's friends, she and Sally had become
brunch buddies with him and Stewart.

Ronnie dropped her mask and blood-smeared
lab coat in the can. "Welcome to the age of
AIDS," she said, obviously trying to move the
conversation away from her apparel. "We used

to eat, drink, and be merry while doing autopsies. No longer." She grimaced. "They're constantly coming out with more protective suits. The way things are going, pretty soon we'll be getting oxygen tanks and be able to survive on Mars."

"They'd better try harder. You've got blood in your hair."

Ronnie groaned. "Oh, shit. I just hate wearing those hoods they've concocted. It wrecks my hair. Remember those dorky hoods that would snap on your coat when you were a kid? Then a draw string would cinch it up tight? And all the kids at school would call you a wimp? Like that. And now I'm going to be streaked like the Bride of Frankenstein." She stretched on clean gloves from a box on the stainless steel counter by the stainless steel sink, jiggered bleach on a paper towel and began dabbing her hair in front of a mirror. A few black strands of hair came out sandy brown.

Since when did Ronnie give a damn about her hair? Recalling Chiligny's speech about the priesthood, Orlando rose his eyebrows innocently, grinned, and asked, "You take these precautions even with priests?"

Ronnie didn't get the joke. She turned and threw a stony look. "You haven't been watching the afternoon talk shows lately," she said dryly. "*Especially* with priests." She did the best she could with her hair, threw away the gloves and towels, then came over to Orlando. "Now, what can I do for you?"

"I need everything you got on the Morant case."

Ronnie arched her eyebrows, now black and sculpted. "I didn't know you were on this case."

"I'm not. And I'm not here. But Briggs brought in the wrong guy and I'd appreciate what help you can give."

"The report hasn't been typed yet, but let's have a viewing and I'll show you the basics." She went to the counter and pulled on another pair of gloves and a lab coat, then returned to the stainless steel tray in the center of the room. Holes on the surface of the table allowed bodily fluids to drain, God knows where. Pipes underneath secreted it off someplace. A hose glugged crystal water onto the table, carrying away any bloody residue. She rolled the sheet down to Morant's feet. A longitudinal cut from the trachea to the penis separated the body. The diener, an assistant to the medical examiner, would be by soon to stitch up the cut with a big curved needle, with thread as thick as yarn. Orlando had learned that all the horrors in the vilest scare films were true. "First, he died of a gunshot wound that entered under his right rib twelve, the bottom rib"—she fingered the small crimson hole—"then went through his liver, lungs, ripped his aorta, and lodged in his shoulder blade. He died fast. We sent the bullet off for analysis, but I'd say it was a .22. No power at all."

Orlando frowned. That explained the blood seeping from under the body the night before. "What about the baseball bat wound?"

Ronnie waved a gloved hand now stained with blood. "That was a love tap. He was already dead. Look at the contusion." She walked around the table and touched the gash at the back of Morant's head. "No ecchymosis formed."

"In English, Ronnie." He followed her.

She pursed ironic lips. "I'm still paying off my million-dollar debt for medical school and you want me to speak common English?" She sighed. "Okay, there's no bruise. No swelling. Dead people have no blood pressure, they don't swell up when struck with an object."

Orlando pondered that, stepped over to the mean wound below Morant's rib. "What about distance?"

"We're talking point-blank. The perp dug the pistol into his gut and fired. We traced gunpowder residue on Morant's shirt around the wound. And on his sleeves."

Groping inside his jacket, Orlando pulled out a pen and pad. He scribbled. So the priest had struggled for possession of the gun with his killer. Then another question hit him. What had become of the murder weapon?

"Another thing," she continued. "At least two shots were fired. The other missed—it skinned his clothes. We found a hole in the shoulder of the priest's jacket that's consistent with a bullet hole. I can't tell you which was fired first."

Orlando chewed his nail. During the struggle, the first bullet must have missed its mark. The second time Morant hadn't been so lucky. If the forensics team found no bullet at the crime scene, that would back Orlando's theory that the murder had taken place somewhere else. He'd check the police report back at the office.

"The angle of the bullet's path is interesting." Ronnie's eyes twinkled. Oddities in murder cases always intrigued her, made an ugly job come alive. "I don't think the perp was standing in front of Morant when they struggled for the gun. They were side to side, as if . . ." she searched for a likely analogy, couldn't find one, ". . . say, standing in a police lineup?"

Orlando knitted his brow. He couldn't picture it.

Ronnie stepped back. "That's all I have for you now, babe. On this appetizing note, why don't you and Stewart come by for lunch on Sunday? Say about two."

"We'll be there." He and Stewart enjoyed the time they spent with the women, and they loved their little girl Amy. But lately Ronnie had begun to wistfully bring up her age, early forties, in every conversation. She'd say how much she wanted a baby. Then she'd stare at Orlando across the dining table with pleading eyes. It wasn't hard to figure what Ronnie was building up the courage to ask.

She pulled off her lab coat, wriggled her nose as if it was the first time she had noticed the foul smell in the room, and walked Orlando to the door. "As far as the baseball bat goes, it didn't do more than make a superficial wound on someone already dead. Nasty, but pointless. As to why, your guess is as good as mine."

Orlando had already guessed. He stuffed his

pen and pad inside his pocket. "To frame Herb Chiligny," he said under his breath.

Orlando leaned back in his chair, feet on the desk, phone receiver hitched between his shoulder and his ear. He punched out his home phone number on the heavy-duty black telephone on his lap, and listened to the ring. Squarely on his blotter lay four manila files. Mrs. Burdict had worked fast. The secretaries must have enjoyed a long coffee break.

Stewart answered on the fourth ring.

"It's me," Orlando said. "I just wanted to let you know Ronnie has invited us for lunch on Sunday." He paused and added, "I think she wants my sperm."

"I don't object," Stewart answered casually. "I'm willing to lend it to her after I'm finished with it. Remember dinner tonight."

Orlando tapped his forehead. He'd already forgotten the dinner party celebrating the publication of Stewart's book. He felt a little ashamed he hadn't read it yet, but a three-hundred-and-fifty-page book analyzing the social, psychological, spiritual, and political ramifications of Bertha Mason, the crazy lady locked in the attic in *Jane Eyre*, wasn't exactly what Orlando wanted to curl up with after a hard day. "I'll be there," he said and signed off.

Orlando sighed, planted his feet on the floor, set the telephone aside, and sifted through the folders on the desk. The preliminary forensics report told him nothing beyond what he'd just learned from Ronnie, except that the bullet was indeed a .22. A strange choice for murder. Orlando puzzled over the fact that there was no mention of the contents of Morant's jacket pocket. Briggs's vague report didn't note it either. An uneasy suspicion formed in his mind that something had already gone irretrievably wrong with this investigation, and he wanted to find out why.

Serra Pritchard had a long rap sheet, one that she was probably proud of. It began with spilling blood in the Pentagon during the Vietnam War, then segued to the grape fields of the San Joaquin Valley, where protests sometimes got rough and strike breakers got rougher. She'd been arrested four times and hospitalized once. Swatting an anti-abortion demonstrator with an umbrella in front of a besieged clinic in upstate New York on a rainy Saturday morning had been her next encounter with the law. That charge had been dropped when a client of the clinic testified that Pritchard had been protecting her from a screaming assault by an Operation Rescue gorilla. Finally, Serra Pritchard came full circle during the Gulf War, spilling blood and oil on the steps of the Federal Building in Manhattan. Last address? Unknown.

No unknowns plagued the case of Susan Krouse. Her husband had killed her, confessed to it, and was serving seventeen years at Rikers. But what the hell did it have to do with Morant?

Orlando pushed back from the desk, grabbed his jacket from the back of the chair, and went for the door. He had questions to ask.

CHAPTER 5

A gauze of bright clouds clamped down over the city, holding heat and humidity captive. Orlando peeled off his jacket but felt no relief from the breezeless day, and wished for rain. His shirt stuck to his back. The grass, strangely bluish the night before, had gone yellow-green. It looked tired from the long summer, scuffed from rough use, ready for autumn rain. White chalk formed a diamond, with each base marked by a canvas pad. A black teen argued a shovel into the rose garden bed that fronted the rectory. Shirtless, his muscular torso glistened with sweat. Father Shea knelt beside him, seized a weed, and urged it from the soil. He held it up in triumph. "You see, Trevor, if you hold firmly you can pull it up by the roots." He spoke amiably but loudly, as if conversing with a person hard of hearing. "Otherwise, it's no use. They just come up again."

The boy nodded glumly, hitched his foot on the shovel, and pried up a clump of dirt. Shea stood up slowly, brushing the soil from his hands. The oxygen tank swung from his belt like a censer during Sunday mass. He squinted toward Orlando. He didn't look the worse for last night's binge. "Detective Orlando," he said. "How nice to see you again. Trevor and I are doing a little gardening, something I can't do as much of as I would like. Trevor, say hello to Detective Orlando."

Trevor looked up, caught sight of the Smith & Wesson holstered at Orlando's left side, and his eyes widened. The kid was probably fourteen. He held out a tentative hand, saw the dirt on it, withdrew it again. "Sorry," he mumbled meekly, looked away, and took another bite of earth with the shovel.

Shea gazed at the young man fondly. "Keep up the good work." He turned to Orlando. "Why don't we take a little walk? I try to cover the perimeter of the field twenty times every morning. I think that's about a mile, don't you?"

They strolled along the wrought-iron fence. Orlando could see it hadn't been dusted for prints. He shook his head. Some investigation Briggs took pains to make. "You may have heard the latest finding in the case," he began.

Shea looked straight ahead, hands folded behind his back. "Yes. Detective Briggs had the kindness to drop by in person this morning. I understand he arrested the guilty party." He wheezed a sigh. "It's all so sad."

"Arrested doesn't always mean guilty. I meant that Father Morant died of a gunshot wound. Did you hear anything like that last night?"

Shea frowned. "No, it was just like I told you. I thought I heard a noise. But not sharp like a gunshot, at least I don't think so." He looked puzzled. "Should I have heard a gun going off in the church? Don't they have those"—he waved a hand to catch the word he wanted—"silencer things?"

Orlando already had assumed the church wasn't the murder scene because of the scratches on Morant's shoes. The forensics report didn't mention any stray bullet found in the church either. Still, there was a lot of wall space; it could have been missed.

"I noticed something unusual last night when I looked at the body," Orlando said. "Morant wasn't wearing his collar. I found it stuffed in his pocket." As they strolled, he scanned the lawn for traces of blood, but he didn't see any.

"Gracious," Shea said, a smile breaking out on his face, his hands cupping together as if in prayer. "Do you think we're born in our robes? It was after midnight. If a noise awakened him, I'm not surprised he wasn't fully dressed."

They had reached the far end of the yard. Brownstones across the street warmed in the hazy sunlight. Turning, they continued to follow the fence. "Yes, but if he rushed outside because of a noise, throwing on his clothes, the collar wouldn't be in his pocket, would it?" Orlando remembered the crackle of plastic deep in Morant's pocket. Nothing fit, and somebody was destroying evidence.

Orlando watched Trevor set his shovel aside, bend, wrestle with a thick root. The root seemed to be winning. "The boy," Orlando said. "Does he live here?"

"Trevor? Oh, no. He lives over on Union. We hired him as a favor to his mother, who attends mass here. She's one of the few blacks in our congregation. She remarried recently and is having a difficult time with the boy. Working here full-time during the summer, it's a good way to keep him busy. I just wish we could do that with all the boys in the neighborhood. Father Morant's baseball team was one of the few ways we really reached out to these boys, and now ..." Emotion rose in his voice and he clutched his throat. He swallowed slowly. "I'm sorry. But you see, I lost more than a fellow priest. I lost a friend."

Orlando reached in his jacket pocket, plucked out his writing pad. He flipped pages. "Ever hear of a woman named Susan Krouse?"

"Let me see." Shea placed his index finger on his chin. "I don't think so. No, it doesn't ring a bell, but you have to understand how many people I come in contact with in my work."

"You would have remembered her. She was bludgeoned to death five years ago."

"Oh, my." His palm went to his cheek. "No, no, I don't remember any—" Then his eyes clouded over suddenly, and he nearly stumbled. He righted himself, turned to Orlando, and said with finality, "No, I don't know anybody of that name. What a terrible thing. Why do you ask?"

"Father Morant kept a newspaper clipping about her murder. Yellowed with age. It must have meant something to him. What about a Sister Serra Pritchard?"

The bloodless lips became a fine line. "Yes, I do believe I remember that name. She is no longer with the Church."

"She left her order? Know what's become of her?"

Shea looked sharply at the detective, his voice brittle. "I'm losing my patience with you, Detective Orlando. What has this to do with any of these murders of yours? Why all this digging into the past? You already have Father Morant's killer in custody, and I can assure you, for all her faults, Serra Pritchard is not the person you are looking for."

Orlando persisted. "Know what's become of her?"

A sigh of annoyance turned into a coughing fit. It doubled him over and stopped him in his tracks. He heaved for a moment, bent, hands on his knees. When it was over, he eyed Orlando crossly and said, "She joined some organization more to her liking. I believe they put out a little paper and criticize canon law. They all live in a tattered commune in Bedford-Stuy and dream of the sixties."

"Does it have a name?"

Shea waved a dismissing hand. "The Catholic Worker, the Catholic Union, the Catholic Front, something like that. These people are earnest but misguided. They don't seem to understand that the Church is a fragile thing: lesbian nuns, priests wanting to get married, abortion on demand—it can take only so much strain." They passed Trevor, who had conquered the root and was now splashing water from a hose into puddles under the rose bushes. Orlando noticed the boy observing him curiously, then shifting his gaze when he realized Orlando had seen him.

Shea shook his head gravely. "I'm afraid we live in the age of the shopping-list Christian, who picks and chooses what he will accept from the Bible. We cannot allow that. Pretty soon we'd have murderers in our church saying murder is okay."

Slipping his pad back into the jacket hung over his arm, Orlando said, "But you do have a murderer in your church. And your policies are allowing him to keep on killing. Isn't that as bad as saying murder is okay?"

Father Shea let out a deep breath—as deep as could be expected from a man with emphysema. "Detective Orlando, I did a little checking. You grew up in this church. You know better than that. I know your mother, who, by the way, is one of the most charming women in the parish. I don't care how long you've been away, this church will always be a part of you. The beauty of confession is that a person who has broken from our community by committing sin can be brought back into the whole through forgiveness." He gave Orlando a look of mock reproach. "Surely every altar boy would know that."

Orlando had never been an altar boy. The boys were recruited only from the fourth grade, with the prerequisite of no grade lower than a C. Orlando had received his one and only D in all his school years in a math class with a particularly cantankerous nun and a particularly mischievous boy he had been enamored with and wanted to impress. After a whipping from his father, Orlando reformed. When the fifth grade rolled around and he received straight A's, it was too late.

Shea spotted a softball nestled in the grass, stooped, and tossed it toward the garden. It didn't go far. "Remind me to tell Trevor to take that ball in. The boys can be careless with the equipment." They walked in silence for a moment, then Shea threw up his hands and continued as if the conversation had never abated. "To be honest with you, there are many Church laws I find difficult to live with, but as an minister of the Church, I must accept them with humility. And I couldn't tell you who that murderer is even if I wanted to. Father Morant was the only one who may have known his identity—and that's a big *maybe:* hearing someone's voice in a confessional does not make for a positive identification—and I'm afraid what he knew is a secret that's going to be buried with him."

"Did you see Herb Chiligny threaten Father Morant?"

"No. I didn't even know it had happened until Detective Briggs told me this morning. You see, Father Morant was the kind of man who didn't want to make others worry. He carried a lot of burdens on his own shoulders. Perhaps he died because of that." He was silent for a moment. The sun had drawn sweat from his bald head. A dog barked in the distance, and birds chattered from the roof of the church. "I did see the disruption of Mass on Sunday, however. It was frightening. I can only hope now that they will stop." His expression went severe. "Though considering the people we're dealing with, I hardly think their anger is yet spent. They came here, with their signs—obscene signs—chanting and yelling. They came in droves with their black arm bands, ridiculing our beliefs. They turned communion into a mockery. One horrible man with a shaggy beard in high heels spewed out blasphemy so vile I can't even repeat it. Right in front of women and children. He screamed in my face like he wanted to attack me personally. It was difficult for members of our congregation to keep their composure. What makes these people so bitter against the Church?" He shook his head again, this time wearily. "We know these people are hurting. But how can we help them when they act like that? The Church has tremendous sympathy for those suffering from their homosexual orientation. We have meetings to help them live celibate lives. Look at all our work with AIDS. We even used to allow the gay Catholic group Dignity to meet and have mass on our grounds. But the pope decided it was not necessary to have special masses for them, that they should join the rest of the congregation. Is that so bad? You should have seen their hysterical reaction. Anyone who disagrees with them is labeled a Nazi. Did you know that Father Morant gave mass to Dignity in Greenwich Village before the pope's decision? Yes, and here those protesters claimed he was some kind of bigot. He had compassion for everyone. And look how they abused him." When he had finished, he looked very tired and very old.

Margarita came across the playing field at a trot. A man in overalls sauntered after her. Shea watched her approach. He turned to Orlando. "Poor Margarita," he said. "She lost almost her entire family in Guatemala. Killed by government forces along with many priests and nuns. Only she and her baby granddaughter survived. If we hadn't gotten them out of the country, she and the baby would have died too."

"The man," she panted when she reached them. "He is here." She stared at her feet. Her eyes were dark, even in sunlight. Now Orlando understood why.

That man stopped in the middle of the field. "Got to get a move on," he shouted, pointing to his watch. "I don't usually make house calls."

"I'll be right there." Shea gave Orlando an indulgent smile. "I'm afraid we have a Mickey Mantle on our baseball team. Hit a fly right over the rectory and directly into the garage window. I know boys will be boys, but it can be expensive. Took all week to get the repair man here, so I guess I'd better go take care of it. Will you excuse me?"

Orlando remembered playing in this field, and the terrible feeling that descended over the team when a pop fly smashed a window in the rectory. The church's stained glass windows had wisely been protected by wire mesh. "Thank you for your time. Could you spare Trevor for a minute? I'd like to speak to him after I look over the grounds."

Shea observed him steadily. "Certainly, I'll tell him. He'll be in the garden all day." He turned and followed Margarita and the repair man down the flagstone path to the garage, the oxygen tank swaying at his side, and stopped to confer with the boy. The cloud layer was thickening to a threatening mass. Orlando didn't have much time before his lunch appointment, and he still needed to search every inch of the yard. He strode the playing field back and forth, focusing on every inch of turf, until he had covered the area. No indication of violence, no blood stains. When he was done he felt damp and scratchy all over. He went to the rose garden.

The shovel was planted in dirt. The hose, tossed aside, spouted water on the grass. Orlando looked both ways. Trevor had disappeared.

Orlando's elbows pressed against the iron railing of the Promenade, his hand grasping a white bag of deep-dish pizza slices going translucent with grease. Despite the mess, Tony's made the best pizza in Brooklyn. Tension was building in the brooding clouds hanging heavily over the sweep of Manhattan skyline across the river. The Statue of Liberty was lost in haze, and the jagged wall of skyscrapers that made up lower Manhattan looked gray and tired. Only the Brooklyn Bridge, sedate and sturdy, spun with graceful lines of wire, retained its wonder in the face of the coming downpour.

The air was perfectly still, the heat oppressive—always a warning. Any moment there would be a break. Orlando looked around, humidity stinging his cheeks. The narrow park of benches, chipped slate, and asphalt was nearly empty. A young couple, tourists who didn't know any better, strolled by arguing over a clumsy map stretched between them. On a bench, a man with a great red beard buried his face in his hands, shoulders slumped. His ragged clothes and the tattered shopping bags at his side declared he had nowhere else to go.

Orlando gazed down, where a double-deck highway was secreted away beneath the Promenade, the only evidence of its existence the rumble of traffic and the smell of fumes.

"I guess my suggestion for lunch in the great outdoors wasn't my best idea today, was it?" a resonant voice asked.

Orlando looked up. The man had kind brown eyes graced with fine laugh lines that seemed to insist everything would be okay. He was well dressed in slacks, a muted tie, and a loose shirt that couldn't hide his erect posture and muscular arms. His hand swept through his wavy dark hair, casually tossing locks in place that had cascaded over his forehead.

"Dr. Phillip Michaels?" Orlando extended his hand. "Doug Orlando."

Michaels smiled easily and the fine lines danced around his eyes. His grip was firm but gentle, as if he knew his strength but also knew he didn't have to show it. Orlando felt calluses on the palm. "Are you so sure I'm not just some strange man in the park?"

"I saw your picture on the back of your book."

"Oh, good. So you've read it?"

"Uh, no, but I have it." Stewart had given it to him, first casually, and then when he didn't read it, the book began to appear on his pillow, his favorite chair, in his briefcase. *Partners For-*

ever examined gay relationships, how to keep them strong. From what Orlando had glanced over, Michaels heavily promoted communication—not always Orlando's strongest point. But what interested the detective was Michaels's bio on the back jacket of the book. The psychiatrist had studied with the late Dr. Arthur Freedlander, a famous pioneer in the study of serial murders. There were plenty of experts in the field, but he needed to talk to a therapist who could cut through the cloud of homophobia and see this case for what it really was. He didn't need more nonsense from the police psychiatrist's ilk. In their phone conversation the day before, Michaels explained he had moved away from working with psychopathic personalities and his practice was now mostly gay couples, but he was glad to help.

Orlando watched Michaels gaze out over the river. Blue Brooklyn Port Authority piers lay silent, fronted by heavy-duty trucks. Older piers, oily and ramshackle, jutted into the calm water, broken railroad tracks running their length. Michaels noted the sky and turned to Orlando. "Shall we eat before the deluge?"

Orlando followed him to benches backed by the spiked fences of houses running along the Promenade. Someone had cleverly posted a sign to a tree behind the fence warning "POISON IVY—KEEP OUT." Still, Orlando wondered if even that would stop intrepid trespassers. The bench they settled in was green, its ubiquitous gang slogans silver. Bees cruised garbage cans flanking the bench.

"I appreciate you taking the time—" Orlando began.

Michaels put down the briefcase containing the files Orlando'd had messengered to him Thursday, and held up a hand to silence him. Orlando guessed the calluses were from working out. "I want to catch this killer just as much as you do. I just hope I can help. It's been a long time since I've dealt with this kind of case, but frankly I don't think psychiatry has made any advances in this area lately."

"The police psychiatrist, Archy Stigler, hasn't been too helpful."

Michaels set the briefcase behind him, and produced a salad and a bottle of juice from a bag. "That doesn't surprise me. I actually took classes once from Dr. Dark Ages when I was going for my Ph.D. It's scary what that man believes." He found a plastic fork, flipped open the salad container, and began to munch. He indicated the salad. "You ever been to Health Nut? The salads are just terrific. And none of that crap they spray on them in the little markets. I guess it's salads for me from now on. I hit the Big Three-five last winter, time to watch my weight."

But it sure didn't look to Orlando like he had to.

Orlando sheepishly drew a soggy slice of pizza from his bag. "So far we haven't got a clue on this killer, except the No Exit connection. I'm going to be there tonight with reinforcements, but I know we'll be powerless to stop that maniac from striking again. Sometimes I think it was a mistake allowing that place to stay open."

No Exit was an illegal club, one of hundreds in the city that operated without required licenses. Close one down, five more would spring up. The liquor board didn't have the manpower to go after them all. It usually took a major fire and dozens of deaths for a crackdown.

"It wouldn't make any difference. The people who go to that bar would just find a new place. And the killer would follow them. Or maybe you'd spook him to a new city, where he'd kill several people before authorities realized they had a problem on their hands."

Orlando had assumed as much. But he couldn't feel good about sacrificing lives now in hopes of saving more later.

Michaels popped a cherry tomato into his mouth, crunching with very white teeth. "I'd heard the rumors, of course, but I had no idea how terrible these killings were until we spoke and you sent me your files."

No one had. The department had kept the gory details of the murders from the press. Bizarre cases brought crazies out of the woodwork to waste police time confessing to crimes they hadn't committed. Media attention occasionally attracted copycats. However, people who had found the bodies told friends what they'd seen, and word had spread in the gay community. But that hadn't stopped the popularity of the bar. And Orlando knew it would be packed again tonight. Especially after this morning's tabloid.

"What do you think?" Orlando asked.

"Well, for starters, it's definitely a man. Women just don't operate this way."

Orlando pondered. "Unless it's all just an elaborate setup by a very clever killer. I haven't ruled that out." Pigeons, heads bobbing, begged at his feet. Orlando tossed them a crust, took a bite himself. "Any idea what personality type I'm looking for here?"

"There are two stereotypes. An emotionally isolated person with low self-esteem, no friends, few personal contacts, who has been in trouble with the law before. The other extreme is the gregarious psychopath, charming and engaging, glib, with a total absence of conscience. Conventional wisdom says these people were abused as kids, often, but not always, sexually. They saw their mothers abused too, and learned to equate sex and violence. Usually they have a history of cruelty to animals when they were young. Often they're drifters, moving from place to place."

Orlando had heard this before. The F.B.I. agent from Thursday night had told him. She had also informed him it didn't always hold true. "You say stereotype."

"Yeah, because I'm not so sure that's the case here." Michaels twisted the bottle cap and took a swig. "All we know is that this character is suffering from incredible rage. The m.o. is unusually specialized for a serial killer."

"I've contacted the F.B.I. No other cases with this m.o. around the country."

"That's good. That means he's just begun. Often these guys kill a few people, then move on. It's almost impossible to track them unless they get sloppy. Some of these individuals are suspected of killing upwards of three hundred people. My advice to you? Catch him before he moves on. Because if you don't, he's just going to keep killing and killing. Nothing will stop him, nothing will quench the fury burning inside him."

Orlando finished the slice, greased up the paper napkin with his dripping fingers, and pulled another pepperoni wedge from the bag. "The police shrink says the killer is gay."

Michaels shrugged. "I suspected that, too, until I read your files. Despite Stigler's homophobia, there is some logic behind that assumption. Some people have homosexual feelings they can't accept. You have to understand that people go through phases of developing their gay identity. This killer could be in the first stage: awareness of homosexual feelings. Some people never develop beyond that stage. They have the feelings and they repress them. It isn't a recipe for mental health. The fundamentalist preachers who seem obsessed with homosexuality and preach against it all the time probably fall in this category. Your killer may be like that; every time he kills a gay man, it's an attempt to kill those feelings in himself. But it never works, so he has to keep on killing."

"But you don't believe that now."

"No. When we spoke, I also considered that we might be dealing with someone who hates nonconformity so much he'll kill. Look at the victims: not just gay men, but gays who fetishize tattooing and piercing themselves. So I began to ask myself, are we dealing with sex here, or just sexual orientation? What a homicide cop sees as sodomy ain't necessarily so in my line. What I find interesting is that there's no semen in the victims. No evidence sex took place. The needle stuffed in the anus means intense hatred of homosexuals. But there is no literal sex crime here. The needle in the ass doesn't have anything to do with sexually stimulating your psycho. I think you have a killer who is heterosexual in orientation but has a bitter feud raging in his mind with the gay community. Think how often homophobic straight men use the slur 'He takes it up the ass.' This psychopath is giving it to gay men up the ass, but not for reasons of arousal. He's telling us how much he hates gay men, in the most graphic way he can think up."

"Herb Chiligny blames the homophobia in the Catholic Church."

Michaels smirked. "If it were that simple. How about the homophobia of Western civilization? But you've got to remember, it's more specific than just homophobia. The focus of his rage is narrow. They have to be male *and* gay *and* into tattooing and piercing. This killer feels terribly wronged by gay men in this subculture. If you find out why, you'll have your killer. When he kills and does his needle act, he's reliving an experience in his past, but this time *he's* in control. The needles symbolize his perceived victimization, but I haven't the foggiest why."

"Could he branch out?"

Michaels pondered. "He could. But my feeling is that he'd do it only if cornered. The funny thing with this is I think he'd be perfectly harmless with a person he didn't know was gay. But let that gay man reveal his sexuality and tattoos, and our killer would be set off. He'd be very reluctant to kill a heterosexual. They don't fit the criterion of what he is raging against."

It wasn't much to go on. And late tonight or maybe tomorrow, someone—a roommate, a friend dropping by, or a landlord—was bound to stumble over the latest victim of the killer. Orlando ran down the list of what he already knew. There was some connection with the Catholic Church because of the confession, and the killer knew a little about drugs. That meant millions of Americans. Not much to go on.

A heavy wad of rain spat on his forehead, and Orlando looked up at the troubled sky. They'd have to move soon. "If I can understand why people are into that scene, I know I'll find a clue to the killer's mind-set."

Michaels had finished his salad and slipped the box back into the bag. "Have you been to Red Demon? Over on West Street in Manhattan? That's the hot place right now, where everybody goes for piercing and tattooing. You should check it out. You'd find it interesting."

"Got any idea why this subculture is so popular right now?"

Michaels grinned. "You need a fashion consultant, not a shrink. People like to belong to a club, to feel special. Being gay used to be a secret club we belonged to, something that set us apart from the rest. With the acceptance we have nowadays, that feeling of belonging no longer exists. Younger gays are finding it in other ways. I don't see anything necessarily destructive in it."

"Except when it attracts a killer." The rain began to patter insistently on the slate and asphalt, turning them from gray to black. The bees had disappeared and the pigeons escaped to the trees. "Want to make a run for it?"

They tossed their bags into a garbage can and strode past the inadequate playground surrounded by a cyclone fence to the deserted street. The clouds let loose and rain thrashed their shoulders in big, drenching drops that fell with a thud. They looked both ways, scrambled up stairs, and took refuge in the doorway of a brownstone. Michaels stood there with the briefcase still over his head. They both laughed, breathing hard.

"I guess I should have shared," Michaels said, winking a merry brown eye and bringing the briefcase to his side, where he carefully wiped off the rain. "Sorry about that." He leaned against the door. "Maybe I'll see you tonight," Michaels added casually. "You've piqued my curiosity."

The downpour slackened after a minute, and Orlando decided to make a break for his car. Thanking the psychiatrist for his help, he flipped up his collar, grasped the neck of his jacket tightly, and trod down the street toward his Chevy.

CHAPTER 6

The rain had stopped, but the shoulders of his jacket were still damp, giving off a faint wet-dog odor. Orlando stripped it off, draped the jacket over his shoulder. Hard sunlight had broken through a moody sky and scared the humidity away. A gentle breeze wafted from the river. The storefront—a plate-glass window and a door squeezed uncomfortably together—was bracketed by two bars Orlando had never heard of. It had been years since he had frequented this stretch of West Street; back then the Ramrod had been his bar of choice. But that was long ago. It was closed down now, gone, like so many friends Orlando had caroused with in his earlier days. Across the West Side Highway, abandoned warehouses and the darkness of the night had hidden his first furtive attempts at finding who he really was. Those frightened encounters now carried the sweetness of nostalgia, but it all made him feel old. The warehouses had been mowed down, leaving piers of sunlight where boys with big radios hung out, kissing with glistening tongues to the beat of rap music. A whole generation had sprouted up, unaware they were trampling on the graves of their elders, raising ghosts for those still alive to remember.

The storefront window didn't mince words. A male mannequin, tits pierced, glinted with a silver chain connecting the nipples to a ring piercing a dildo set strategically between the dummy's legs. Orlando grimaced. Window displays were getting more graphic every day. Above the plate glass, crimson lettering proclaimed: "RED DEMON ON WEST STREET." Orlando pushed a door labeled No Smoking and stickered Visa and American Express.

The man and woman behind the glass counter didn't look up when he entered. The room was narrow, with a mauled couch along one wall facing the counter spanning the other. A red curtain hung in a doorway in the back. A magazine rack displayed the literature of the culture, and sample tattoos plastered the walls. Earrings and chains graced the display counter.

The woman's blond hair, shaved to a quarter-inch length, revealed tropical fish tattoos swimming on her scalp. The rainbow colors seemed to glow. Countless earrings speckled her ears, caught light, hung like miniature wind chimes. A stud protruded from her lower lip and needles emerged from her forehead. Orlando couldn't tell exactly how they were grounded, but the area looked a little inflamed. It bothered him to look, and he found himself turning to the man. His brown hair was artfully streaked with blond, and he had a diamond in his ear and a ring in his nose. They studied order forms on the counter. Orlando cleared his throat.

The man didn't look up. "Can I help you?" His tone was peremptory.

"I need information." Orlando reached for his badge.

"Don't bother with that." The man wasn't more than twenty-five. He glanced at Orlando, then went back to his paperwork. "I know a cop when I smell one. Or a journalist. They call, or come in, wanting to understand the *phenomenon* of piercing and tattooing. For their tacky tabloid stories."

"You have to admit a lot of people are doing it now. That makes it news."

The woman opened her mouth. Her tongue was pierced with a silver bob. "It's always been popular, piercing and body art. But now it's coming out of the closet. We're growing like crazy."

"Maybe you can help me," Orlando said. He couldn't help averting his gaze from the woman's forehead. It hurt in his gut to look.

The man extended a long finger toward the rack. "Buy one of the magazines. That's what I tell the clowns from the newspapers. If another person asks me *why*, I think I'm going to commit murder."

"That's what I'm here about. You know about the murders?"

"They screamed at me from every newsstand this morning. But all I know about them is that it hasn't hurt business. Excuse me for a sec." He disappeared behind the red curtain.

The woman gave him an apologetic smile, and Orlando saw that, despite the hardware, she was pretty. "Don't mind Peter," she said. "He gets like that. I'll help you if I can."

"I need to know more. Understanding why people do it, what it means to them, may make the difference in solving this case. Is it political to you, just a fashion, what?"

The woman blinked. "It's not even that. I just do it because I like it. I think it's neat, like, getting back to your primitive nature, you know?" She pondered for a moment. "For other people, it depends. I do the piercing here, and my clients are a mixed bag. The straight men get a nipple pierced for decoration. They don't see anything sexual in it. Gay men, they do it for sexual stimulation purposes. They like to tug on the ring during sex. The only thing I draw the line at is when people come back again and again to have the same spot pierced. It took me a while to figure out what was getting them off." She seemed suddenly indignant. "I'm a professional. I take this business very seriously, and I'm not catering to anyone playing games with me. I can tell a lot about a person by what he or she wants here." She stopped and analyzed Orlando. "You know, I have the perfect tattoo for you." Her finger landed on a tattoo on the wall. "This is perfect for a cop, kind of fascist. Shows power. It circles your biceps." She pointed to a heavy link chain, black with blue highlights.

"I'll consider it." Orlando dug into his jacket pocket and laid two photos on the counter. "You recognize these men?"

Her hand went to her throat and she let out a

little gasp. "Are these dead people?" Tiny gold rings clung to each knuckle.

"Sorry," Orlando said. "I should have warned you." In one of the cases, photographs of the victim while alive had not been available. In the second case, pictures provided by the family—a straitlaced college student with bangs—held little resemblance to the goateed, shaved-headed, sideburned, tattooed victim Orlando had encountered.

She didn't look again at the pictures, and she didn't touch them. Her voice had risen to a higher pitch, taken on a strained quality. "Jimmy came here. I did his piercing. He came several times. I remember him because he was so funny, so nice. He hadn't been here in, oh, a month, I guess. The other, I'm not sure. We get so many people coming in."

Orlando handed her a card with his office and home phone in case she remembered anything else. "You keep records? Maybe with your clients' names?"

Peter slipped from behind the curtain and carried a black box filled with earrings to the counter. "We're a business, not a counseling service," he said shortly. "We don't ask for people's names when they buy an earring from us." He drew open a door in the counter and began transferring the jewelry from the box to the display case. He avoided the photos.

"I see you take credit cards." Orlando gestured to the stickers in the door window. "Don't you keep your copy of the receipt?"

"Yes. And they are available for snoopy cops

to peruse. As long as they come armed with a search warrant. You got one?"

"Young men are dying. Do you really want me to waste the time getting one?"

The red curtain billowed, then a thin and pale teen, close-cropped head tied with a red kerchief, loops in his ears, emerged. He walked as if he'd just received a shot, and not in the arm. He grinned sheepishly at the woman behind the counter. "Bye, Tisha, see you soon." He hobbled his way out the door.

Tisha fought a grin. "Butt tattoo," she explained, pointing to a coiled snake on the wall. "I warned him not to do it all at once."

A hairy hand drew back the curtain, and a grizzly of a man peered out. He had the wild beard of an Old Testament preacher, thick and black. His eyes were black, too, eyes that swallowed light and kept no prisoners. He looked like he belonged on a Harley. But his voice was gentle. "You want me to stick around? No more appointments this afternoon."

Peter studied his watch. "Why don't you stay for a while? We might get some drop-ins." The grizzly disappeared. Peter added slyly, "Who knows, maybe our friend with the P.D. might get off on a tattoo."

"I just might."

Tisha brightened. "I was telling ..." She looked questioningly at the detective.

"Orlando. Detective Orlando."

"I was telling Detective Orlando how terrific he'd look in the bicep chain." Now she was getting excited. "You should see what incredible work Salamander does. He's really an artist. Most of the designs here are his originals. It's really kind of an honor, like having Michelangelo paint you! He did my fish. Aren't they wild?" She ran her fingers through her crewcut.

Peter finished with the earrings, slapping the box shut. He looked directly at Orlando and his eyes shone mockingly. "Yeah, I think you'd look great with the chain tattoo. And ya know, I think I could trust a cop who had the guts to walk through that red curtain and get some body art." Amusement played on his lips, but he didn't smile. "I think I could trust a cop like that with my records, right, Tisha?"

"Do it!" Tisha enthused. "It'll be great. Your wife will freak. She'll love it." She added reassuringly, "Don't worry, it's all safe. We're really careful. We use sterile needles; it's not like the old days."

Peter boomed, "The door to manhood—and to my records—lies behind that curtain." It was a challenge, watered down with humor, but a challenge.

Orlando wavered, then made up his mind. What the hell? He'd been complaining how old he felt. Why not try something new? Somehow, being branded struck him as a simplistic solution to his problems, but why not? He and Stewart had joked for years about doing it, and he knew Stewart would get a kick out of it.

"In the meantime, take a look at these." Orlando tapped the photographs with his finger. "Maybe it'll motivate you to care a little." He strode over and stripped back the curtain.

The little room was clinically spotless and brightly lit, with what looked like a barber's chair before a mirrored vanity. White shelves covered the walls, holding large bottles of cotton tubes and little bottles of dye. A copy machine dominated one corner, and a water cooler squatted in another.

Salamander straddled a stool, puffing a cigarette, and watched the detective. "I don't talk with cops," he grunted.

Orlando stepped into the room, snapping the curtain closed behind him. "Make an exception. I'm a client."

Salamander crushed the cigarette in a glass tray on a shelf, blew smoke out with a skeptical snarl. His hairy arms sported smears of faded blue shaped like reptiles. His belly hung and rested on his thigh. He looked to be in his mid-forties. "Back when I used to ride, there were a lot of times I almost got killed by cops. Just remember this time I'll be holding the gun."

Orlando saw the device on the vanity. More like a tiny hand-held sewing machine or an electric ink pen on steroids, but intimidating nevertheless.

"I'll keep that in mind."

Salamander rose and took Orlando's jacket, tossing it through a doorway by the water cooler and onto a chair in what was obviously a dressing room. He found what looked like a sheet of carbon paper from a pile on a shelf, and sauntered past the detective, throwing open the curtain. Squeezing behind Tisha and Peter, he outlined the chain tattoo onto the paper. When he came back, he pulled the curtain closed.

"You knew which one I wanted," Orlando said. "Are you perceptive or is this the required tattoo for cops?"

"I was listening. It's right for you. Simple, direct, classic really. Strong lines. Take off your shirt." He fed the paper into the copier in the corner. "This is a thermo-fax. We use this to transfer the image onto your arm."

Orlando laid his shirt over the back of the barber chair and settled in. He decided on his right arm. Salamander came around, said, "Raise your arm." Orlando did and the tattoo artist pressed the paper over his bicep, leaving an outline of the chain.

"Yeah, back when I used to ride I spent some long nights in jail with some mean motherfucker cops. You can relax your arm."

" 'Used to.' What happened, did your Harley insurance run too high?"

"Nah." Salamander picked up the tattoo gun, fitting in a needle from a sterile plastic pack. "I just figured I had to change my life. Too many drugs, too wild a life. The bike was just one of the things that had to go. That, or I'd end up dead. I had the Mexican mafia after me in California. So I packed my bags and I left it all behind." He put on rubber gloves, opened a jar of dye, and dipped the needle in. "I had a good name in L.A. Movie stars would come to me for their tattoos. Worked for years on Sunset. I had a real following."

The tattoo gun buzzed to life and Orlando

glanced away. It felt like a serrated knife stroking his skin. His jaw clenched.

"This is gonna hurt some, and you'll have inflammation for about a week, but nothing bad."

Second thoughts scrambled through Orlando's brain, but couldn't compete for attention with nerves yelping from his bicep. He let out a deep breath and tried to find the place he escaped to when in a dentist's chair. It didn't work. His grim expression haunted the mirror.

"Don't worry." Salamander laughed. "We only got about ninety minutes—or, say, maybe two hours to go."

"You're a real pal."

Salamander stopped, dipped, continued. "I heard your conversation with the kids out front. You're investigating the No Exit thing. Scary. I been there."

Orlando raised his eyebrow. "You don't look the industrial music type."

"Lift your arm. I'm not really. The kids drag me there now and then. I never stay long. My ears nag me to leave."

"Yours too, huh? It must be a generational thing."

"Shit, I'm a child of the sixties. My eardrums should be like leather by now. You can put your arm down for a sec." He dipped the needle in dye. "But, man, half an hour in that place and my ears are begging for mercy. Okay, raise it again."

They were silent for a minute. The only sound was the tattoo gun screaming like a barber's shears gone rabid. "No," Salamander finally said.

"I go to see the tattoos. Helps me get ideas. Sometimes I see my own babies there, and that's always a blast."

"I'd like you to see the pictures I have up front, of the murder victims. Maybe you'll recognize them. So far the only connection between them is they both went to No Exit the night they were murdered."

"If all you got is faces, I don't know if I can help you. See, a lot of people come through here. I don't get names and it's rare I'll remember a face. Those guys they mentioned in the papers, hey, I coulda done them last week, but I don't look at faces."

"Tisha said she recognized Jim Stoker. He was in here a month ago."

"Could be. You got pictures of their tattoos?"

"I have every square inch of their bodies on film."

"Bring in all you got with their tattoos. Forget the faces. I'll tell you whether they were here or not. I may not know much, but I know my designs."

By the time Salamander was done, Orlando felt a fever sweep through him and wiped a sheet of sweat off his brow.

"You did it, my man. You're no longer a virgin. But you may be needing this." Salamander found a bottle on a shelf and toppled some aspirin onto the vanity. He filled a paper cup from the cooler and set it before Orlando. "You should be okay, I don't think you'll have any infection, but call if you have any problems beyond the usual pain and agony." Pulling a red Sharps container from a cabinet under the vanity, Salamander deposited the needle.

Orlando downed the pills. They seemed too small and too few to deal with what he was feeling right now. "Gee, thanks, Salamander."

"My pleasure. Cops are my favorite people. I got a feeling this is just your first taste of body art."

Orlando rose, steadied himself, grabbed the shirt, and stepped into the front room. Tisha looked up. "Oh, like, wow, does that look fantastic! I told you Salamander was an artist. That is so *you*. Peter, isn't that just great?"

"Peachy."

Orlando had been so caught up in his frenzied nerve endings, he hadn't given the tattoo proper notice. He looked down and nodded. Yeah, it did look pretty good. He thought about tonight with Stewart, and for a moment it took the pain away. He put on the shirt and slipped a credit card onto the counter.

"About our deal," Orlando said. "I'd like to see those receipts as soon as possible."

Peter rang up the sale. "I can't believe you really did that," he said, shaking his head. But he looked grudgingly impressed. "I don't keep the receipts here. But I can get you copies by Monday, if you'll pay for the photocopying."

"I'll pay."

Salamander finished cleaning up in the back room and appeared at the curtain. "I'm off," he said.

"I'll go with you," Tisha said. "See you tonight, Peter." She came around the counter and gave Orlando a pat on the back. "Your wife's gonna love it!" Salamander handed Orlando his jacket, and he and Tisha stepped out the door, flipping the Closed sign toward the window.

"I need those records of yours tonight. Can you handle that?"

Peter handed back his card and gave him a slip to sign. "I'll be at No Exit tonight. I'll have the copies. You gonna be there?"

"I'll be there."

CHAPTER 7

Lazy trees gently shaded the brownstones on this short stretch of Charles Street bracketed by the arty boutiques of Greenwich and the grunts and wheezes of traffic on Seventh Avenue. Leafy shadows played on the red brick faces of the buildings, soothing the savagery of the late afternoon sunlight and swelter. The heat had been rising since the sun banished the storm clouds. Orlando took the stairs of a building in the middle of the block, pushed the old-fashioned door aside, and punched the button for the third floor. The brass plate for the intercom speaker was missing, a confusion of wires peeking through the hole. After a moment he was buzzed through a modern glass security door, then hiked the stairs.

The door on the third floor gaped open. The sweat on Orlando's brow suddenly cooled with conditioned air pumping from a unit plugged into a window. The living room was small, just space for a puffy beige leather couch, which had been rolled out into a bed of twisted sheets, and a TV between tall windows that looked out back. An informal dining room furnished with dark maple met the living room. There was no one here. He shut the door to hold in the cool.

"You're late, Cesar," someone yelled from the bedroom. The voice, masculine and throaty, carried remnants of a lisp.

"Yeah, you lazy bitch!" a high-pitched voice cackled.

Over the drone of the air conditioner, Orlando also heard the peck of typewriter keys. He moved down a hall toward the front of the building. It was narrow going. Gunmetal gray shelves lined one of the walls, housing cut-down cardboard boxes holding tax forms, both common and exotic. He stood in the doorway of a room that was all computers, video display terminals, and electronic gadgets. The bedroom had been transformed into an office.

A man leaned back in a wooden chair, telephone at his ear, legs crossed and resting on a desk. A stockinged foot exposed a big toe. He was dressed in faded Levi's and a T-shirt that had suffered too many washings. The man looked up. His face was open, with a round jaw, a shaggy mustache, and dark circles around his eyes that made him look like a bandit. Plugs of hair sprouting from the top of a bald head cried "hair transplant in progress." They stuck up like rows of carrot stocks springing from a desert. He put his hand over the mouthpiece. "Sorry, we thought it was someone else—intercom's been on the blink all week. I could fix it in ten minutes, but the co-op board prefers to fork over a few hundred bucks to a professional who keeps, day after day, promising he'll be here tomorrow. Be with you in a sec."

A black teenager, stringy and tall, was perched on a swivel chair, tapping away at a keyboard with machine precision. Green numbers radiated on a black screen. He looked Orlando up and down, doubtfully. "Honey, I don't think you have an appointment." He went to the desk, waved the man's feet off, and flipped through a book. His long fingers moved like poetry. "Baby, you're not in the book. Unless your name is Mrs. Miesner, and she isn't supposed to arrive for half an hour."

"You weren't expecting me." Orlando showed his badge.

The young man gaped, then his mouth puckered in a circle, and his long fingers rested demurely on his chest. He turned to the man in the chair. "Boss man, you in *big* trouble." He looked Orlando up and down again, then went back to his keyboard and began to type. Faster.

The man mumbled something into the phone and hung up. "I'm Rick Dunham." Paper began to shriek out of a printer, and he glanced over at the boy. "Maybe we should talk in the other room," he said quickly. "It's time for my break anyway. Jonathan, keep inputting those figures till I get back." He led Orlando down the hall and to the kitchen. Pots hung from a wall, and appliances crammed the counters. Dishes and glasses were piled in the rack by the sink. They still didn't look clean. It was a kitchen of utilitarian necessity, with no attempt at color or beauty.

"I guess you know why I'm here."

Dunham bent and rummaged in the refrigerator vegetable bin. "I read about Father Morant in the morning paper. It's all very sad." He set an armload of goods on the counter. "You don't mind if I have something to eat, do you? I've started a new workout program, and I have four meals a day." His arms showed the workout was working.

Orlando recalled Reilly's concoction this morning and Phillip Michaels's meager lunch. "No problem. It's going around."

"Can I offer you anything?" He observed Orlando's sweaty shirt, then assessed the detective's face. Orlando had seen that look from gay men before. Dunham's vague smile said he knew Orlando's story. "Something to drink? I have apple juice."

"That'll be fine. Looks like you have a busy office here."

Dunham poured juice from a pitcher into two spotted glasses and handed one to Orlando. "I keep busy. You should see it at tax time. This time of year, audits and accounting, isn't so bad. I keep the boys hopping March and April." The intercom by the front door coughed and sputtered. "Speaking of which ..." Dunham said, slipping past Orlando to the front door. He pressed a button.

The stairs groaned, then a handsome Latino boy appeared in the doorway, apology sketched on his face. "It wasn't me," he said. "There was smoke on the tracks. They held us forever at the station."

"You'll just have to stay twenty minutes late," Dunham said sternly, eyeing his watch. The boy nodded deferentially and disappeared down the hall. Dunham shook his head and returned to the kitchen. "You gotta be strict with them. They're really good workers, but they have to know what it's like in the real world. I spent years on Wall Street before opening this business. We can be casual here, but they've got to understand what will be expected of them."

Jonathan shrieked down the hall. "You're late, bitch," he cackled. A mumbled response. "Don't give me no excuses. I seen your picture in the papers. You was out being a little ho' last night, weren't you? The cops are here to take you away, tramp." Another mumbled response. "No, *you* do the envelopes. That's the job of the office slut."

Fine disapproval lines creased Dunham's mouth. He grunted and shook his head. Jonathan was referring to a series of prostitution exposés in one of the tabloids. The editors had decided to rid the city of the oldest known profession—a daunting task. The campaign had begun with the paper publishing photos of suspected johns cruising 42nd Street. That had brought threats of lawsuits. Now they concentrated on the hookers, but only after vice had moved in for an arrest. Children's advocacy groups cried foul when the paper printed pics of kid prostitutes. The pictures were a regular feature in the paper now.

"Where did you find these kids?"

"From the Harvey Milk School." He built a sandwich from wheat bread flecked with grain, bulging tomatoes that bled with juice when he sliced them, ruffled dark green lettuce, and shavings of turkey so thin they bordered on transparent. He cut the sandwich carefully in half, then observed Orlando again, appraisingly. "You know it?"

Orlando nodded. The Harvey Milk School had been created for gay kids who had dropped out of other schools because of harassment from students and teachers. This way they could get their diplomas in a supportive environment.

"I thought you might." The thin, knowing smile played again beneath the shaggy mustache. "After all those years in the closet on Wall Street, it's great to be openly gay. Almost all my clients are gay. I'm having the time of my life." He opened wide and took a bite of the sandwich. "I actually ended up hiring these kids because I was trying to get rid of an old television set. Someone on the gay bulletin board suggested I donate it to the school. One thing led to another and now I hire two kids a year, from August till June, when they graduate. This is the third time I've done it."

"It's terrific you do that."

"No, it's not. They're good workers and I need the help. This is no charity. It's totally a business thing." He ate with his mouth open. "These kids live over in a home they have for them in Astor Place. Some have been in trouble, some not."

Jonathan whooped from down the hall. "That's *your* job Cesarella. I'm busy."

Dunham rolled his eyes. "Jonathan was on the

street at age thirteen. His father threw him out when he found him in the bathroom decked out in his mother's Sunday best—lipstick and all. I think you can guess how he had to make his living. On the street, they push the boys to play butch or femme roles." Dunham sighed. "I'm hoping he'll outgrow it. I try to be a role model."

"Maybe he just came that way," Orlando said.

"Nobody comes that way," Dunham countered. "Compared to Jonathan, Butterfly McQueen would sound like Katharine Hepburn. You want to talk out on the deck?" A glass in one hand, a plate in the other, Dunham led the way to a windowed door covered with wrought iron. The narrow windows facing the back were also protected. Dunham obviously wanted to keep his equipment. It was cooler out back than on the street, with a breeze that tickled the leaves of a tree dominating the small yard below. Behind the foliage, sun hammered twisted chimneys and haphazard slanting roofs on the back sides of buildings from the next street. Orlando leaned on the railing and set his glass down.

"People are always amazed that I have this little oasis in my backyard. I swear, this is the last privately owned tree left in Manhattan."

"How well did you know Father Morant?"

"I knew him pretty well. We met when he was at St. Mary, here in the Village, several years back. I had grown up a Catholic, but drifted away from it in my college days." He grinned, swallowed the last bite of the sandwich half. "Actually, I went to mass because a Saturday night trick asked me to go. I never saw the guy again, but I really enjoyed the service. All those gay men. It was fun."

"It must have been a little more than that. You were president of the Manhattan chapter of Dignity when Morant was at St. Mary."

Dunham shrugged. "I go gung-ho on everything. I just did it for a year. And after a while the shine wore off." He slugged down some juice and started on the rest of the sandwich. "I don't go to mass much anymore. Just Christmas, Easter. But I still care about it deeply."

Orlando sipped his drink. Salamander's pills were beginning to wear off: his arm started to reproach him for getting the tattoo. "Herb Chiligny says Morant was gay."

Dunham waved a hand in disdain. "Oh, please. You ever read his column? That catty queen claims everyone's gay." He shrugged. "To tell the truth, I'm really not sure. We speculated about it at first. I mean, when a priest gives mass to Dignity and supports gay rights, you sort of wonder. And he was handsome. But I never saw any evidence to back it up—and believe me, I would have heard."

Orlando leaned forward. "How closely was Morant involved in gay issues?"

"As much as one can be and remain celibate. Why do you think they dragged him kicking and screaming over to Brooklyn? The pope pronounced: 'No more mass for faggots,' and they whisked Father Morant off to someplace across the East River where nobody speaks English anyway. It was a punishment, to shut him up. Those Queer Nation brats don't know what

they're talking about when they call him a
bigot."

"What was he, then?"

Dunham chose his words carefully. "He was a
. . . compromised man. He was given a choice:
shut up or leave. He chose to shut up. It wasn't
the choice I would have made, but it doesn't
make him a bigot."

A bird with a ragged caw took up residence in
the lone tree. It preached to smaller birds in the
branches below. "It's something I've always wondered," Orlando said. "Why gays stay. When I
left, it wasn't particularly political, I just wasn't
interested. I went to church because my parents
made me, and when I was old enough, I didn't
go anymore. Why stay? Why take the grief?"

Dunham stared at the water rings his glass
had left on the railing. "Because it's ours too."
He looked up, blinked thoughtfully. "Some old
man over in Italy doesn't own the Church. We
all do, it's ours. Gays love this Church. We're
not going to abandon it because of the blindness
of its leaders. I was raised a Catholic, that's what
I am, and I'm not leaving."

"What about Morant keeping mum when he
knew the identity of the No Exit Killer?"

Dark eyebrows furrowed. "It wasn't his fault.
It's impossible for people without faith to understand," Dunham said slowly, "but I felt sorry for
him. He must have been in terrible agony. What
a burden."

"Did you see him after he was transferred to
Brooklyn?"

Dunham shook his head glumly. "No, he might

as well have been sent to the moon. We thought about visiting, but we figured it would just make things more miserable for him." He fingered the crumbs left on the plate.

"So I take it you didn't join the protests."

"You kidding? Those people hate the Church. They're only interested in tearing it down. I want the Church to open its doors."

"You think that'll ever happen?"

Dunham gave a sad smile and knocked back the rest of his drink. "Maybe in about five hundred years."

CHAPTER 8

Orlando pulled his jacket off gingerly, then put it on a hanger in the front closet. Horowitz danced the piano keys on the CD player, the speakers booming, and Poindexter stood in the living room barking along. Orlando slipped off his holster and slung it over the doorknob. He was tired and hungry, and his arm throbbed with the gnawing ache of a rotten tooth, but excitement welled up in his gut. It was going to be fun surprising Stewart. A grin surged on his face with the sudden inspiration to strip off his shirt right now. As he draped the shirt on the knob, the strong smell of food wafted from the dining room. Terrific. Stewart had gone for take-out.

He buried the grin, sauntered nonchalantly to the arched doorway of the dining room, spread his arms in a "ta-dah!" gesture, then stopped in his tracks.

Stewart sat at the table in his pale blue gabardine suit, his chopsticks nimbly pinching a coil of sushi. Plates on oriental placemats were set around the table, and Japanese beer bottles were wet with droplets. An Asian man in a white shirt and black bow tie put a plate of tempura at the center of the table. Then open mouths gaped raw fish at him.

"Oh," Orlando said.

Stewart's reminder this morning of his book publication dinner swamped Orlando's mind. There was the head of the English department, Professor Maximilian Fahrglass, or as Stewart called the grumpy elderly gentleman, Maximum Fart Gas. His wife sat next to him, a gaunt and prim woman who always seemed to get specks of food sticking to her upper lip whenever she dined with Stewart and Orlando. There were other colleagues around the table from different departments, too, and a few of Stewart's students.

Stewart went red and seemed to swallow a sushi whole. "Doug, where's your—" He leaned forward, squinted. He wasn't wearing his glasses; he never did at dinners where everything interesting was close up. "Good grief, what's that thing you've got on your arm?" The chopsticks clattered on the table and a piece of sushi rolled on the floor.

Orlando looked down at his hairy chest, back at the staring crowd, then turned on his heel and strode to the front hall. Embarrassment swept through him like a flash fire, leaving a stinging heat. He heard Stewart's feet clatter on the parquet floor as he whipped on his shirt.

"Have you gone totally bonkers? Didn't you remember tonight is—" Stewart began, but his curiosity got the better of him. "Wait a sec! I gotta see this!" Stewart placed his hands on Orlando's shoulders.

"Don't touch it, Stewart. It still hurts," Orlando said crossly. "I'll show you later."

"What on *earth* made you decide to get a tattoo?"

"My fevered mind, I guess," Orlando said grimly. Thick fingers savagely buttoned his shirt.

"Well," Stewart said, his face returning to its normal color, "this may not have been the proper time for your unveiling, but I like it. It's neat." Out of the side of his mouth, he whispered, "Later, we'll have our own party."

Orlando remembered what Tisha had said at Red Demon: *It's neat, like, getting back to your primitive nature, you know?* Was that all there was to it? For Orlando, yes, but for the people devoted to this culture, he wasn't so sure.

Once Orlando was properly attired, Stewart steered him back to the dining room, took a chair from the wall, and looked for a place to squeeze it. Everyone said hello and had mercifully passed to another topic of conversation.

"Oh, I insist you sit next to me," said a forty-something woman with dark straight hair parted down the middle and ending in an inward curl at her neck. Orlando recognized her as an assistant prof in the film department, remembering only her first name, Angela. She liked to throw people off guard with her enthusiasm and audacity, but sometimes only came across as annoying.

Stewart wedged the chair between her and one of his students, and Orlando settled in. Angela offered him the platter of sushi, and he plucked a couple with chopsticks and arranged them on his plate.

"What a marvelous tattoo," she exclaimed. "You really must show us after dinner. I think they're so extraordinary. It's so, how should I say, *aboriginal*, don't you think? I have one, just a little one, on my ankle. I really do love it."

Across the table, one of Stewart's students, a young black man with a handsome face, stylish haircut zigzagged with lightning bolts, and shirt unbuttoned far enough to show shiny kinks of chest hair, grinned at Orlando. The detective had forgotten the young man's name, but knew he was one of the English undergrad groupies following Stewart around at school. "I don't have a tattoo," he said, his eyes shining. "I've got something wilder." He pulled up the right short sleeve of his shirt to reveal a brand in the shape of a Greek letter. "It's for my fraternity. Kappa Alpha Psi. It's a national all-black organization."

Angela admired the colorless, risen scar. "Lovely. I once saw a film done by one of the professors in the Anthropology department on a tribe in New Guinea. The artistry of the tattoo designs was absolutely stunning." She waved her hands. "People in all cultures around the world have had a desire to decorate themselves, from the beginning of time. It seems to be a human need." She leaned across Mrs. Fahrglass to her husband and touched his sleeve. "Come on, Max, fess up. Admit you got a big tattoo when you were in the merchant marine! Show us!"

Suddenly her smile vanished as if she recollected something terrible, and she drew her hand to her lap. An embarrassed silenced descended suddenly over the room, and Orlando caught Stewart's eyes questioningly. Stewart shook his head, scratched his sandy mustache nervously, and looked at his plate. This evening seemed to be offering more bumps than he had bargained for. Some bright person at the end of the table started up the conversation again by saluting Stewart and the publication of his book, and table talk moved smoothly after that.

As the guests were leaving and Orlando shook Maximilian Fahrglass's hand goodbye, he understood what the tense moment had been about. As the old man raised his hand and placed it in Orlando's, his sleeve pulled back to reveal small numbers in smudged blue tattooed on his wrist.

Once the guests were gone and the caterer had cleaned up and left, Stewart cuddled next to Orlando on the couch and suggested there was time before going to No Exit tonight for an unveiling of the tattoo in bed. He regarded his watch, and further intimated that there might also be time for additional activities as well.

As Stewart took a shower, Orlando went to the bedroom and pulled back the cover sheet. He lay naked on a mountain of pillows, studying his tattoo. He liked it, despite his sizzling nerves, but something disturbed him. He had always been fascinated by tattoos and piercing, and yet somehow repulsed too. Perhaps the permanence was scary, the never going back. Also, there was a dark side, an unknown, just under the surface that he couldn't quite shake off or explain away: that blurred line between pain and pleasure.

He meditated on the basis of its appeal, especially to the young, and pictured shocking countenances of the kids he had seen at No Exit. They seemed to willingly mutilate themselves, with no thought of the future. He wished he could understand them; maybe it was all a matter of where individuals decided to draw the line.

Orlando heard the shower nozzle shudder and turn off, and Stewart appeared in the doorway toweling down. Stewart let the towel drop and climbed up on the bed, straddling his thighs. He examined the tattoo closely, placing his hands gently around it.

"Does it hurt?"

"Yeah, some, but not that bad. I should take another aspirin before we go out."

"How did it feel when he was doing it?" Stewart leaned back on a pillow beside him, but he didn't take his eyes off the tattoo.

"It hurt," Orlando said. But he felt pride when he said it. It was as if he had gone through a manhood ritual and could now tell the fascinating story. It suddenly occurred to him that he had felt that same pride and excitement at the tattoo parlor, that he had crossed a line that only a minority ever steps over. And he liked it.

The warm night still held the threat of a cool edge. Orlando's leather jacket over a ragged black T-shirt and Levi's seemed right for the evening and the occasion. He unlocked the Chevy door, dumped a camera and film in the back, and slid over to unlock the passenger side. Stewart got in and set a thermos full of coffee under the seat. The Chevy coughed and rumbled to life.

Orlando geared the car and they sped down Sackett.

"Your mother called," Stewart said. "She wants you to take her to church this Sunday. She says she's afraid to go alone now."

At first Orlando felt annoyance. His mother was great, but whenever she needed anything she always depended on him or Stewart. All the maintenance in the houses she owned along the street fell on them, and he spent late nights repairing plumbing or painting bathrooms when he preferred to be with Stewart. His sister and brother, with kids of their own, had abandoned Brooklyn for Jersey and upstate New York, leaving him to contend with the demanding widow. He sighed and said, "I'll call her in the morning."

He turned left onto State Street and headed for the Brooklyn Bridge. The notion of stepping into that church again, especially after last night, didn't particularly appeal to him, and he remembered the dull masses in Latin he had suffered through as a kid, a permanent form of aversion therapy. Then it struck him that it might not be such a bad idea to check out the congregation after all. "Can I interest you in joining us?" He glanced over at Stewart.

"My Jewish intuition tells me to pass." He smiled stiffly. "But have fun."

CHAPTER 9

Orlando could hear the screams from the parking lot—frenzied, guttural shouts, like a mob attacking its prey. But he didn't react; it was just the music. He pulled the car into a space and twisted around to get the camera case from the backseat.

"There's already a new roll in it. Thirty-six exposures." He opened the case and flipped the lid off the lens. "I have ten more rolls here. That should be enough."

Stewart took the camera, looked through the viewfinder, and twisted the zoom lens into focus.

"I want to get a picture of every person who leaves this place—especially those who leave in pairs. They have to pass by here on their way out."

Two men in leather strolled by, glancing in the car on their way to the entrance around the corner.

"You're going to have to be very subtle taking the pictures because people can see in here. But if you lean back, I don't think anyone will notice." He gave Stewart a kiss and said, "Thanks, hon, I appreciate this."

Orlando shut the door and turned the corner of the squat black structure. The parking lot was still almost empty, but within a half hour cars would be double-parked and a leather-clad line would snake from the entrance around the building. The front door opened onto a dead-end alley that stank of yesterday's piss. Scaffolding topped with a crazy curl of barbed wire loomed above rusty accordion gates pulled back to reveal a heavy black door. The big-gutted doorman in a leather vest and cap nodded as Orlando passed, then recognized him as the cop who'd interrogated him the week before and looked away contemptuously.

A blond woman with harsh red lipstick and long black fingernails sat behind the counter. Her tight black dress and attitude said bored chic. "Ten bucks tonight."

"I thought it was six." Orlando reached for his wallet. The nerves in his arm jumped and he squelched a wince.

"We got a slide show, then a live band. Dr. Period's Blood Garden is playing tonight." When his face didn't register appreciation, she tossed her hair to indicate a poster of a sideburned, shirtless anorexic male flanked by three women with dyed black page-boy cuts in leather shoulder harnesses that didn't hide their breasts.

"I'll look forward to it." He handed over a twenty.

Her nails made it hard to handle the cash. She fiddled in a drawer, then gave him change and a tight smile, stamped his hand with a smeary "Fag!" and said, "Have fun."

Smoke hadn't choked the long, narrow, and
dark room yet, but it would; it was still early.
Tacked-up Hefty trash bags served as wallpaper,
billowing as people passed. A pool table stood at
the far end, a bar with stools in the center, and
a small dance floor of sticky parquet by the entrance. A steep wooden staircase, painted black,
led to a small loft with a d.j.'s booth that overlooked the dance floor. The incessant beat almost
drowned out shrieks from the hanging sound system. Orlando had come prepared. He stuffed sil-
icone plugs from a packet in his pocket into his
ears.

Leaning against the bar, he ordered a Bud-
weiser. A young bartender with a shaved head
gave him an appraising, appreciative look and
set the beer on the counter. Orlando had been
noticing that a lot lately. Younger men giving
him that look.

"It's on the house." The kid gave him a wink
and a smile of crooked teeth.

Orlando nodded, surveyed the bar. Almost
empty. A couple of middle-aged men with pool
cues lazily hit balls under a yellow light—this
scene must be repeated in almost every bar in
the country; only the rampaging music made it
seem different. Orlando glimpsed a bulky man
behind a group of leather boys, hunched over the
end of the bar, his face turned away. He could
catch only snatches of the man, but he looked
vaguely familiar. His clothes were all wrong: a
polo shirt, khakis baggy in the butt, white socks
and dress shoes. He stuck out even in a place
as eclectic as this. You didn't need to be in the

department to smell a cop. Orlando regarded his watch. It was too early for the backup men he'd requested. Well, it wouldn't be the first time Orlando had run into other cops in dark hangouts— men who wore wedding bands at the station house. These encounters usually produced a sheepish grin, embarrassed, downcast eyes, vague explanations about stumbling into the bar, and wasn't there maybe something funny going on here? He didn't need it tonight; he wasn't in the mood. Orlando looked away and swigged the Bud. He strolled to the dance floor to give the guy a chance to avoid the hassle.

A song that mimicked the ravings of a fundamentalist preacher to the banging of drums sent two leather-bikinied girls with Louise Brooks hair into a writhing frenzy on a pedestal at the edge of the dance floor; their matching dragon tattoos danced along on their wobbling midriffs. A mobile with the words "WHIP-BEAT-TOUCH-HOLD-FUCK" dangled above them. The bar began to fill—mostly men, but a lot of women. Some dressed ordinarily, others sprouted mohawks stiff and green, bangles in their noses, pierced earlobe holes stretched to hold wine bottle corks. Shaved heads glistened with sweat on the dance floor. A boy in red high heels, a black body net and black silk stockings, head shaved except for a platinum blond circle on top, climbed the pedestal and began dancing with the Louise Brooks sisters. Strobe lights cut the images into garish stills, and amyl nitrate fumes wafted by on feeble air currents stirred by a grunting air conditioner jutting out of a wall.

A battered screen that hung from the d.j.'s booth, and boasted a Coca-Cola stain resembling a malevolent amoeba, flashed slides: a young man, tarred and feathered and strapped to a post, snarled at the camera. A gleeful smile from a naked middle-aged woman with clamps on her nipples that supported lit candles. Pliers yanked an anonymous tongue. A gaunt leatherman with skin the color of old newspaper sprawled on the floor smeared with something dark brown. A close-up of a man with lips sewn together like a shrunken head. A blood-spattered woman gripping a cat-o'-nine-tails danced close with an obese man. They couldn't part: their nipples were sewn together by a complex web of threads.

Orlando turned away. It made him depressed and furious. He understood they were deliberately teasing limits, but his visceral reaction was revulsion. He had already seen too much torture investigating these murders to have tolerance for self-inflicted misery. They played around with pain and suffering as if it were a game. They danced and they laughed and they flirted with the tools of violence as though they were party toys. They mutilated themselves, then acted surprised when their diversion turned fatal.

Nobody really cares about people like that.

Orlando remembered Briggs's words and he felt angry with himself. It was so easy to divorce himself from the brutality he saw every day by blaming the victim. It happened in the department every day, a survival technique for homicide cops. The victim shouldn't have been doing that, the victim shouldn't have been there. Heaping blame on the victim always made a barbarous crime easier to take. He was beginning to think like a cop, and he didn't like it. He stared into the crowd.

"That one looks like he stuck his finger in a light socket," a familiar voice said.

Orlando turned and found Phillip Michaels standing next to him, nursing a bottle of mineral water. He wore a form-fitting T-shirt, Levi's, and cowboy boots.

"Glad you could make it." Orlando shook his hand. "Yeah, I've been wondering how people, who start out as babes only wanting a cookie from their mother, manage to develop into this." He had to shout to compete with the music.

Michaels shrugged. "Not my area of expertise. I'd guess it's an extension of the punk aesthetic, reflecting the ugly state of the world. The world is not beautiful, so why pretend? They may feel like something that just crawled out from under a rock, so they deliberately look that way."

That was far from Orlando's experience in his twenties, when few lengths had been spared to look as good as possible in the bars he frequented along Christopher Street. He recalled the gasping tight Levi's to show off vigorously toned buttocks, skin-tight T-shirts expressing every chiseled curve, and posture so stiff mannequins could have taken lessons.

Michaels swigged his mineral water and continued, "If you want to go a little deeper, I think a lot of this has come about because of the danger of AIDS hovering over this generation." He had to press close to Orlando's ear to be heard. "Re-

member, we had at least a little time of utter
spontaneity in our younger years. These kids
have grown up in the shadow of a monster. We
were the generation of sex, drugs, and rock 'n'
roll. These people don't have the sex, at least not
without anxiety. No one believes drugs are
mind-expanding anymore. What's left? Just the
music. They've taken the S&M out of the back-
room and brought it into the nightclub. They go
wild in a safe way, but still break societal taboos.
This is exhibitionism at its height—when you
think about it, all these kids have left is
exhibitionism."

Peter, Tisha, and Salamander appeared in the
entranceway, and Orlando excused himself and
threaded through the crowd toward them.

"You're not helping business wearing that
jacket," Salamander pronounced. He and Peter
were dressed in the same casual garb as this afternoon; Tisha wore layers of wrinkled black
rags dubbed the Holocaust Look. The needles
protruding from her forehead weren't so disturbing in the dark.

"Yeah, man, take off that jacket and show us
what you got," Tisha laughed. "We hear you got
some fantastic art on your bod."

Orlando smiled. "Today I learned what they
mean about suffering for art."

"No pain, no gain," Salamander said,
scratching his belly.

"You cops are all such sissies. Every cop we
tattoo is a whiner," Tisha scolded. She turned
to Salamander. "I love this song. Let's dance."

Orlando watched her lead him to the parquet

floor. Salamander danced like someone from the
sixties. Tisha writhed with the rest of the young-
sters to the shouts and sneers vibrating from the
loudspeakers, gyrating in hellish anxiety right
out of Hieronymus Bosch.

"I brought the receipts," Peter said. "They're
in a box in the trunk of my car."

"Thanks. Why don't you hand it over to me a
little later?" He wanted to watch the crowd.
"Let me know what I owe you."

Peter looked down at the sticky floor. "Forget
it. It was shitty of me to act that way. Anyway,
I didn't have time to do the copying. You're getting the originals. I really want you to catch this
guy."

Orlando placed a hand on Peter's shoulder. "I
will, I will." He said it with resolution, but he
knew already that it was probably too late to
save tonight's victim. He scrutinized the crowd,
reading faces, as if he would instinctively know
the killer once he spotted him. As his eyes
panned the room, he jolted in surprise. Anthony,
the activist from the Queer Nation protest at the
police station, leaned against the railing at the
foot of the stairs to the loft, a scowl on his face.
He was in full regalia: leather, cuffs, boots. Jeans
had replaced the cutoffs and net stockings. His
shirt announced, EVERY TENTH JESUS IS A
QUEER. Orlando made his way over to him.

"I think you and I ought to talk," Orlando said.
A line of shirtless, sweating refugees from the
dance floor jostled past them to the stairs, pushing them together.

He looked Orlando up and down. "Sure. Mind

if I hit the head first? I gotta go." His hand
pinched his crotch. Teeth bit the tip of his
tongue in a tired parody of Marilyn Monroe sala-
ciousness. "Wanna join me?"

"You go ahead. I'll wait here."

Feigned pout. Shrug. "Whatever."

Orlando put his empty beer bottle among others on a cigarette machine beside the men's room
door and waited. The music wasn't as penetrat-
ing here, but Orlando knew that despite the
plugs, his ears would be wailing all night. Two
leather boys, arm in arm, walked by. After a
minute he glanced toward the men's room doorway, then looked at his watch. He waited another minute, then stepped into the can.

It smelled like you'd expect a toilet used by
hundreds of beer drinkers to smell. One of the
urinals was taped over with newspaper and
someone stood in front of the other one. It wasn't
Anthony. The door to the single stall lay open.
So did the window inside. Orlando stuck his
head out and peered into the alley. A line had
formed at the front door and reached around the
corner. Orlando cursed and angrily pounded his
fist on the windowsill. Anthony had to go, all
right.

"I'm taking off," Tisha announced as she abandoned the dance floor after an hour, carefully
dabbing sweat from her forehead with a Kleenex
while avoiding the treacherous protruding barbs.
Peter and Salamander had long since tired and
leaned against the Hefty trash-bag walls watching her dance. "I got a nine a.m. appointment for

a perineum piercing." She winked at Orlando.
"Bet you didn't even know that part of the body
existed. Is there a gentleman who will escort me
home?"

Salamander grunted and raised his hand.
"Might as well. My eardrums are confetti. I
didn't see a single decent new tattoo tonight."
His face broke into a grin. "But I did see several
of my babies."

Tisha kissed Peter goodbye, waved to Orlando,
and pulled Salamander through the crowd
toward the door.

Orlando discovered several familiar faces bobbing in the dynamic crowd: the backups had finally arrived. They didn't do a bad job of
blending. Mostly Levi's and T-shirts. There was
Bill Shaw, a black sergeant Orlando counted as
a friend, one of the few on the force. Shaw had
turned his back on Orlando during those difficult days after his testimony, and his rejection
had been the hardest to take. Eventually the sergeant had come around and they had become
friendly again. But it had never been the same.
They joked as they used to, slapped each other's
backs, but something was missing, something
they had taken for granted before. Sometimes
trust can come only once in a relationship.

Orlando slipped through the crowd to Shaw,
who leaned against a shelf populated with empty
cans and bottles.

"Glad you're here," Orlando said.

"This is quite an experience." Shaw grinned.
"I stationed a man out front to take pictures."

"Good. That means Stewart and I can go home

and get a little rest. Good luck." Orlando laid
ear plugs from his pocket in the sergeant's hand
and winked. "Wouldn't want you to have to go
out on disability after tonight."

Making his way through the crowd, Orlando
spoke with each of the other men. But without
any real clues to the killer's identity, they could
only sit back and watch while one of the people
in this room picked up another for a night of
mutilation and murder. He spread the word that
they were to meet Saturday afternoon at headquarters. By that time they probably would have
received word of the next carnage of the No Exit
Killer.

When he passed the bar, he noticed the cop in
baggy khakis still hunched at a stool nursing a
drink. The face in the mirror reflected back to
Orlando. Briggs. He should have known. Reilly
the jokester. At least he had sent some humans
with the orangutan.

Orlando dropped into the next stool. "What
are you doing here, or do I have to ask?"

Briggs grinned an ugly grin. "You asked for
backups, right?" He tapped his glass on the
counter. Slumped shoulders and the way he
propped himself against the bar for support
showed this was definitely not his first shot of
whiskey.

"Backups, not fuckups. You look like a cop. A
cop with bad taste. And if you expect to get paid
for this evening's work, I suggest you roll off
your stool and work the crowd."

As Orlando slid off his stool, he caught a
glimpse of a dark blue blur on Briggs's ankle,

between his loose, hanging white socks and the high-water cuffs of his slacks. At first it registered as a birthmark, big and ugly, but no, the shape revealed artifice. It was a tattoo of swirled letters. A.B.? Initials? No, Briggs's first name didn't begin with an A.

Later, when Orlando asked him to hand the receipts over, Peter decided it was time to go, anyway. Orlando spotted Phillip Michaels on the loft above the dance floor and waved goodbye to him, glanced back to see Briggs had disappeared from his stool, then he and Peter strolled out to the parking lot. Peter opened the trunk of a black Toyota Celica convertible. The roof was down and a red bar clutched the steering wheel. "Yeah," Peter said. "Not the kind of car one should own in the city. It stays in the garage at my parents' place in Connecticut nine months out of the year. Then I spend my summers arguing with the insurance people over the weekly break-ins and slashings. This car has seen more roofs than an old house in cyclone country." He hoisted a cardboard box from the trunk and set it in Orlando's hands.

"Thanks."

"Just get 'em back to me when you can." He ran his fingers through his blond-streaked hair. "Oh, one more thing. Remember Jimmy Stoker? The first guy killed? Well, I sort of knew him a little. We hung out a lot. I don't know if this will help you, but he didn't go with many guys. He would come and dance, but he wouldn't go home with anyone. Unless they were really hot. I mean

really beautiful. Guys on the A list. And you
don't see much of that in this scene."

Peter slid into the driver's seat, found a key,
and jiggled the red bar until it came free in his
hands. "Good luck. I hope my records can help."
He revved the car, shoved it in reverse, and sped
to the parking lot exit. Orlando watched the Celica hover there, then shift and zip back into the
parking space.

"Why the hell am I leaving?" Peter asked. "I
ain't got laid in forever."

"Be careful." He watched Peter join the line
twisting around the corner. Peter hadn't turned
out to be such a bad guy after all, he thought.
Orlando stowed the box in the Chevy trunk. He
got into the car and looked over at Stewart, who
sipped coffee from the thermos but still looked
very sleepy.

"We can go now. Backups are all in place. You
doing okay?"

"Sure. I'm already on my sixth roll. Some people saw me, but they didn't seem to care. Probably used to voyeurs. This place makes me feel
like I'm in a time machine. A lot of the guys look
just like leather bar patrons from fifteen years
ago," Stewart said. He added a tired grin. "Except some of them have bones in their noses."

Orlando turned the ignition and pulled out of
the parking lot. Glancing back at the line waiting
to get into the bar, he felt a helpless chill run
through him. There was nothing to do now but
wait.

*   *   *

Orlando saw them from the car window, just down the block from No Exit.

Boys. They leaned against a faded brick backdrop, studied casualness in every gesture. T-shirts tight, trying to show off budding adolescent musculature. Whenever a car passed, their faces went stiff with whatever expression they were trying to sell. Tough top: not very convincing. Innocent with wide eyes: that was a laugh. Only the swishy kid in shirttails bunched in a knot at his abdomen, with short shorts that let the bottom of his pert buns peek out, seemed to convey his true self.

Briggs's shadow fell over them, a long shadow from the streetlight at the corner, and at first they thought they had a potential customer. They put on their expressions again. Then their faces fell and fear crept into the void. They'd been on the street long enough to know what Briggs was.

Orlando pulled to the curb across the street, told Stewart he'd be a minute, and climbed out of the car. He strode across cobblestones covered with patchy blacktop. What the hell was Briggs up to now?

"Show me your rubbers," Briggs demanded. "Show them to me now. All of them."

The boys meekly dug in their pockets and held plastic wrappers in outstretched hands. Hands that trembled. Briggs whipped out his wallet and extracted a two-inch needle. He grabbed each boy's wrist in turn and ran the needle through the condom wrappers.

The fleshy lips smiled and the brown eyes

shone meanly. "You're through for the night. Go home." The needle bled. So did the boys' palms. Briggs carefully wiped the needle on the swishy boy's shirt, replaced it in the wallet, and slipped it into his back pocket. Tears ran down the kids' faces. All but the swishy one. He had the look of a killer.

Orlando reached the sidewalk and gripped Briggs's shoulder. "Leave them alone."

Briggs swung around. "I'm already done here," he growled. He looked Orlando up and down. Then a knowing grin spread on his face. A wink. "They're all yours, pal." He sauntered over to his Plymouth.

The swishy kid narrowed dry eyes and set his hands on his hips. "Whatsa matter? You don't love me no more?" he called after Briggs as the car sped away. The other boys laughed, but it was a forced laugh. They stared at their bloody palms and knew what it could mean.

Orlando felt old rage burn inside; he didn't notice his hands had become big fists. "Why don't you kids call it a night?" he said gently. "Time to go home."

But he knew these kids probably had no home to go to.

Stewart was staring fixedly out the windshield when Orlando climbed back in the car. Apparently he had found a pack of stale cigarettes in the glove compartment, because he had a Marlboro dangling out of his mouth and he'd pressed the lighter in the dashboard. He usually only smoked during finals weeks, while under pressure grading exams.

Orlando pulled the car into traffic and felt silent tension between them as Stewart brought the glowing lighter to the cigarette. He didn't have to guess what this was about.

"You didn't tell me Briggs was back on the force," Stewart said finally.

"I just learned about it yesterday," Orlando answered. "I didn't want to tell you because I know how upset you get. His six-month suspension is over."

"Six months," Stewart said bitterly, expelling a plume of smoke. "Six months for killing a kid. Some justice we have in this country."

Orlando didn't tell him the suspension was for falsifying the police report, not for gunning the boy down in the back. Some things were better left unsaid. He braked at a light and flipped the turn indicator.

Stewart cracked the window for air. "Briggs is fucking crazy. I saw what he did to those hustlers. Shit, that could have been you."

Orlando didn't say anything. He couldn't contest the truth. The indicator clicked like a metronome, measuring the silence between them. The light went green, and Orlando gassed the car and swung around a corner.

Stewart looked his way. His eyes were cool blue. "You've known this since yesterday, and you pretended that everything was okay." He flicked an ash out the window and shook his head angrily. "You made a deal."

Orlando hadn't forgotten the deal. Back in the

dark days before Briggs's suspension, when harassment at the station house had been especially tough, Stewart had promised to stop nagging him to quit his job if only Orlando wouldn't shut him out. It had been easier to share his experiences with Stewart in the months of Briggs's absence, because things had gotten better. Several cops had come around, and though many would never forgive him for testifying against one of their own, he was no longer completely alone on the force. Stewart and Orlando's mother had eased their suffocating concern, and things had returned almost to normal, despite Reilly's attempts to dump the ugliest murder cases in Orlando's lap.

He didn't know why he hadn't confided in Stewart. Maybe he was afraid of his reaction; maybe he was afraid that things were going to go back to the way they used to be, both at work and at home. Whatever the reason, he acknowledged he'd been a bastard not to tell Stewart.

When they reached the Brooklyn Bridge, steel grate zinging beneath the tires, Orlando glanced tentatively over at Stewart, who studied the beam of the headlights on the bridge. "Hey," he said. "I'm sorry, I should have told you. My mistake. I won't let it happen again."

Stewart reached over and squeezed Orlando's thigh. He had that weary, sad expression on his face that Orlando had seen so often in the last two years. "You'd better not," he said. His voice was only half forgiving. "Or you'll be sleeping with Poindexter."

CHAPTER 10

A paper target, a silhouetted figured impaled by concentric circles, ran the course of the firing range on a buzzing electric track, then came to a stop and shuddered, as if it anticipated the assault to come. Orlando gripped the nickel-plated Ruger in both hands and squinted at the bull's-eye. It was an old gun, not the Smith & Wesson he carried while on duty. The handle was worn and fit his hand snugly. His father had given him this six-shooter on his sixteenth birthday, and they had spent leisurely Sundays shooting cans on his uncle's farm in upstate New York. It was just a .22 without much power, but his father told him it could kill a bear, as long as you shot him between the eyes.

The gun's smell always brought back memories of his father, an unassuming man who had never said much but left an indelible impression of integrity on his son. Orlando remembered strange things about his father, little things. The details had remained vivid in the ten years since his death while the bigger picture blurred to soft focus. He recalled the odor of grease on his father's rumpled overalls, soiled from long days at the garage, and how his mother's washing could never quite get the smell or the stains out. He remembered the scratchiness of his father's cheek when wrestling with him as a kid, and the bent tubes of oil, kept in the bathroom cabinet, that he rubbed in his hair.

His father hadn't encouraged Orlando in his choice of a career in law enforcement. Because Doug was the first in his family to finish college, his father had hopes his son would choose a profession. A mechanic who never quite got the grease from under his nails, even when in his Sunday best, he dreamed of better things for his boy. But he accepted his son's decision to join the police academy with characteristic laconic truisms: "Son, if it's what you want, do it."

No, his father had not encouraged him to become a beat cop. But his death had pushed Orlando to transfer into homicide. Salvatore Orlando's unsolved murder, over a decade ago, had been the catalyst for becoming a homicide detective. He didn't often find the job fulfilling, but it had become a part of him, something he could never extricate himself from and still be the same person. Like a war wound, both a curse and a sense of pride. And he knew he was needed on the force, a steady hand to balance the crazies like Briggs.

Orlando stroked the trigger in rapid succession, not sure whom he saw in the target's black silhouette. In the past he'd always spied the murky, featureless face of the man who had killed his father. After the abuse of those hustlers the night before, however, the form's aspect was becoming clear. This morning the figure he was pulverizing began to look more and more like Briggs.

"That's five for five, right in the heart. Who you mad at?"

Orlando looked back, pulled the sound muffler off his ears, letting it hang around his neck, and found Sergeant Bill Shaw standing behind him.

"What makes you say that?"

Shaw gave a hint of a smile. "You're up mighty early and you're shooting to kill." He planted a friendly slap on Orlando's back. His kinky hair, touched with gray, was cut short. A tweed sports jacket snugly fit his broad frame. "And you know how late we were out last night."

"Anything happen?"

"Not that I noticed. Briggs split a little before you did."

"Yeah, we had a rendezvous."

Shaw grimaced but didn't ask.

"And what about you?" Orlando asked. "I don't see you sleeping in on a Saturday morning."

The hint became a wide grin. "You know me too well. Patricia's on the warpath. Last night I went and bought a p.c. that was on sale, without consulting her. You'd think I was a wife-beater. I'm steering clear of the house, at least till to-night." Shaw pushed a button and the target made its way to them, like a sheet on an electric clothesline. "Five through the heart. Not bad for someone who ought to be asleep."

Orlando holstered his gun. He glanced down the line of men shooting at targets, sound muf-flers on their ears. They couldn't hear, but he spoke in a low tone anyway. "I need to know something. I saw something last night I didn't like, and I want to know what it means. A tattoo on a cop's ankle—I just saw it in a flash—that looked like initials. A.B."

Shaw's handsome face grew rigid. "Shit." He swallowed, then looked nervously both ways. "Forget it. Leave it alone."

Orlando leaned toward him. "It was on Briggs's ankle. Tell me. I have to know."

Shaw shook his head angrily, and his voice went corrosive. "You know, I'm one stupid motherfuckin' nigger to associate with you. You never learn, do you? Stay out of things that don't affect you. After all they put you through, you never get it in that thick skull of yours just to leave things *alone*."

Orlando grabbed the tweed collar. "Tell me. What does it mean?"

Shaw yanked away, stumbling backward. His eyes were savage. "It means if you don't leave it alone, you're fucking dead." He turned on his heels and strode past the other marksmen out of the firing range, slamming the door behind him.

Orlando stared after him, then pulled the target down. Leaving it alone wouldn't save him. Briggs wasn't going to be stopped, not this time. Somebody was going to have to die, it was only a matter of who and when. Orlando looked blankly at the ragged hole in the center of the target.

Most New Yorkers open their door only a slit to a stranger's knock, if at all. And usually with

a taut steel chain standing guard. Zachary
Barnes threw his open wide, then took up the
whole doorway with his broad, confident frame.
He crossed beefy black arms, the sleeves of a
red sweatshirt rolled up to hug enviable biceps.
Baggy shorts couldn't completely cover muscular
thighs. "Okay, what's he done this time?"

"Your son? Trevor?" Orlando asked. "You
know something I should know?" It was only ten
o'clock, but the sun beat down hard on Orlando's
shoulders, and the back of his neck felt hot. He
didn't have a chance to go for his badge.

"Look, I'm a guard at the D.A.'s office. I know
a cop when I see one." An Errol Flynn mustache
hovered above his mouth; chestnut skin shone
over high cheekbones, and his wide-set eyes
squinted in the sunlight.

"I need to talk with your son. I don't suspect
him of any crime."

"Well, you're the first cop to come here with
that line." He pushed open the screen door.
"They're always polite, and he's always guilty.
C'mon in. You should talk to his mother." He
turned and shouted into the house. "Hey,
Adrianne!"

Orlando stepped inside. It was a new town
house, one of three built in a row on a vacant
lot on Union. It wasn't as roomy as the older
apartments on the block, but it didn't have
cracked walls, creaky floors, or spitting radiators
either. A Formica bar with stools divided the
living room from a kitchen of matching avocado
appliances. The furniture, nice but a little worn
around the edges, didn't quite fit the squeaky-

clean profile of the building. The mortgage payments must be killers.

A baseball game occupied the television, staccato-voiced announcers analyzing the last play.

"I won't take long," Orlando said, glancing at the TV.

Barnes waved a dismissing hand. "No problem. It's a tape." He turned it down but not off, then motioned for Orlando to take a seat. "Trevor isn't here now. He ran off this morning, but he'll come back. Sooner or later. He always does." The voice said he'd long ago written the boy off. "What's the problem this time?"

Orlando sunk into a comfortable couch. "No problem. I just hope he might be able to answer a few questions. Since he works down at the church, I thought maybe he might have seen some of the people going to confession."

Barnes nodded, fitting his bulk into a recliner. A can of Miller and a pack of Salem sat on a lamp table beside him. "You're talking about that priest murder and the whole serial killing thing. Yeah, I read all about that. We knew Father Morant, you know. Fine thing to happen at a church. First you have these goddamned queers in there raising hell so people can't even worship in peace, and now you have a murder. My wife came home from Sunday mass scared to death. Some sick faggot killed Father Morant, I saw it on the news that they arrested him. And I'll bet it's another sick faggot doing that needle thing. What's the world coming to?" He took a gulp of the beer, made a face. "Warm," he explained.

Jumping to his feet, he bent the can in his fist. "Can I bring you one?"

Orlando's original marginal approval of the man had turned to sudden dislike, but his tone didn't change. "I'll pass this time," he said. "That's unusual, isn't it, for a black to go to a Catholic church around here?" The St. Agatha congregation was almost exclusively Italian and Latino.

Barnes grinned proudly. "My wife is an unusual woman." He drained the remains of the can in the kitchen sink, then slam-dunked it into a plastic garbage can with a swivel top that was color-coordinated with the appliances. "She's out back with the little ones. She'll be in in a sec. Let me get my beer." He pulled open the fridge, found what he wanted, yanked the tab. He seemed satisfied by what he tasted. "Trevor is not my son," he explained. It seemed important to him that he let Orlando know this. "Adrianne and I just married last year. And in every marriage you got to take the good with the bad."

Barnes came around and plopped in the recliner. "I guess you could say Trevor's been the bad. The two girls, now, they're good as gold."

"That's quite a responsibility to take on."

Barnes shrugged. "When you marry late, it comes with the territory. And I got somebody pretty special in the deal."

"You say you work for the D.A."

"Yeah. Adrianne too. She's a paralegal in Appeals. But someday she's going to be a lawyer. Takes classes nights. We're all mighty proud of her. I thank the Lord every day she's mine."

"Well, it looks like you've done very well."

Barnes eyed Orlando. "Excepting Trevor, that is. Right from the start he was trouble. Like, my first date with Adrianne, that was something else. Trevor greets me at the door, says his mom's still getting dressed. I take a seat and the kid kicks me, right in the shin."

"What did you do?"

"I kicked him right back."

Orlando wondered if the physical violence in the relationship had continued. Zachary Barnes's dislike for the boy was palpable.

"So anyway, I don't mean to bore you. I just want you to understand I didn't mean to bite your head off at the door. I'm just getting tired of the antics of that kid."

"I saw him briefly at the church. He seemed a little grim, but he wasn't kicking anybody."

"Well, he don't kick me no more neither. Once he learned who was the boss around here, he took his tough-guy routine out on the street. I've tried to reach him. We've tried to get him involved in family things, but he don't want no part of it. Won't have nothin' to do with sports. When I was a kid, I lived for baseball. Guess we should just be grateful he's stayed away from the gangs."

He stared at the TV screen for a moment, transfixed by a triple play, then fingered a cigarette from the pack on the table. "I dunno, maybe this church work will straighten him out." He scratched a match against a matchbook and the cigarette came to life. "I don't go myself. Went for a while when Adrianne and I were courting, you know, to please her. Just didn't do it for me. I was raised in the Baptist tradition, lots of hosannas and sweat. All this swinging of incense seems a little too sedate for me." Smoke curled from his cigarette and he exhaled with a sigh. "Church don't seem to do much for Trevor neither. We sent him to visit my mother in Philly during spring break. She raised six boys and none of us got into trouble except the youngest, and I got a feeling he was born bad. I thought maybe a little fire-and-brimstone preaching might scare the hellion out of the boy, but he came back as bad as ever. You can sure tell he's not my flesh and blood." He drew smoke into his lungs. "You got kids?"

Orlando shook his head. He was curious why Barnes had such a need to disassociate himself from the boy.

"Lucky. Sometimes I long for that freedom. Still, those girls, they're the sweetest things and I love them like my own. Look just like their mother. Beautiful." He took a quick swig of his beer, then pushed up from the chair. "Let me see what that woman's up to." He went to the door at the back of the kitchen, and called into the yard, "Hey, Adrianne!" Orlando followed him and they stepped outside.

Sunlight bleached the narrow backyard of color. A patch of lawn held a swing set, where a little girl sat, and behind that, rows of struggling vegetable plants clung to leaning sticks. Adrianne Barnes knelt by a tomato plant, doctoring a reluctant stake. She had a high Nefertiti forehead and short hair brushed back. Her nose was wide, and her voluptuous lips shone red with lipstick. She looked up and her eyes said worry. "Oh, God," she sighed. "What has he done now?"

Orlando entered the garden. "Nothing. I just need to find him."

"Well, when I mentioned he had to help out in the garden this morning, he made a beeline for the front door and he hasn't been back since. I guess he gets enough gardening all week long at the church." She straightened and wiped the soil from her hands on a handkerchief. "Zack, would you take the girls inside?"

One of the girls wandered between a row of plants. "Look, Mom, this one's ripe. It's red."

"No, honey. Not yet. It's still a little hard. In another week. I want you to go inside with your father, dear." She watched her husband take the girls by the hand and lead them into the house.

"Mrs. Barnes, I'm Detective Orlando, Homicide. Trevor hasn't done anything wrong. I just need to question him about whether he saw anything unusual at the church, anything that could help me in investigating these killings. Have you seen a change in him lately?"

"He hasn't been very happy since I married," she said. "Zack's a very good man, and he's tried with Trevor, he really has, but the two just lock horns." She bent, found a small shovel, and troweled the earth. "Trevor needed a real man long before Zack came into our life. He doesn't know how to react now that he's finally gotten what he's needed all along. Zack is very macho;

he thinks a boy should be involved in sports activities, and Trevor doesn't want any part of it."

The problems between Trevor and his stepfather seemed deeper than that, and Orlando wondered what Zachary Barnes found so repellent in the boy. The sun scorched his neck and he shaded his eyes with his hand. "Mrs. Barnes, have you seen any mood change in Trevor since Father Morant was killed or the serial killings began?"

Adrianne Barnes leaned on the shovel. "He's been taking Father Morant's death hard. Oh, he won't say anything to me. He has to show how tough he is. But it's tearing him apart, I know it. Trevor and Father Morant had a special bond. When the father talked, the boy listened. Last night Trevor woke the whole household screaming. When I rushed into his room, he denied he'd had a nightmare. But I know he's devastated."

Or scared, Orlando thought. The boy knew something, Orlando was positive, but what? "Have any ideas when he'll be back?"

"Come by late in the afternoon. He never stays gone long, and he never tells me where he's been."

CHAPTER 11

The Catholic Freedom Union House drooped among a row of narrow turquoise houses hitched together, a steeply pitched roof over each front door, with iron gates in the design of a spider's web. The homes had surely been charming once, but now they overlooked the dingy trestle of the elevated F train; their owners must have given up in despair and moved to more desirable digs long ago. Moss ate at the tar shingle roofs, and paint curled on the windowsills. The whole block spoke of decades of low-income rent.

Orlando rapped at the front door and saw a man approach through the dimpled window above the brass doorknob. He had long hair dyed blond and wore a loose-fitting flowered shirt. As he opened the door, the wrinkles on his face told Orlando that he was well in his forties. His blue eyes, though, were curious and young.

"Can I help you?"

Orlando extended his badge. "I'm looking for Serra Pritchard, I believe she lives here."

The man looked at the shield, then at Orlando. "Oh, she lives here. But you're going to have a hell of a time finding her." He put his hand on the door and called back into the house. "Anybody know what Serra is up to today?"

A moment later a young woman appeared in a doorway and said, "She's not going to be back till tomorrow. She's up in Albany."

Orlando reminded himself of Serra Pritchard's arrest record and the announcement by Operation Rescue that they'd be trying to close clinics in Albany that afternoon. Even though he had never met her, he could picture the feisty ex-nun swatting religious fundamentalists with her umbrella.

The man grinned. *If* she's not arrested, she'll be back tomorrow. She'll be at the kitchen."

"The kitchen?"

He explained that the house ran a soup kitchen and gave the address. Orlando scribbled on his notepad. He thanked the man and turned down the cracked cement walkway to the sidewalk. As he opened the gate, the man called after him in amused warning, "But knowing Serra, I wouldn't count on her being there."

Marie Orlando and Stewart sat at the kitchen table rummaging through the receipts Peter had handed over the night before, searching for the names of the two murder victims. Under her coffee mug Marie had placed a morning tabloid. The headline screamed of child prostitution, and the blurred faces of scantily clad girls being herded into police cars stared from under the wet circles made by the mug. At least the No Exit murders had been relegated to the back pages—no garish pictures, no interest. Orlando wished his lover wouldn't buy such trash.

Stewart looked up as Orlando settled in the chair next to him. He was still nibbling on ruga-lach and schnecken, pastries from Feldstein's, where they bought their breakfast goodies. "We found receipts with the names of the two vic-tims. Looks like Stoker was a tattoo and piercing addict," he said, and handed him the receipts.

According to the receipts examined so far, Stoker had gotten four tattoos and numerous piercings at Red Demon. No wonder Tisha and Peter had remembered him. Carter had been there for a tattoo, and the price on the receipt made it clear it had been a small one. Orlando remembered Carter's naked body'd had many tattoos, and figured he'd find more receipts bear-ing Carter's name in the box.

Marie took a break from flipping through the floppy pink pieces of paper and took a sip from her mug. "Dougie, Stewart says you'll go to church with me tomorrow." Her voice rose hope-fully at the end of the sentence. She was wearing a shapeless blue cotton flower-print dress, the style of choice for Italian neighborhood housewives since the fifties. Their working daughters followed the latest fashion trends, but it looked like the older generation would die out before they'd update their wardrobe.

"Yeah, Ma, let's get together a few minutes before ten."

"Will they be back again this Sunday?"

"Queer Nation? I doubt it. Now that Morant's dead, I don't think there'd be much point."

"He was such a nice man," Marie said, her eyes anxious. "He was always so polite." Marie Orlando put a big store in politeness. She loved renting her apartments to gay couples, who she insisted were such nice boys and took better care of her buildings than other tenants. She reached over and put her hand on Orlando's. "I feel bad sometimes: I don't like the way the church treats gay people, I don't like how they act toward women. But I don't know what to do. I've gone to church all my life, it's a part of me."

Stewart pointedly glanced up from the receipts, ran his hand through his blond hair, and said, "Don't mind me, I'm just a Jewish infidel, but you know what I think you should do."

Marie nodded and Orlando wondered if Stewart had been prodding his mother to leave the church. He couldn't see it; Marie Orlando had gone to church every Sunday from when she was a girl in Italy right up to the present. Despite his ambivalence toward the church, Orlando could never feel comfortable asking his mother to make that sacrifice.

Stewart rose and went to the fridge. "You feel like something cold? Juice, seltzer, iced tea?"

"Tea is fine." He read his watch; he'd have to go in a minute to the station house for the task-force meeting. Orlando started to file through the receipts, deciphering the scribbled signatures to see if they were familiar. Suddenly he remembered Tisha had commented the night before that the parlor had a lot of cop customers. Would he find any names from the department? It occurred to him that perhaps the killer had been a client and had been to Red Demon on the same day as the victims. Could the killer have sized up his intended victims at the tattoo parlor, then picked them up later at No Exit? Orlando would have to laboriously check dates on all the receipts to find who else had been to the parlor on the days Stoker and Carter had.

Stewart returned to the table with two glasses clinking with ice, and took another stack of receipts from the box on the floor. He sifted through them for a moment, then froze. Staring over at Orlando, he said softly, "I found another name I recognize." He slid a pink receipt across the table, and Orlando knew the name from the expression on Stewart's face.

"Briggs," Orlando said.

The newspaper clipping was taped to the open door of the lounge. Orlando had come to grab some coffee before the task-force meeting. He stopped and observed the picture of a grumpy, obese black teenage girl in handcuffs. Orlando knew the case. The young woman had been arrested earlier in the week for bringing a loaded rifle to high school and threatening other students. Under the photo, someone had written in blue ink: "I DIN DO NUFFIN WRONG. PO-LISE OUT TO GET ME. I BE FRAMED."

Orlando tore the clipping down and crumbled it in his hand. As he stepped into the room, he spotted Bill Shaw at a table, stirring a cup of steaming coffee. He nodded, filled up a styrofoam cup of his own, and walked over.

"Thanks," Shaw said broodingly. "I've been

waiting for a white cop to tear that down. It's been up since this morning."

Orlando pulled back a chair. "Maybe nobody noticed it."

"Maybe they agreed with it."

Orlando shrugged. He didn't need to explain to Shaw what it felt like to be black in the department. Minority people were expected to be cops first, and nothing else second. It didn't leave much room for fighting bigotry in the department without making yourself an outsider. He took a cube of sugar and plopped it into his cup. "So, are we on speaking terms again?"

Shaw shook his head apologetically. "Look, I'm sorry about this morning. That wasn't right of me. You just don't seem to understand that sometimes a man's got to look out for himself and his family first."

"Are you ready to tell me what Briggs's tattoo means?"

Shaw looked down at his steaming brew, tapped a plastic spoon on the edge of the cup to remove excess liquid, and set it on the table. "You're always ready to get me in trouble, aren't you?" he said, but his tone was friendly. "Well, if I gotta go, I guess this cause is good as any." He leaned closer to Orlando and his voice was a deep whisper. "There's been a rumor going around that a loose umbrella of white supremacist groups have been infiltrating police departments all over the country. These neo-Nazis were responsible for killing some liberal radio talk-show host, and I heard some were arrested recently for planning to bomb a gay bar in Seattle. They call themselves the Aryan Brotherhood, and they tattoo their ankles to show their allegiance to the group."

Shaw's revelation wasn't surprising, considering Briggs's past relations with minorities, but it made Orlando go cold inside. Briggs wasn't working alone, he was part of an organized network of like-minded fanatics.

Orlando blew on his coffee and told the sergeant what Briggs had done to the hustlers the night before. Briggs's hatred of gays, and his needle attack on those poor kids, made him a prime suspect in the No Exit murders. And now it was clear Briggs could have had help. Shaw whistled and shook his head incredulously.

Orlando grappled with the new information. How many cops had been recruited into the group? Probably not a lot, or Orlando would have heard of them before. But a few sick men in the right positions could do a lot of harm. They might just be responsible for the No Exit murders. Cops wouldn't have to pick up victims at the bar; they could bang on any door, wave a badge at a peephole, and demand any potential victim to open up. Everyone in the police department knew how to kill and cover their tracks. Then another idea struck him.

"We could have members of our task force who are a part of Briggs's group. That means any lead we get on the case goes directly to Briggs's ears. He can always stay one step ahead of us." They stared at each other over steaming cups and realized what that meant. "It means we can only trust each other."

"You're some pal," Shaw cajoled. "Always prodding me to make decisions I know I'm going to regret later."

Orlando shrugged. "What are friends for?" He glanced at his watch. "Look, we're late for the task-force meeting. I'd like you to handle it for me; there are some things I want to check out. Give the rest of the officers general info about the case, but nothing we don't want Briggs to hear. I've asked a psychiatrist to stop by who's got an idea or two about the psychological profile of the killer. Until we get word about the next murder, there isn't much for us to do but wait."

Orlando asked Shaw to follow him to his office, and handed over the box of receipts Peter had given him. He explained finding Briggs's name among the papers and suggested Shaw scan the receipts looking for other cops' names. It was possible Briggs's entire cult of hatred had been to Red Demon. He requested the sergeant cross-check the dates the victims had gone to the parlor against the days Briggs or other cops had. Orlando believed the dates would match up with some unexamined receipts.

Orlando locked his office, wished Shaw luck, and went to pick up the developed photographs Stewart and the officer stationed outside No Exit had taken. He had dropped Stewart's rolls off after going to the firing range, marking them *rush,* and assumed they would be done by now. In the hall he ran into Phillip Michaels, who grinned broadly.

"I see you chickened out and went home early. You missed the live band. It was . . ." he searched for an appropriate descriptive word and gave up, ". . . an experience."

"Sorry I missed it," Orlando said. "Look, I'm going to have to miss this meeting, but I'd like you to go over your theories with the rest of the officers. So far we haven't gotten a call about last night's victim, but I know it's coming."

"Maybe our killer has moved on," Michaels said, but he didn't look like he believed it.

Orlando considered what he'd just learned about Briggs and the Aryan Brotherhood. "Not a chance. This is only the beginning."

CHAPTER 12

The Barnes family was sitting down to dinner when Orlando arrived. All except Trevor.

"He's in the yard," Adrianne said, her face tight with strain. "With that puppy." She led him through the dining area and pointed to the back door in the kitchen.

Orlando thanked her; he had a notion he'd just walked into a family argument, and probably not the first on the subject. The little girls, already settled in chairs, stared nervously at their empty plates.

"He should be in here, eating," Zachary said from the head of the table. It was more a demand than a statement. He took a platter from the center of the table and slid fish fillets on each of the plates.

Orlando passed through the kitchen and opened the door. He paused and heard Adrianne wearily say, "You said if he didn't get that dog trained, you'd send it to the pound. And I can't make him eat if he doesn't want to. I'm doing the best I can, Zack."

"I want to know where he's getting all those things," Zachary Barnes said angrily. "A gold chain. Those things cost. I saw that goddamned earring. I know a real diamond when I see one."

As Orlando slipped out the back door, he heard Zachary continue, "It just ain't right, something's funny with that boy. It ain't right and you know it, Adrianne."

The sky had clouded up, darkening the back-yard, promising rain; dusk would come early to-night. A German shepherd bolted to the foot of the stairs, an overgrown tail wagging his entire backside, and thrust heavy paws on Orlando's chest. A long pink tongue breathed dog biscuits in the detective's face, stealing a slobbery lick. Orlando steadied himself and wiped his face.

"Veska, you get over here! You get down, right now!" Trevor stood across the yard in a green sweatshirt and jeans, shouting and waving fran-tically. Frustration creased his face. "Damn you, behave!"

Orlando gripped the coarse paws and set the dog down on all fours. Veska circled him as he crossed the lawn, yapping playfully, nipping at his heels, searching for a foothold for another assault.

"You have your job cut out for you."

Trevor yanked the choker chain, momentarily gaining control. "You retard," he scolded. "Now sit!" He dangled a biscuit above the dog's nose.

Veska panted, looked stupidly at the treat with merry eyes, tail swinging. But he didn't sit. Maybe he was deaf, or maybe he was just en-joying his last moments of savagery before the yoke of conformity settled on his shoulders.

"Sit you brainless mutherfuc—" Trevor struck

the dog's flank. Veska jumped, bounded in a circle, and let out a series of barks.

Orlando crouched, patting his knee. "Let me show you something." He collared the dog, placed one hand gently on Veska's throat as the other pushed down firmly on the dog's hind. "Sit," Orlando said in a gruff tone learned in the police academy. Veska plopped into sitting position. "Now you can give him the biscuit."

Dripping jaws shattered the biscuit, half of it falling into the grass unnoticed. Orlando straightened, brushed his hands. "You just have to do it that way, again and again. It takes patience."

Trevor tried it, and it worked. He looked thankfully at Orlando, then quickly averted his gaze. The kid had a hard time with eye contact. Maybe his dealings with Zachary Barnes made him that way. The detective wondered what in the boy's manner so enraged his stepfather. Trevor seemed like a rather ordinary, sullen teen. A possibility struck Orlando based on Zachary's obvious contempt for gays and his puzzlement over the young man's lack of interest in sports. Could Barnes suspect the boy was gay? Orlando recalled the secretive looks Trevor had given him in the ball field the day before. Had Trevor been inquisitive because he knew Orlando was a cop, or was he looking for another reason?

Orlando said, "Maybe you'll get him trained after all. Why aren't you having dinner with the rest of the family?"

Trevor shrugged, a diamond sparkling in his ear. "Not hungry." He found a brush in the grass and put it to the dog's coat.

"Your parents seemed concerned. You got to eat."

Trevor made a dismissive noise. "They don't care. And they're not my *parents*. My mom is my mom. Zack, he's not my dad. He's just someone my mom married. Don't got nothing to do with me."

"He doesn't seem like such a bad guy." Orlando tried to hide his dislike for the man, and spoke with an even voice.

"You don't know him."

Orlando couldn't argue with that. The sparring that went on between the two men in the family must make Adrianne Barnes miserable. "I missed you when I was at the church yesterday. You cut out before I had a chance to talk with you."

"They got me runnin' all over the place," he said glumly.

"Trevor, you can be honest with me. Did you leave because you were afraid to talk to me, or did Father Shea tell you to go?"

As the brush caught a snag of hair, Trevor yanked, and the dog whimpered. Trevor gripped Veska's collar and tried again. "I'm not afraid to talk to nobody."

"I suppose it's pretty unpleasant there right now, with the murder and all. That must be tough for you, knowing someone who was killed like that."

No response. Trevor hadn't looked at him twice in the entire conversation.

"You liked Father Morant, didn't you?"

"He was okay."

"Trevor, if you saw something related to these murders, you can tell me. Don't be afraid. I'm here to help."

Something akin to fear flickered on Trevor's face as he glanced up at the detective, then it was swallowed up by the dour mask the boy wore. "I didn't see nothin'."

"Do you remember what any of the people who went to confession in the last few weeks looked like?"

"A lot of people go around there. It's a church."

"Maybe someone out of the ordinary, an unfamiliar face?" Orlando sighed. He didn't want to say it, but the boy had to know, for his own safety. "Trevor, I want you to understand something, and I'm not doing it to frighten you. Don't you understand that if the killer of those gay men saw you around the church when he went to confession, he might see you as a threat? Even though you may not be able to identify him, you probably saw him. That's going to make the killer very nervous."

"I don't notice stuff like that."

"That's not going to convince a killer. I bet you could remember if you tried." Orlando decided to take a chance. He already suspected Briggs in one series of murders, why not the Morant killing too? He couldn't come up with a motive, but he knew Briggs was destroying evidence that could lead to the priest's killer. "Did you see the policeman that came by before me on Friday morning, Detective Briggs? Big guy, short dark hair that's kind of wavy and going gray. About fifty years old."

Warily, Trevor said, "Yes."

Orlando leaned forward. "Did you ever see him before, Trevor? Around the church in the last few weeks?"

The boy stared down at the dog and said, "I don't remember seeing anybody."

Orlando tried a different approach. "Were you in the churchyard when Queer Nation had an altercation with Father Morant?"

"Alterwhat? Oh, yeah. A whole bunch of fags started yelling at him. Some of 'em was dressed pretty funny."

Orlando pictured Anthony in his come-fuck-me pumps, teaching America's children to respect homosexuality. Orlando wondered if his suspicions about the boy were correct; after all, the kid had just used a homophobic slur. Then he realized that kind of behavior wasn't uncommon among gay kids trying to disassociate themselves from their sexuality.

"Who was there? Think back. I want to know every person who saw it."

Trevor stopped brushing. He looked at Orlando thoughtfully, his fear seeming to diminish. "Nobody. There was just Father Morant, the kids he was teaching baseball, and all these faggots. One of them grabbed this baseball bat like he was going to smack Morant up-side the head, but he put it down. There wasn't nobody else there."

Orlando studied the boy. If Trevor was gay, Orlando didn't envy his predicament. With a hostile stepfather, a church that wouldn't accept him—as well as his probably negative experiences in the fire-and-brimstone Baptist church he'd attended when visiting Zachary's mother—the boy had a tough road ahead.

"I'm going to give you my card. I want you to call me if you want to talk." He scrawled on the back. "I'm putting my home phone too. If you remember anything unusual, please give me a ring. And if you ever want to just talk, I'd be glad to make the time."

Slipping the card in his back pocket, Trevor said, "I gotta walk Veska now." He attached a leash to the choker chain, and the dog pulled him to the gate at the side of the house. Trevor flipped the latch, and before the dog dragged him away, he turned and said quietly, "I'll call if I think of anything."

Orlando hoped Trevor would, but he doubted it, which it made him very sad.

CHAPTER 13

The poster on the streetlight proclaimed "ABSO-LUTELY QUEER" above the grainy photograph of a recent Academy Award winner. Below, in smaller letters: *Actor. Former Disney Moppet. Oscar Winner. Fag.* Similar posters of various celebrities graced the telephone poles and street-lights down 13th Street off Seventh Avenue in the Village, like a bread crumb trail in a fairy tale leading to the community center. Orlando paused in front of the double doors to take in the building. Big, old-fashioned, it looked like a high school from another era, with a facade of red brick and brownstone, and long, narrow cor-niced windows to the third floor. He stepped in-side and made his way through the entry hall, furnished with tables stacked with flyers and bulletin boards announcing various activities, to the main meeting room. The combat of tense voices split the air.

Orlando leaned in the doorway, unnoticed. About fifty men and women sat in a lopsided circle of folding metal chairs on a checkered green and black tile floor dimpled with age. Most were young, but Orlando spotted a couple of gray heads. Slender Corinthian columns, unevenly placed throughout the room, partially obstructed his view. They looked like they'd been employed to fortify a sagging ceiling long after the building had been constructed. Murals on symbolic and mystical themes, painted by a variety of artists, adorned the walls. Ceiling fans whirred, each at its own pace, some gyrating as if on speed, others paddling gently. A few hung still and silent— dead or waiting to be born. None did more than push the heat around.

The woman from yesterday's protest, lean-faced, with a Dutch-boy haircut and pointed glasses set with rhinestones, had the floor. "You still haven't convinced me there's any reason for another action at that church. Morant's dead. He's not going to tell us anything. What's the point?"

"The point is," Anthony spat out, "Morant was never the problem. Our enemy is the Church, and we shouldn't stop protesting until it is as dead as he is." He slouched in a chair, arms interlocked at his chest, legs spread wide apart. He had exchanged his high heels for cloddy boots, but they didn't look any more comfortable. "If you don't want to join in with the action, Jennifer, you really don't have to. The vicious policies of the cardinal, that drag queen on Fifth Avenue, have done more to foster hatred and violence against us than the Klan."

"Then why Brooklyn and not Fifth Avenue, Anthony?" the woman said sharply. "You're trying to use this group for your personal vendettas. Thank God we never announced why we chose

St. Agatha over all the other Catholic churches in the city. And this is the last time I support an action based on your word without corroboration from the source. I can't say I really believe you even know what you're talking about."

"Believe it," Anthony hissed.

A squat woman with a low, conciliatory voice said, "I think we should examine very carefully whether we need to continue any more actions against the church in Brooklyn. This could get very heavy. We already have the press against us in this thing. I say we better wait awhile for the dust to settle."

Fingers began to snap around the room, a sign of agreement. Anthony's face went red with their betrayal. He rose and kicked back his chair. "Okay," he muttered. "Sit around and do nothing, but don't come crying to me when more people die. I gotta go take a leak." He sauntered away from the circle as the assemblage stared in silence. After he disappeared through a doorway, a gray-haired man who looked like a school teacher said, "There was a snooty article in the *Village Voice* last week that I think we should address. . . ."

Orlando pursued Anthony up worn slate stairs, the activist's footfalls pounding angrily on the next landing. The detective quickened his pace. A door swung open on the next floor, and he caught a glimpse of the back of Anthony's leather jacket slip inside. Orlando followed.

The men's room was a work of art a museum curator might admire, but he'd never be able to convince the board of directors to install one like it. It was just an old bathroom—and it smelled like it, despite an open window—with five wooden stalls and an old-fashioned, tub-like sink, but the walls made it art. Before his death, Keith Haring had splashed the upper walls with vivid line drawings of orgiastic penises in various states of carnal involvement. The room elevated elimination to the sublime.

Orlando clutched a leather shoulder and felt Anthony flinch and spin around. His arms shot up and he bounced on his knees in a fighting stance.

"Oh, it's you." He seemed almost disappointed that a fight was not in the making, and dropped his fists. But they remained fists at his side.

"You're sensitive tonight."

"When you have 'faggot' bumper-stickered on your back, you have to be."

"Then why wear it?"

The fists softened and stroked the long, tangled hair. "I can't control it," he purred. "You see, I'm just a slave to fashion."

"Well, at least you're learning. Your footgear has become more sensible since yesterday morning."

"And what, if I may be so bold to ask, do you have against stiletto heels?"

"Nothing, on Halloween."

"Every day is Halloween when you're queer. But then, you know that, don't you, Officer Closetcase?" Anthony dug into his pocket for a cigarette pack and knocked one into his palm. He found a match and flicked it into flame with a thumbnail. He inhaled deeply, then blew smoke into Orlando's face. "I've always wanted to do that to a cop. And with you, I can do it safely."

"Don't be so sure." Orlando waved an annoyed hand at the smoke.

"Aw, c'mon, Officer Butt-fuck, admit you're one of us. Cruising the bars in your Stanley Kowalski T-shirt. Are we going to have to plaster your picture all over the Village with the headline *Absolutely Queer*?"

"You're new in town. That wouldn't be news. Tell me, why did you cut out last night?"

This time Anthony shot the smoke toward the humping penises on the walls above their heads. "I was bored. The d.j. must have left all his new records at home. You got a problem with that?"

"Let's talk about your problems first. Start with the Church."

"My problem with the Catholic Church," Anthony mused. He shook his head with incredulous amusement and leaned against the white tile on the lower wall. "With a name like Orlando, you ought to know. Isn't being a parochial school survivor enough? C'mon, didn't you have your very own Sister Nosewart rapping your knuckles with a ruler or refusing to give you permission to go to the can when you just couldn't hold it? Surely you remember that terrible feeling when the piss started to run down your leg and the dark spot grew in your groin? And the shame you felt, the shame they count on to keep you in line. They shame you as a kid and they use it to control you the rest of your life."

"Not you."

Anthony dropped the cigarette and mashed it with a heavy heel. "Like I said, I'm a survivor. Mind if I take a leak?"

"Be my guest. I'll stand guard at the window." Orlando walked to a sill of chipped paint and glanced down at the street below. In the early evening darkness, the street lamps shone soft circles of light on the cracked sidewalks. Rain began to patter down gently. He'd called Stewart and told him not to hold dinner, that he would grab a burger in the Village. "You're the one who talked Queer Nation into protesting at the church, aren't you? It was on your word they staged the disruption of mass last Sunday. That means you're the informant, or you know who was."

"Not me, fella. If Morant had admitted to me he was shielding a serial killer, I would have beaten the identity of the killer out of him. No, I'm afraid your informant wasn't satisfied with your handling of the situation, so he/she/it came to me."

Orlando already knew it was a man. He remembered the muffled, distorted voice. "I need to know who the informant is." The stalls obstructed his view, and that made Orlando nervous. Anthony was a magician—he knew how to disappear. Orlando came around and pressed against the wall opposite the stalls.

"It wouldn't help you." Anthony stood over the toilet, the stall door open. "He/she/it doesn't know who the No Exit Killer is. All he/she/it knows is that Morant did. I mean really knew. Could identify the face and knew the name. But you see, catering to church superstition and dogma is more important to Catholic priests than people's lives."

"I could drag you down to the station house for a very long and unpleasant night."

Anthony glanced back at the detective. "That would be a waste of your time and mine. I gave my promise, Queer Scouts honor." He raised his hand, middle and index fingers together. "Trust me, your informant told you everything he knows."

"Except if he was really telling the truth at all."

"Oh, he/she/it was telling the truth. As a matter of fact, you couldn't come across a more reliable source." Anthony tapped his penis and zipped. "Forget the informant. Start thinking about Herb Chiligny. He's innocent, you know." Anthony stepped over to Orlando, hips swaying like a gunslinger's.

"What makes you say that?"

"You wouldn't be here otherwise." He paused and pulled at his beard. "And I was at his apartment that night."

"What did the good sister tell you about lying?"

"It's the truth." Anthony scowled. "I didn't say I was *inside* his apartment, I said I was *at* his apartment. Outside, on the street. And in the hall. I was there most of the night."

"Sure. Like Freddy in *My Fair Lady*. Maybe the sister had the right idea rapping your knuckles."

Anthony glowered. "I was there. I saw him go

in, and he never came out. I got no reason to lie."

"Except to create an alibi for yourself. What were you doing there?"

"You wouldn't understand." He stood with arms crossed.

"I'm a very understanding guy. Try me."

Anthony stared at the floor for a moment, scuffed at his cigarette butt. "I wanted to talk with him. I've been back a month and he hasn't said a word. It's like I'm not there. We go to the same meetings, sometimes we even pass on the street. He pretends I'm not there. We were lovers once. We had a great relationship and I trashed it being stupid. I got on a plane and I threw it away. We made a mistake we shouldn't have made, and I wanted to ask him Thursday night if he was willing to start again."

"That brought you back to New York."

"Pneumocystis brought me back." He fumbled for another cigarette, then laughed sourly and stuffed the pack back in the pocket of his leather jacket. "Under the circumstances, I don't think I need these." His face went somber. "I may not have too much time left, and I know who I want to spend it with. I love Herb. We fight like cats, but I love him. I hung around that night trying to get up the guts to tell him, but I just couldn't. I even got to the hallway of his apartment and stood at the door. I could hear him clanking on that old typewriter of his. He was there. He didn't kill Morant."

"You got no argument from me. Unfortunately, he was also at the church Monday afternoon wielding a baseball bat. You were there. Who saw him do it?"

Anthony tugged at his beard again, shrugged. "Just us. Us Queer Nationals, Morant, and some very surprised little kids. Nobody who would have wanted to frame him."

"Why didn't you go to the police with your alibi for Chiligny?"

"I did. Men in high heels don't have much credibility in this society. I told the guy in charge of the case. Prigg, Pricks, Piggs, Briggs, something like that. The one who tried to kill me yesterday. He wouldn't listen. Why do you think we had that demonstration?"

"Herb Chiligny says you were there for your own ego. Something about always being the center of attention."

"I've changed," he said. "I'm off the booze. I've been clean for a year this July. For the first time in my life I'm thinking clearly. I know what I want." He sauntered to the door, swung it open, looked back. "And I'm going to get Herb back before I die. Excuse me, but I've got a meeting to attend." The door swung closed in Orlando's face.

"Good luck, Anthony." But his tone didn't hold much hope.

Through the apartment door Orlando could hear the clack of typewriter keys. Not the gentle rattle of a terminal keyboard, but the heavy clanking of an old-fashioned typewriter that built the finger muscles. He gave the door a pound. There was a pause, the sound of paper being yanked from the platen, the quiet thump of a cane on carpet, then Herb Chiligny appeared at the door.

"If it isn't my favorite boy in blue," he said. His smile was tired, and he looked pale under his sunlamp-induced tan. "Come in. I was just about to make tea."

Orlando closed the door behind him and let Chiligny thump his way to the kitchen. The journalist leaned the cane against the yellow range and limped to the sink with a teakettle. The kitchen was small and bright, with a nook big enough for an antique table and two chairs. No windows. Windows are a premium in New York kitchens. "Why aren't you home on a Saturday night? If I had a husband who looks like yours, I would be."

"I'm trying to make sure you don't get sent over for the next twenty years. I see you made bail."

"The paper coughed up the money. In exchange I'm writing a hot exposé of the city jail system. The whole story of my thrilling arrest and captivity. It has everything but the obligatory rape scene. That I did not experience. I'm afraid phlegm balls were the only bodily fluid my little Puerto Rican friend in the next cell was shooting at me." He clanged the kettle on the range, twisted a knob, and blue flames jumped. "I'm also going to write another article, one that you're not going to like." His journalist eyes narrowed. "About how the police didn't bother to warn the customers of that bar of the danger. That's criminal irresponsibility."

Orlando felt suddenly defensive and his back went stiff. Because he still wasn't sure he had taken the right course. "Then you're going to have to say some very ugly things about me, because it's my investigation. The murders were all reported in the press. We just withheld the m.o. of the killings, which is not unusual and you know it."

"Yeah, but some m.o. And you failed to mention the No Exit connection. It wasn't until yesterday's paper that the public was informed. You think anybody would have gone to that bar if they knew what was going on?"

"I know they would. I was there last night," Orlando snapped. He wanted to believe it, needed to. Otherwise, those punctured faces would haunt him forever.

Chiligny raised surrendering hands. "Don't take it so personal. You're a cop, I'm a journalist. I believe in full disclosure. Don't expect us to agree on everything. I know the narrow line you have to tread. Geez, you have a murder in a hetero bar and you have a hundred witnesses. You have one in a gay bar and everyone was in the rest room. I call it the Silence of the Lambdas."

Orlando didn't have to be told. The managers of No Exit, when he finally tracked them down, had been less than helpful. 'Vague' was the best word to describe the recollections of the doorman and the bartenders. Nobody knew, nobody saw, nobody heard. Monkeys all in a row.

Chiligny searched a cupboard. "Let's see. I got Cinnamon Spice, Apple and Cinnamon, Natural Lemon, Blackberry Delight, Orange Pekoe or—"

Orlando was glad for the change in subject. "Anything's fine. You stockpiling for the deluge?"

Chiligny pursed amused lips. "One needs such *accoutrements* for those occasional—make that rare—Saturday night tricks who stay for Sunday brunch. Let's go for the Orange." Chiligny set tea bags inside the kettle and found blue mesa cups and saucers. Propping himself against the counter, he grew serious. "I didn't tell you that I appreciate your support in this. It means a lot to me that you know me well enough to realize I could never do what was done to Morant." Pause, grin. "Much as I would have liked to."

Orlando settled in an antique chair that creaked under his weight. "Considering he died of a gunshot wound, a frame-up with the baseball bat seems pretty obvious. Besides, you have a witness to your alibi."

Chiligny frowned. "But I was alone. All night long. Tapping away on my old Smith-Corona." The used typewriter his parents had given him at sixteen.

"A little fairy was watching over you. One in high heels and a scraggly beard."

"You got to be kidding."

Orlando shrugged. "That's what he told me. He was playing Romeo to your Juliet, if only you'd looked out on your balcony."

Lines appeared between his brows as Chiligny poured steaming tea into the cups. "Let's go into the living room where it's more comfortable. Will you carry the cups?" Chiligny caned his way to a stiff white couch while Orlando followed and set the teacups on an oval glass coffee table. The ceiling was studded with track lighting that focused on framed movie posters. The posters leaned heavily toward Crawford and Davis during their scream queen years. Bad movies, good posters. A wall of shelves housed a library of videos—more than three thousand, Chiligny had once said. A big desk huddled in the corner by the door held an old black typewriter. Chiligny eased himself down and Orlando sat beside him.

"Why in heaven would Anthony do that?"

Orlando handed him a cup and saucer. "He says he loves you and wants you back. He says he's changed. He's off the booze for good."

Chiligny blew at his tea and looked skeptical. "Don't believe it. I know Anthony. I know him better than anybody on this planet. That queen is the Joan Crawford of the gay set. A total mess."

"Any idea what made him that way? I couldn't get a straight answer when I asked him about his relationship with the Church."

"He has every reason to hate the Church, but Anthony takes everything to operatic excess. He can't get over the past or focus on the real issues."

"Which are?"

Chiligny's eyes hardened as he prepared his mental list. "The Catholic Church has a history of oppression against gays." He took a sip of tea. "Oh, I should have asked. Do you want sugar? I don't usually have anything with my tea, and I always forget others don't have my problem."

Orlando rose. "I'll get it."

"No, no, I can manage." Chiligny struggled up and limped to the kitchen. "I need the exercise anyway. At least that's what the doctors I rarely listen to say." He came back with a honey bear and spoons and set them on the table. "Honey's better for you; I think I'll have a taste myself." He squirted in both cups. Spoons clinked. "Where was I? Oh, our friend the Catholic Church. Well, should I go back to the Church's early days and talk about stoning, castration, and burning at the stake, or would you prefer contemporary issues?"

"Let's narrow it to the present."

Chiligny settled back into the couch. He sounded like he was reading from his column, "Chiligny Maligns," clippings of which hung framed on the walls. "The Church campaigned for years against the Gay Rights Bill. The official position of the Church is that many people are *born* gay, but they want to make it legal to fire people from their jobs and throw people out of their homes because of the way they're born. They have worked actively to keep sodomy laws on the books. They want to put us in prison for having sex they don't want us to have. In short, they want to take away our lives and replace them with lives they have chosen for us."

Chiligny took another sip of tea as his cheeks took on color. Orlando had seen him like this before. He was getting into it and there was no stopping him. "Gay bashing has skyrocketed in recent years. What does Cardinal O'Connor say to that? He announces 'People shouldn't be surprised when a morally offensive life-style is physically attacked.' And so the baseball bats continue to swing with the sanction of the Church. They've lobbied against sex education so that more teens can die of AIDS. They've fought against support services to help gay teens despite the fact that thirty percent of the teen suicides in this country are gay kids. And it's not just a gay thing. That Church believes if a thirteen-year-old girl is gang-raped at gunpoint, she should be forced by law to have her rapist's baby. That's the kind of barbarians we're dealing with. Their whole focus in life is on other people's dicks and asses and uteruses. If Catholics want to follow the dictates of their Church, that's fine, but we're getting tired of them trying to force the rest of us to be good Catholics.'' The tea had cooled, but Chiligny was steaming. "Sorry,'' he said sheepishly. "Politics makes me humorless.''

"That's all right. I think you just wrote yourself next Wednesday's column. What makes you think your attitudes are so different from Anthony's?''

"I want the Church off our backs. I want them to stop trying to legislate their religious beliefs. Anthony, he won't be happy till every last Catholic church in every last backwater is razed to the ground. Call it a grudge.''

"You were with him for a long time. Ever figure out why?''

"He told me. Frequently. You could say it tainted his whole life.'' Chiligny set his cup on the coffee table and spread his hands wide. "Picture Anthony an innocent twelve-year-old. I know it's hard, but use your imagination. Picture him as an altar boy. Picture his proud parents in the congregation. Picture the local priest tickling little Anthony's pickle and queering his rear every Sunday morn. Get the picture? Anthony told his parents and they went to the priest's superior. Suddenly the priest had been transferred to another congregation in another country, where he no doubt raped and pillaged every boy he could get his hands on until they moved him again and again. It's called the geography cure—when a priest molests a child, keep it quiet and move him to a new parish."

"His parents didn't go to the police?"

"Deep down, I think they blamed Anthony. You know, thought he must have done something to cause it to happen." Chiligny took up his tea again. "We're talking the dark ages of sensitivity to rape and molestation victims. Back in those days, you didn't get booked on *Geraldo* and sue the Church for a million bucks. You kept the shame hidden; you shut up for the good of the Church. That's what Anthony's parents did. They were good little Catholics, and they let a child molester get away with abusing their only son because the priest told them the Church was a fragile thing and couldn't withstand the scandal. Anthony hated his parents for that. He never forgave them. They live right in Brooklyn and he hasn't spoken to them in twenty years. That's why Anthony hates the Church, and when I come to think of it, I can't blame the poor guy." He slammed his cup on the table and tea sloshed onto the saucer.

"Do I detect a sympathetic crack in your armor? Why not talk to the guy? See what he has to say." Orlando grinned. "To tell the truth, you two are made for each other."

"A yenta you're definitely not." Chiligny crossed his arms, then became thoughtful. "But you know, after all these years, I don't think a day's gone by that I haven't thought about him and missed being held by him. We had something very special, despite all the fights. Who knows, maybe because we were so close we had to fight. He certainly was great sex. The problem was what came after." He sighed humorously. "I guess you could say I lost everything in the post-coital depression. I dunno. I think I've given up on relationships. They never work. Put me in a room with another person, the result is grief. For me. How do you do it? You and Stewart have been together forever."

Orlando shrugged. "I guess we just work things out."

"Yeah," Chiligny said dreamily, "I loved him, I just couldn't take the grief."

Orlando guessed, despite the harsh criticism, Chiligny still loved Anthony. Clearly he had known Anthony was the one who had alerted the rest of Queer Nation that an informant had revealed Morant knew who the killer was. Yet Chiligny hadn't told Orlando that when they'd spoken at the jail cell. Chiligny loved his ex, perhaps hated him a little, but above all wanted to protect him. "Come again?"

"He was fucking around behind my back every chance he got. And I'm not talking about the days when it was 'in' to have an open relationship. This was *after* we knew about AIDS. That last fight we had, at the political meeting, it was really over his wandering dick. He swore to me that night that he wouldn't trick out anymore, that he wanted to start over, but ..." Chiligny stared down at his teacup with regret. "The next morning he was on a plane to San Francisco."

"You couldn't forgive him?"

He looked up, and his doe eyes were sad. "Would you have?"

Orlando wasn't sure how he would react if Stewart was unfaithful to him. But he knew he'd never want to be without him. "If you still love him," Orlando said, "I'd at least agree to coffee."

CHAPTER 14

When Orlando put his key in the front door, he heard the telephone ringing. Once inside, he ran to the phone on the table by the easy chair and grabbed the receiver. The apartment was quiet and dark, except for the light in the front hallway. Stewart must be out with Poindexter, he thought.

The voice on the line was hysterical. It took Orlando only a moment to recognize the sobs were Tisha's. "Oh, God, oh, God," she kept saying.

"Tisha, this is Detective Orlando. I want you to take a deep breath, then tell me what's happening." He heard a muffled whimper, as if she were strangling a wail with her hand. "He's dead," she gasped out. "Oh, God, please come, Detective Orlando. For God's sakes, please come." Through tears she told him the address and he scribbled it on a pad by the phone.

He didn't have to ask whose address it was.

A glass coffee table inches from the floor fronted a stylish low-lying beige couch threaded with parallel gold stripes running its length.

Oversized art books lay flat on the table to smooth conversation. Potted vines crept around squat lamps on each side of the couch on teak wood tables with stunted legs. Primitive masks bearing long lips and slanted eyes hung low on the walls. Rain pelted the black windows, pastel blinds open, at an angle. Everything in the room accentuated the horizontal.

Even the naked body lying on the carpet.

Only the needles protruding from all angles spoiled the motif. But that wasn't the decorator's fault. Orlando stooped over the corpse, observing every detail, but trying not to see. It hurt that much. For the third time in as many weeks he didn't have to close his eyes to see the needles. Here they were, in the flesh. In Peter's pale, firm flesh. Mocking, hateful. And he'd been powerless to stop it. The boy's face looked like a tortured Christ, eyes puzzled, asking why he had been forsaken. Orlando turned his head away.

An ugly thought haunted him. Was this another random killing, a pickup like the others, a meaningless murder whose symbolism was clear only to the killer? Or was the No Exit Killer running scared? Had he seen Orlando with Peter last night and been threatened? By what? What could Peter have known that he hadn't told him?

Tisha crouched in a ball on the sofa in the alcove, head down, legs tucked under her, arms hugging her purse as a child embraces a doll. She rocked back and forth, sniffling. Salamander sat next to her; he gently touched her shoulder, but she cringed and he pulled away. He looked helpless in dirty overalls that couldn't hide his big belly. His gruffness of Friday afternoon was gone. The big man's eyes held the sorrow of a madonna in a Byzantine mosaic. He blinked hard and clenched his jaw to hold back tears.

Orlando walked across the carpet to the open alcove. He felt relief just being out of the same room as the body. "Forensics will be here soon. It's best we talk now and get you home before they come."

Tisha nodded but didn't look up. Despite the rings piercing her knuckles, she wiped a tear away with the back of her hand.

"How did you find him, Tisha?" Orlando said it slowly, soothingly, deep-voiced, like music. He wasn't sure she could hold it together, and he didn't need a breakdown—not with what he was feeling now.

She looked up, but she didn't stop rocking. Her cheeks were stained red. "I have a key. He was supposed to drop by my apartment tonight. We had invitations to the opening of a new dance bar. When he didn't answer my calls, I got worried and came over and used my key."

"When did you last see him alive?"

Her lips puckered and her eyes narrowed, brimming. "With you!" she burst out. Now the tears overflowed and ran down her face. "Last night," she added, "at No Exit." She averted her gaze from the body in the next room, resting her eyes on Peter's jumble of clothes on the rug. Black Levi's, black T-shirt. The clothes he had worn last night to the bar.

"Wasn't he supposed to work at the shop today?"

She shook her head but couldn't speak, her features twisted misery. In her black rags Tisha looked like a waif out of Dickens.

"He doesn't work on Saturdays," Salamander said dully. He grimaced. "Didn't."

"You two arrived together?" Orlando slipped a notepad from his jacket.

Tisha's expression went apprehensive. "I couldn't be alone here. I phoned Salamander after I called you." Her voice wobbled like a top spinning out of balance. "Was that okay?"

No, it wasn't, but he couldn't blame her. The more people bumbling around, the less pristine the crime scene. "Did you touch anything?"

Tisha shook her head quickly. Salamander placed his big hand on her shoulder again, like a big brother, and this time she didn't flinch. "You must have, Tisha. The front doorknob. The telephone." He said it with the tenderness of someone reminding an Alzheimer's victim of a forgotten fragment of the past.

"Yes . . . yes, I touched the door when I came in, and the phone." She stared, eyes unfocused, at the telephone.

"Tish called me, frantic," Salamander explained. "I live just three blocks down. I found her huddled here, on the sofa." He looked appraisingly at her, leaned forward, and said to Orlando, "Can I take her home soon?"

"In a minute." Orlando wanted her out of the apartment, and quick. He wasn't afraid she would touch anything else. He was afraid of the gut-wrenching knot contorting his stomach every time he looked at her. And the steadily building anger that had no vent. He quickly searched the rest of the crime scene. Decorator kitchen, decorator bath. Dishes done, towels hanging neatly. Glinting gold faucets in the sink and the tub. Nothing to indicate the killer had been here. He stopped in the bedroom doorway. The bed was made, but that was about all that wasn't a mess. Drawers yanked from the bureau, tossed about the room. Clothes heaped. The bedroom had served as an office too; green metal files and a high-tech black-and-chrome desk filled one wall. All drawers ripped out, papers everywhere. Ripped, crumpled. The detritus of a frantic search. For what?

Orlando tugged his mustache, pondered. No other crime scene had suffered this violation. This time the killer had been looking for something. The receipts Peter had given the detective the night before? That would fit his theory that the killer had been a customer at Red Demon and wanted to destroy the receipts to hide any connection with the victims. That meant the killer's name was somewhere in all those receipts, and Orlando already had a prime suspect. But how could he prove it? Briggs and his cohorts would be too clever to leave any evidence.

Orlando returned to the living room. "Tisha, I know this is hard. But I need you to ask you a few more questions." He remembered Briggs had left before Peter. But, of course, Briggs didn't have to use sexual attraction to get in any door. He had a badge. Orlando decided to cover all bases. "What kind of man would Peter have gone home with?"

She looked up and her lips were puffy and red, like someone had bitten them. "The same kind of guy I like. Hot men, nice bods. He liked successful guys, that turned him on. He liked guys with originality, just like him, maybe a tattoo, pierced some but not a real lot—" She stopped, looked at the punctured body on the carpet, and her face dissolved.

Salamander looked away. "I think he usually went for the strikingly handsome type." He watched Orlando for a moment. "You were there. Didn't you see who he was with?" His eyes, black pools, were accusing.

"He went back in after I left." The words seemed feeble and his failure weighed heavy. He swallowed hard.

Tisha poked in her black leather purse and found a Kleenex. She blew, looked up, blinked. "He was picky, really picky. They had to be something or he wouldn't waste his time."

Orlando went into the living room and examined the pile of Peter's clothes by the body. As Orlando pulled a black wallet from the back pocket, a scrap of paper fluttered to the carpet. He put down the jeans and bent to pick it up. It was a telephone number of the precinct house, and an extension. Orlando knew it. His lip tightened.

It was Briggs's.

"Uh," Tisha moaned from the alcove, feeling her stomach. "I think I may be sick."

"Go ahead, take her home," Orlando said. "We'll need you both to come down to the station house tomorrow to give your prints." Salamander nodded, took her elbow, and ushered her out the front door and onto the landing. He paused, then came back. He gazed at the body impassively, then at Orlando still crouched on the floor.

Salamander looked both ways, as if he didn't know how to say what he wanted to say. "I didn't know Peter that long. He was more a boss to me than a friend. But he was okay. He was fair." Then he trembled, his face went savage and his fists flailed. "I want you to nail the bastard who did this. I want you to nail this guy's balls." His voice boomed and he looked like a thundering Old Testament prophet. "And then I want you to give him to me."

"I'll nail him," Orlando said.

He tightened his grip on the slip of paper in his hand.

Orlando battered the door with his fist, an angry echo resounding through Briggs's house. Despite his stinging hand, he kept pounding until locks unbolted and the door parted a crack. Briggs stood in the threshold, a density of shadows in the dark living room. Only the dim yellow flame from the light post in the cement yard revealed that he'd thrown on trousers, belt still unbuckled, and wore a wrinkled white T-shirt. The door fell open farther and Briggs stepped forward.

"Yeah?" Briggs looked like a badger awakened from a deep sleep.

Orlando held the scrap of paper in Briggs's

face. "What the hell is your connection with Peter Nelson?"

Briggs squinted at the paper, as if he needed reading glasses. "Peter . . .?" he said stupidly. Then, "Oh."

"Yeah, oh," Orlando said. "He was murdered last night after leaving No Exit. He looks like a human bed of nails. I found this in his pocket. You got some explaining to do."

Briggs's mouth dropped open, then he pulled his face up tight. "I got nothing to say to you. Go home, Orlando. You've already woke up me and my wife. Don't do it again." As he pressed the door closed, Orlando charged with all his weight. His tattooed arm screamed as his shoulder assaulted heavy oak. The door gave way and Briggs stumbled backward into darkness. When he regained his balance, he strode forward brandishing a .38 from his back pocket. In a flash he had the barrel rammed in Orlando's nose and a grip on his ear.

"Nice and easy," Briggs cooed as he yanked Orlando into the yard and kicked him down on all fours. Briggs pounced on top of him, and cement, wet with rain, greeted Orlando's face with a gritty kiss. He tasted blood. The pistol barrel toyed with his ear.

"While I have your attention, let's set some ground rules," Briggs said, his breathing labored. "Don't ever come to my home again. Next time I'll kill you. Stay the fuck out of my way and stop prying in my cases. I'll be dropping by St. Agatha on Monday morning to tell Father Shea that Father Morant's killer, Herb Chiligny, was set free on bail and he'd better be careful. I don't want to see your ugly face in that church ever again, so make sure you're out of the neighborhood. Still listening?" He ground Orlando's face into the cement. "You still awake, pal? I hope you are, 'cause I got news for you. I didn't have shit to do with that kid's death. He runs a tattoo place. I know 'cause I been there. I wanted a quote on a custom-made tattoo for some friends, and he said he'd call me. So don't try dragging me into this case, I got nothing to do with it." Briggs paused for a moment, as if he was mulling something over, then chuckled. "But I do have something for you to think about." He seemed to wrangle with something in his back pocket, then Orlando felt his face slam-dunked again into the cement as a sharp pain pierced his lower back.

Briggs stood up and sauntered to his front door. "If you must drop by in the future, please be so kind as to call first," he said, smirking. The door slammed and bolts slid into place.

Orlando lay still a full minute, then propped himself up on shaky hands. He staggered to the Chevy, slumping against it as he unlocked the door. Slipping behind the wheel, he realized that he no longer had the piece of paper. Not a shred of proof to connect Briggs to Peter. He cursed himself; he'd let his hatred of Briggs get in the way of solid police procedure. As he leaned back in the seat, he jumped and winced. A sharp pain radiated from his back. Reaching around, he felt for its source. His fingers touched a cold, narrow shaft of steel.

There was a two-inch needle in his back.

*   *   *

It was late when Orlando arrived home, but Stewart was still up, settled in the easy chair, staring at the floor. Poindexter lay curled at his feet on the carpet. Stewart looked up hopefully as Orlando closed the front door and stowed his jacket in the hall closet. Stewart's glasses lay on the lamp table beside the chair; he looked tired and worried.

"Geez," Stewart exclaimed as he put on his glasses, rising from the chair. "What happened?"

"Briggs and I danced cheek to cheek. He hadn't shaved."

Stewart blurted, "You've got to get out—" He caught himself and mumbled a despairing apology.

Shaking his head, Orlando said, "It's all right, Stewart. You don't have to censor your opinions. You think I ought to get the hell out of police work now that Briggs is back, and you're probably right." He flopped on the couch, exhausted. He ached like he'd had the shit beaten out of him, and come to think of it, he had. Stewart sat beside him.

Orlando told his lover what had happened since they last spoke, and Stewart, remembering Peter from spotting him and Orlando together in the parking lot the night before, went pale. When Orlando recounted his adventure with Briggs, the color came back to Stewart's cheeks.

"Next time you go up against Briggs," he said fiercely, "I'm going to be there. Don't try to stop me. From now on, include me in." Stewart rose from the couch. "You're bleeding," he said, his voice quiet now. "I'll get something to clean you up." He went to the bathroom and Orlando heard water running. Poindexter struggled to his feet and moseyed over, resting his nose on Orlando's knee. He affectionately wrestled with the dog's floppy ears, then pushed him away when Stewart returned with towels and a bottle of rubbing alcohol.

"Let's see," Stewart said, sitting beside him. "I think this may hurt a little." He gently rubbed a soapy hand towel on the abrasions on Orlando's face, then followed with a clean, wet towel. Stewart frowned. "It looks like you've got grit in the cuts." Orlando wasn't surprised—he recalled staring into the pavement. Then Stewart applied the alcohol.

Orlando winced. "Ouch," he said.

Stewart splashed more alcohol on a hand towel. "Get used to it, I'm just beginning. You're going to have scabs on your nose and chin tomorrow." Applying the towel again, he said, "Bill Shaw called. He went through all the receipts, but he didn't spot any other familiar names."

Orlando clamped his teeth down as his nose and chin stung and burned. The pungent smell of alcohol got to him, and he leaned back for a breather, holding up his hand for Stewart to stop. "I got the idea tonight Briggs was just planning to send his friends to Red Demon."

"Another thing," Stewart said, coming at him again. "The dates are all wrong. Carter went to Red Demon a week after Briggs's only visit. Stoker missed him by a month."

That was disappointing, but it didn't clear

Briggs. "That leaves us without a paper trail, but he could have visited the parlor other times and bought with cash." Tisha or Salamander might remember if Briggs had been to the parlor more than once. He would have to scrape up a picture of Briggs to see if they recognized him. It was unlikely, though, that they would recall dates.

When Orlando and Stewart made it to bed, they didn't sleep. The plate of pastries from Feldstein's lay between, the cellophane pulled back, and they nibbled as they worked. Orlando handed Stewart half the packages of developed photographs he'd picked up earlier at the station house. They went through them, searching for a picture of Peter leaving No Exit. Who had he gone home with?

Orlando flipped quickly, occasionally recognizing the faces of the cops who had been at the bar last night, and also some of the more outrageous characters whose getups he wouldn't soon forget. Here was Phillip Michaels strolling from the bar, hands in his pockets, by himself. Eventually, Stewart found the photo they were looking for and stared at it, puzzled. He handed it over to Orlando.

"Peter left alone," Stewart said.

CHAPTER 15

Clouds still ruled the sky early Sunday morning, but the brightness of the day predicted they'd burn off by noon. Orlando and Bill Shaw looked at each other, shrugged their shoulders, and let the knocker drop on the big white door. The terraced lawn and sculpted bushes in the yard showed impeccable care, and the huge house itself was newly painted. They'd called beforehand, requesting a meeting, and the chief of police had grudgingly agreed to a brief interview before he took his family to church.

Chief Sorensen was still in his bathrobe when he opened the front door, a speck of pancake in his white mustache. "This better be good," he said in his stentorian voice. "Sunday is my one day with my family."

They had decided earlier that Shaw would do most of the talking. His stature in the department would lend credibility to their story. Considering Orlando's standing in the P.D. popularity polls, the less he said the better. Sorensen waved them into a chandeliered entranceway with a shiny slate floor.

"This is worth your while," Shaw assured. He

explained the background of the Aryan Brotherhood and his fears that they were recruiting in
police departments around the country. Describing the tattoo initiation into the group, he mentioned that a similar tattoo had been spotted on
Briggs. Watching the sergeant, cool and articu-
late under pressure, Orlando could see why he
had gained the respect of the men in the
department.

The chief's eyes darkened as Shaw spoke, and
before the sergeant could bring up Briggs's possible connection with the No Exit murders, Sorensen raised a hand to stop him.

"Wait a minute. Is that what this is about?
You're accusing some of my officers of being
Nazis?" He loomed menacingly, rocking wrath-
fully in his stockinged feet, and Orlando could
imagine what a threatening presence he must
have seemed when he was younger and on the
beat. "You'd goddamned better have proof before you come up with an accusation like that."

Shaw and Orlando stared at each other. Orlando decided to make a try with Sorensen.
"Look, Briggs has the insignia of the organization
on his ankle. What more do you want?"

"A.B.? You call that proof? As far as you
know, those are his mother's initials."

Orlando swallowed the anger building in him,
and coerced calm into his voice. He was fed up
with department leaders who dug trenches at
any criticism of an officer. "I witnessed him
using needles to harass male prostitutes, and his
phone number was in the pocket of the latest No
Exit victim. We have a possible conspiracy of

Nazis killing gay men in this city, and we need your help to root it out."

Sorensen nodded as if he just now understood. "I know who you are. You're the one who testified against Briggs a couple of years back. You claimed he was unjustified in shooting some punk, and the grand jury found no evidence of wrongdoing. I have to ask myself, what kind of a vendetta are you trying to pull on that man this time?"

An iron ring of rage tightened around Orlando's chest, and Shaw put a warning hand on his sleeve. The sergeant's tone was conciliatory. "Chief, we don't want to believe this any more than you. We didn't come to this conclusion lightly."

"If something isn't done soon," Orlando charged, "this is going to blow up in all our faces."

"I've heard about enough from you. Don't come here again wasting my time," Sorensen stormed, "until you've got proof. You bring me evidence that this group exists, you bring me names. And then we'll talk." With that, he ushered them through the front door and slammed it behind them.

The service bored him, but at least it was no longer in Latin. Even so, he enjoyed just being there, the odor of the burning candles bringing back memories of when he was a little boy and his father would give him a coin for the box and he would be allowed to light his own candle. The flames fluttered in their black iron holders, fascinating the children, as they had for generations. There was peace here, in the cool solidity of the wooden pews, in the worn leather of the hymn book he held but hadn't sung from in twenty years, in the droning of Father Shea's sermon.

He scanned the faces of the assemblage, some pert with attention, others stifling yawns. He spotted faces he rarely saw in the neighborhood, of contemporaries he had played baseball with in high school, now jowly and surrounded by teens of their own.

This was a community, with a sense of its history and place, and there was something beautiful in the commonality of experience here that he had forgotten in his rejection of the rituals of the church. In his own life, he missed this sense of togetherness, a fragment being part of a greater whole. But he also knew he could never be a part of it again.

He turned to his mother and touched her hand. She glanced over from her hymnal with a smile that said she was glad he had come. With his sister in Jersey and his brother in upstate New York, Marie Orlando rarely attended church with family anymore.

Marie had seemed nervous when she came by to pick him up that morning, as if she had a difficult decision to make. Seeing the scabs on his face from his altercation with Briggs made her all the more edgy. While he put on his tie, he heard her and Stewart talking in muffled tones in the living room, and he knew they were discussing her discomfort with her church's stand on social issues. He hoped Stewart hadn't been trying to make her feel guilty for going to the church; she had little enough to do with her time as it was.

Worshipers passed collection plates down the pews, with adult hands laying in folded bills and little hands dropping coins with a clink. Marie opened her purse and held a bill in her hand as the plate came to her. She hesitated, looked up at her son with loving, shining eyes, and passed the plate to him without putting anything in. He held the plate for a moment, staring, understanding what she had done. They held hands until the mass ended.

Father Shea stood in the front doorway, shaking hands, exchanging pleasantries with the congregation. The mass had been somber and reflective, the death of Father Morant weighing heavily on people's minds. Shea had spoken words of forgiveness, forgiving oneself, forgiving others.

As Orlando and his mother waited in line to give Shea their regards, Orlando saw Adrianne Barnes hurriedly step up to the priest, clutch his elbow, and whisper in his ear. She wasn't dressed for church, and Orlando hadn't seen her or Trevor among the congregation during mass. She looked wan and agitated, as if she had been up all night. Shea spoke in low tones to her, cocking his head toward the back of the church, and she nodded thankfully and strode down the aisle and through the door at the left of the altar.

Watching her go, Orlando once again wondered what secrets the boy could tell him.

The living room had been worked over into an artist's studio. Wide, tall windows that threw down northern light made it a good choice. Paint and turpentine smells drenched the room, despite open windows that invited a gentle breeze. Spattered easels supported spattered canvases. The canvases were supposed to be art, but they suspiciously resembled drop cloths strewn on the floor. Sally stood in a smock that matched the canvases and the drop cloths, a palette daubed with paint hooked with one thumb, a bulbous brush drooling cool blue acrylic in the other hand. Wavy red hair cascading down her shoulders caught light with each curl, dazzled. No twisted tube of pigment lying on the scarred wood table behind her could match that hair.

Broad smile. "Hi, guys."

Orlando and Stewart stepped into the room and produced a spray of gladioli. "Want me to leave the door open?" Orlando asked.

"Those are beautiful, thanks. There's probably a vase in the kitchen. No, go ahead and close the door. The stench in here makes me feel like an artist." Sally made her living painting *faux* marble in people's bathrooms. Her artistic ambitions hadn't made it past a showing of her work at a hole-in-the-wall East Village gallery run by friends. After seeing the exhibit, Stewart had commented under his breath that Sally should stick to bathrooms. Orlando didn't know. The colors were nice.

Orlando left Stewart discussing color combinations with Sally and took the flowers to the kitchen. Ronnie was at the stove; she had on designer jeans that accented what hips she had, and a pale green crepe blouse with droopy sleeves. She wore light makeup. "Hiya, Doug. Oh, how nice. There's a vase in the cabinet under the microwave." She waved him into a light-flooded kitchen. Knotty pine cabinets spanned from a Spanish-tiled floor to a beamed ceiling. A butcher block island dominated the center of the cooking area. An oval pine table with pilot chairs looked out sliding glass doors onto the backyard.

Orlando found the vase, stuck the flowers in, then filled the vase with water. He brought the vase to the kitchen table. "Can I help?"

"Sure. I can use you on the cutting board. You haven't seen the kitchen since we finished it. We always wanted a country kitchen. We had an all-girl construction crew come in and do it."

"I bet that was fun. Looks good." Orlando found mushrooms, scallions, and cheese waiting for him on the butcher block, along with a Norman Bates knife. He stripped the cellophane off a blue cardboard carton and rolled plump white mushrooms into his thick fingers. "Tell me, what's with the new get-up?"

Ronnie cracked an egg on the side of a bowl, let the contents ooze out, and tossed the shell in a bag under the sink. "I knew you'd have to ask," she said reproachfully.

"When someone talks about the tyranny of lipstick lesbians, my curiosity is piqued. You look great."

"Which, translated, means I used to look terrible."

Orlando showered the mushrooms with water from the double sink. He grinned. "I would have chosen the word *distinctive*. What's this all about?"

Ronnie scowled and smacked another egg against the bowl. "It's all about getting old and becoming a pathetic old fart that everybody laughs at."

Orlando winked a knowing eye. "You'll have to do better than that. Since when do you give a damn what anybody thinks?" He shook the mushrooms and set them on the cutting board. "A woman who wears combat boots and Levi's to work at the medical examiner's office ain't my idea of hypersensitive."

Her smile was thin. "I do care what young women think, though."

"Don't tell me your construction worker gals came in skirts and blouses."

"No, but I wouldn't be surprised." She began to beat the eggs. Mercilessly. "Sally got a job doing *faux* columns in this new women's bar in SoHo. It's called"—her mouth puckered like she'd sucked a lemon—"Club Clit. They actually call it Club Clit. And it's not a women's bar. It's a girl bar. That's what they call it, a *girl* bar. We went to the opening. They had go-go dancers in bird cages. They wore bustiers, long pink gloves, and net stockings. The women in the bar, who were all dressed like hillbilly sluts, stuffed money between their breasts. The music was a nonstop screech. It was astonishing. It was like I had died and gone to hell." Ronnie set the bowl down and fretted a hunk of cheese over a grater. "I heard these young women talking. About this disgusting old lesbian. They were giggling. They said she looked like a diesel dyke out of a Jesse Helms nightmare." She put the cheese down and looked at Orlando. "It took me awhile to realize they were talking about me."

"You let a couple of kids bully you like that?"

Ronnie shook her head dejectedly. "It wasn't that. It was the whole thing. They didn't get it. The didn't get my point. The way I dressed was a statement. It said we wouldn't be told by men what was beautiful. The whole thing was lost on them. They have no awareness that we even existed, what we went through for them. How much we sacrificed so they could feel good about themselves. They feel entitled to have all the good things we had to scramble for. I guess I expect them to be grateful. No, not grateful, but at least aware of what we went through."

"Is that really so bad? They're young. Let them have their fun. They'll find out soon enough." He set the sliced mushrooms aside and went after the scallions. "I was down on West Street Friday. I couldn't get over how much things had changed. There were ghosts there, and I felt like one of them." He grinned sheepishly. "I even got a tattoo. Just on the spur of the moment. Like a kid."

Ronnie pulled open the refrigerator door and found a stick of butter. She lopped off a piece in a skillet and twisted a knob on the range. "I hate it that the innovations of our generation, the *revolutions*, are considered corny by these young kids. They snicker at the idea of women's music festivals." She looked sadly at Orlando and gave a wry smile. "I can't believe a generation of lesbians has sprung up that doesn't consider Holly Near to be a saint." She frowned thoughtfully. "To tell the truth, I long for the days when you couldn't be a sister if you wore makeup."

Sally pushed through the swivel doors, and she and Stewart poked their heads into the kitchen. She had a spot of blue on her nose and exasperation in her voice. "Good God, are you still lamenting the passing of the Birkenstock and L.L. Bean generation of lesbians?"

Ronnie snatched a slice of mushroom from the cutting board, tossed it in her direction. "Go away, you traitor, you ... *assimilationist*. We're talking serious business here, sitting on the ground and telling sad stories of the death of kings and queens."

Sally's eyeballs rose ceilingward, her hands cupped like a beggar. "Doug, please, take this woman away and don't send her back till she's normal again." She shook her head. "I can't take it." She retreated from an assault of mushroom bits, taking Stewart with her. Ronnie should have been a major league pitcher.

"Hold it," Orlando scolded playfully. "I had to slice all those little buggers. They're mine. Now, if you want to use eggs, fine, they're your domain."

Ronnie put what was left of the mushrooms in the skillet, where they crackled and spat. She mauled them with a wooden spoon. "I guess it's my own fault," she said grimly. "I'm the one who made the appointment with the beautician."

"It's made you popular, hasn't it?"

Ronnie added the scallions. "Yeah," she said slowly, "that's what's bothering me." She gave a devilish grin. "Think of all the years I've wasted! I coulda had it all!"

"Stop it. You're breaking my heart."

"Just kidding." She churned the sizzling scallions. Good smells drifted to Orlando's nose. "But isn't there something very wrong when caking makeup on my face makes me a hot property? I just don't feel good about it."

"Have your fun while you can. It won't last. Nothing does."

"You're full of cheer today."

Orlando looked up from the butcher block. "Things aren't going very well with the No Exit case. We have another body."

Ronnie shook her head. "God, not another. I'm sorry."

"That's what I wanted to talk to you about. I need the autopsy results, and I can't wait until tomorrow. Will you be a pal and spend your Sunday afternoon in the morgue for me?"

Ronnie's shoulders sagged. "Buddy, you're asking a lot. Especially with that case. Yuck. Man, seeing that is enough to make me lose my lunch. For about a week."

Orlando began humming Dionne Warwick's "That's What Friends Are For."

"Oh, all right," Ronnie muttered irritably. "But you gotta do me a favor some time." She gave him her I'm-forty-years-old-and-my-clock-is-ticking look.

"Anything you want, Ronnie," Orlando said, then added, "Within reason."

CHAPTER 16

It looked like a pile of garbage on the sidewalk, but it wasn't. There was method in the mess, maybe even skill. It was someone's home, at least for a night. A slanting gray plastic tarp, tied on one end to a chain-link fence, provided a makeshift roof for a construction of walls consisting of a shopping cart loaded to the brim and cardboard boxes probably rummaged from a grocery dumpster. The toothless inhabitant peered out at Orlando as he walked by, then receded into the gloom within.

Orlando stopped, crouched. "You know where the soup kitchen is?"

The dirty face appeared again, squinting in the sunlight. A shaking palm pleaded for money. "Can you gimme a dollar?" An audacious toothless grin shown on a face tough and dark as leather. "For booze and drugs?"

Orlando peeled a bill and put it in the outstretched hand. It was something he just didn't do. Money to charities, yeah. Food drives for people with AIDS, yes. Handouts on street corners, no. He wasn't sure why he did it; the guy just had a winning smile.

A finger with a broken black nail pointed.
"Just down the block. Pink. You can't miss it."
He disappeared back into his cave.

Ragged quilts hung along the fence, drenched
from last night's rain, taking in the morning sun.
Their colors, faded from wear, had lost their
cheer. Black and brown men milled on the street,
leaning in doorways and against the fence, waiting. Waiting.

Orlando walked down the block past the men.
He had left Stewart in the company of Ronnie
and Sally, telling him he would be home in the
early evening, enigmatically suggesting he save
his energy for a little breaking and entering.

The one-story cement-block building was new,
painted beige with pink double doors. Well, the
man had been close. It was the only place in this
neighborhood that had seen paint in years. No
sign to let on what it was. Orlando rapped,
waited, then tried the handle. Locked. He knocked
louder. The door swung open, and a gentle-faced
woman stood before him with hands dripping
wet. Her hair, black and gray streaks, was simple
and pulled back. Large glasses rested on an upturned Irish nose and magnified spirited eyes.
Her green cardigan sweater, sleeves rolled up to
the elbows, hung over another sweater, which
hugged large breasts that hung low on her short,
wide-hipped frame.

"Serra Pritchard?" Orlando showed his badge.

She examined it, then gave him an evaluating
look. "I can give you fifteen minutes tops," she
announced flatly. She had a voice that said she
knew how to deal with people. "And only if

you're willing to follow me around the kitchen while I work. But you have to leave by the time we serve lunch. Our guests don't get treated with much dignity in their lives, and we're determined to give it to them here. And quite frankly, if I'm not comfortable around cops, how can I expect them to be?"

Orlando followed her into a bustling kitchen peopled by a dozen workers of different ages. Several surrounded a large cutting board in the center of the room, chopping lettuce in haphazard rhythm. Pots banged on a black stove the size of a hearse. Serra stooped over a cardboard box packed with heads of lettuce. Taking one in hand, she stripped off shaggy outer leaves, then tossed it in a stainless steel sink where others bobbed in water. The resulting splash covered a Latino teen rinsing celery in an adjoining sink. "Sorry, hon," she said. She looked mock serious. "Now you know a vegetable can be a deadly weapon." He grinned shyly and went on with his work. She looked up at Orlando. "We give the high school volunteers a hard time, but they always seem to come back. Never get quite enough of our little loony bin. Now, what can I do for you?"

"I'm looking into the murder of Father Morant. You knew him, didn't you?"

She stiffened momentarily, then seized another lettuce. "Oh, yeah. I knew him." Her tone said volumes. She peeled off the outer leaves, went to the sink, and dunked it. She leaned on the sink for a moment, as if an old wound had suddenly torn open.

"Was it that bad?"

She stared at him sharply. When she spoke again, she'd lowered her voice so only he could hear. "It was pretty bad, but one learns to forget. I don't pretend to be on the level of Christ, but I try to forgive. It's taken time, but I've made my peace with the situation. You have to or you die inside." She seemed to regain her strength, yanked a slurping plug, and rolled the heads of lettuce into a tilted colander. Hoisting it against her formidable waist, she waddled to the cutting board and said to the volunteers, "So you thought you were through chopping, well, think again, folks." She waved Orlando over. "C'mon out back. I think I deserve a minute for a cigarette break."

Blacktop covered a backyard with rows of wood-grained Formica tables formed in neat lines. Collapsible metal chairs, flattened, leaned against the building. A high chain-link fence stood guard. In a far corner a hut carried the sign "CLINIC." Serra Pritchard leaned against beige cement blocks, fished a cigarette out of a sweater pocket, and lit up. She offered the pack. "They'll be lining up in a minute. Still got a lot to do."

Orlando declined with his upheld hand. "Quite a setup you have here," Orlando said. He looked at the tables. "You feed, what, fifty, sixty people?"

She let out a puff of smoke. "Honey, where have you been? We hand out seven hundred meals on a busy day. Our guests move fast. They eat, then move on so the next guy can take his place. Five hundred on average. Of course, some of our guests go through two and three times. We get more people toward the end of the month because their relief checks have run out."

Orlando scanned the operation in admiration. "May be the only balanced meal they get."

She gave a sad grin. "Balanced, well ... We go heavy on the starch, the point is to fill bellies. We give out soup, sometimes with a protein base, beans, bread, salad. We're about the only kitchen that gives out salad. Tuna runs out by the middle of the month."

"Wouldn't it be best to save that for when they need it most, after their relief checks run out?"

She drew on the cigarette, pondered her answer, shot a plume of smoke skyward. "As unchristian as it may sound, we would have chaos here if we did that. I think seven hundred is about all we can handle at a time." She watched him for a moment, then said, "You know, I had no idea you came about Michael. When I saw you at the door, I assumed you wanted to question me about one of our guests. You see, I haven't spoken to Michael in a good five years."

"You must have left an impression. He kept your letter."

She peered closer at Orlando, as if in disbelief, then shook her head and stared off into the distance. "By God, maybe there was hope for him after all. I never would have thought it."

"Suppose you tell me what it was all about."

"Suppose you help me set up the chairs. It won't take long." She snuffed the cigarette under her shoe and took a couple of metal chairs over to the tables, and set them up. Orlando brought several over, snapping them upright.

"Thanks," she said. "I appreciate the help. I met Michael Morant at a pro-choice rally in the early eighties. This was in the days when we thought we could take on the Church hierarchy and win." She kicked one of the chairs in line with the others. "We were naive enough to believe we were the true Church, and the clowns in the Vatican would topple off their pedestals any day. Unfortunately, we underestimated the ruthlessness of our opposition." She smiled tightly. "And here I am today."

They went back for more chairs.

"You left the Church."

"No, I never left the Church." She grabbed three chairs, tested their weight, took two. "Smoking is doing me in. I could lift twice this many not long ago." At the tables, she continued, "I'm still in the Church. I am just no longer a nun. The work I do is the same. Well, pretty much. Helping people is helping people. And we help a lot of people here."

Orlando glanced over her shoulder. "I see you even have a clinic."

"Had." Serra sighed. "Had, Detective Orlando. We *had* a nurse. In tough times, contributions drop and fewer people volunteer—people get more concerned with personal problems. Nurses included. Now we *have* aspirin. And Tylenol. And we refer to clinics that still have nurses." She grimaced. "It's a sign of the times."

When she went back for more chairs, she was out of breath. She leaned against the building. "I tell ya, getting older is for the birds," she panted. Then she lit up again.

"Tell me about it," Orlando said. "And tell me about Morant."

"He was a caring priest. Complicated, tormented, and in the end, gutless, but in those early days I would have said he was a nice guy. He had a congregation in the Village, gave mass to Dignity." Something stirred in her memory and she shook her head. "I will never understand the Church's stand on homosexuality. Back when they had the hearings for the Gay Rights Bill, I went and testified for its passage. I condemned the Church's male hierarchy for its obsession with"—mischief parted her lips in a smile—"*homogenital activity*. My exact words." Her face shone briefly, then irony took over. "You can just imagine how that went over like a lead balloon with the big brass. Yeah, in those days Michael and I saw eye to eye just fine."

"What happened?"

Serra's face soured. "Our friend the pope came to visit. A number of priests and nuns felt it was time to bring about a dialogue on the abortion issue, so we placed full-page ads in major newspapers pointing out there was diversity of opinion on the subject by Catholic lay and clergy. The bigwigs were not amused." She dropped the cigarette and crushed it under worn shoes. A line had begun to form along the fence, passive faces, wary eyes. "We'd better get a move on." She gripped more chairs.

Orlando followed her, chairs dangling from under each arm. "You must have known."

She stopped, flipped open a chair. "That's the funny thing. We were so wrapped up in our causes, the migrant workers, racial equality, women's issues, that the men who control the Church seemed far away. We surrounded ourselves with people who thought like us, and we really believed our ideas could sway the Church. When the Vatican demanded a retraction, our response was 'drop dead!' "

"What did they do?"

"Nothing. At least to the nuns and priests who belonged to supportive orders. Most are still where they were, doing what they did."

"What about you?"

"I was head of a house for battered women. We were funded by the Church. I'll bet you'll never guess what they did to try to make me recant."

"Pulled your funds?"

"Bingo." Serra snapped open another chair, and settled it on the blacktop to make sure it was sturdy. "My order was borderline supportive, but no way could we replace the lost Church funding. It was me or the abused women who used our facilities. I decided it was me that had to go."

"How does Morant fit into this?"

"Michael did as he was told. He shut up and they carted him off to Brooklyn. No more masses for Dignity, no more pro-choice rallies. He was afraid of losing his job." Her face began to show its age, betraying old wounds. "Better to stab your principles in the back than brave it in the real world."

"You remember Susan Krouse?"

Serra shut her eyes. When she opened them again, they were moist. "How could I forget? Every day I think of her and that beautiful baby."

"Go on."

Her lips tightened and bitter lines creased her mouth. "They died. Thanks to the Church." She leaned against the table for support, and a tear ran down her cheek. "And thanks to me, I guess." She quickly wiped her eyes, gave an apologetic smile. "Sorry. This isn't easy for me."

"Take your time."

She breathed in deep and continued. "Susan was a lovely young woman. Gorgeous wavy hair. Freckles on her nose. She came to us with a problem. Her husband wanted to kill her. He'd come close, too, on several occasions. It wasn't an unusual story for us. Thing was, we had to send her away. We were closing our doors to new clients. No more funding from the Church, no new funding in sight. She and the baby went back home. Her husband was waiting with a baseball bat. You know the rest."

"It wasn't your fault."

"Maybe not. But there is a sin, Detective Orlando, the sin of pride. If I had resigned from my order right away, our service for battered women never would have suffered the funding cut. I stayed on because I knew I was right. I would fight the Church all the way. Only thing was, I forgot who I was supposed to be helping. Pride, Detective Orlando, pride."

"And Morant's connection?"

She looked beyond Orlando to a man who stuck his head out the back door. "I'll be right there," she called. "I really have to go soon. Michael? He was on the board that allocated funds to us. I begged him to put in a word in our behalf, to stand up for what is right."

"But he didn't."

"He wouldn't even return my calls. I was furious. Maybe I wanted to blame him because I felt so guilty. I sent him that clipping from the paper and the note. Lot of good it did. I never heard another word from him."

Orlando shrugged. "He kept it. It was on his dresser the night he died. That means something."

"Yes," she said softly, "that means something." She looked into Orlando's eyes. "But I certainly didn't kill him, if that's what you think."

"Thanks. But I didn't ask."

The man peeked out the door again, waved her over.

"Coming," she called. She looked back to Orlando. "A funny thing. Before all this happened, I really thought Michael was going to become a leader in the progressive movement. I thought he'd come out, really make a statement."

"Come out?"

"Yeah. Michael was gay. I remember he was terribly in love with one of the men in Dignity. He couldn't stop talking about him. I can't remember the fellow's name, but"—she put her hand to her mouth and laughed—"he was one of those middle-aged body-building enthusiasts. He

had a sort of lisp, and I remember he was so
concerned about going bald."

Orlando stared. "Not anymore," he said. "He
fixed that." Walking back to his car, he fit the
pieces together; he had a pretty good idea who
the informant was.

CHAPTER 17

"I'll be with you in a second," Rick Dunham said, leading Orlando into the computer room. "I just have to sign off on the bulletin board." He plopped into a chair in front of a terminal and rattled the keyboard using the hunt-and-peck method. Jonathan sat at another computer, fingers primly raised, inputting address blocks from a list scrawled on a yellow pad. He flipped a page on the pad, gave Orlando a nod, stifled a yawn, then went back to typing at breakneck speed.

Orlando leaned against a dusty fireplace mantel stacked with tax forms and A&W root beer mugs stuffed with pencils and pens. A series of dustier framed diplomas hung above the mantel.

Dunham signed off, flipping the rocker switch at the back of the computer, and leaned back in his chair. "I've become one of the founders of this new gay body-building organization, B.I.G., which is going to compete in the next Gay Games. B–I–G. Bodybuilders in Gotham." He grinned with satisfaction. "You wouldn't believe the guys who showed up for the first meeting. I mean, we're talking world-class. It was incredible." He gestured over to the young man. "Jonathan is doing a little overtime for me, typing all the names and addresses of these guys for the mailing list." He drew his fingers together, brought them to his lips, and made a kissing sound. "Hot." He slapped his knees and said, "Anyway, enough fun, I should get some work done this afternoon. You don't mind if I do some filing while we talk? Here I am, the boss, and I end up doing the filing around here because Jonathan types eighty words a minute and Cesar is a genius with numbers. I'm the only one I can spare to do the menial jobs." Dunham stopped himself and gave Orlando a look that said he knew he was babbling nervously. He saw the expression on the detective's face and grew serious. "I'm sorry, I didn't mean to go on. How can I help you today? I think I told you all I know."

"You failed to mention your affair with Morant."

Jonathan swirled around in his chair and dropped open his mouth. Dunham frowned and ran his fingers through the reforestation project on his scalp. "Jonathan, maybe you should take off now. I'll pay you for the full four hours. You can leave the machine on for now."

Jonathan looked curiously from Dunham to Orlando, eyes theatrically wide, and back again. He shrugged and showed teeth in a wide yawn. "Sure, boss man." As he left the room, he mumbled loud enough so they could hear, "Just when the dirt gets good, massah sends de house nigger out to de field." A moment later they heard the front door close.

"Like I told you," Dunham said apologetically. "He thinks that's how a black gay kid is supposed to act. He thinks he's a comedian."

"Looks like he needs a little rest anyway," Orlando said.

"That kid." Dunham shook his head. "He sneaks out at night to see his old friends on the street. He doesn't do anything wrong, but you can imagine how he's upset the people who run the school." He crossed his arms. "Now, what's this nonsense about Father Morant and me?"

"You may have been discreet, but not discreet enough. People talk. And you left a paper trail. Morant didn't completely burn your letters. There were fragments of your handwriting in his waste basket. Do I need a warrant to confiscate samples of your handwriting, or can we just talk friendly?"

Dunham seemed to ponder what the detective had said, then picked up a manila file and went to a gray metal cabinet across the room and pulled open a drawer. His face was hidden from Orlando when he finally spoke. "He never answered them, you know, any of my letters. At least I know now he read them. It means he knew how I felt."

"It also means you were the informant," Orlando said. "Only someone as intimate as a lover could get a man like Morant to tell about the confession. It was you who called to tell me Morant knew who the killer was, right?"

Dunham turned and swallowed hard, his Adam's apple doing a jig on his throat. "Someone had to," he said bleakly. "People are dying."

Orlando surveyed the equipment in the room. "I should have guessed it must have been you, with your interest in gadgets."

"If you're asking what I used, it was a device that attaches to the phone and distorts voices." He returned to the desk and found a cylindrical object in a bottom drawer that screwed onto the speaker end of a telephone receiver. He let it clatter on the desk. "Like they use sometimes on TV news shows to change the voices of people they interview who want to remain anonymous. I actually got it from a little ad in a magazine to joke around with friends. I like my toys."

"Now that we've established your concern for Morant's 'burden' was bogus, suppose you tell me what went on between you two."

Dunham leaned forward, his hands grasping the edge of the desktop. "I loved him," he said emphatically. "I loved him like I've never loved anybody before or since."

Orlando laid his arm along the mantel, atop the uneven stack of documents. He fingered the handle of a root beer mug. "Unfortunately, in my profession you learn love often turns to hate. You sicced Queer Nation on him, didn't you? You called me, then you phoned Anthony."

"Only after I didn't see any results from you," Dunham said quietly. "I had to do what I could to stop Michael from letting this maniac keep on killing."

"Meaning, only after you realized how angry you really were with Michael Morant for dumping you. You were interested in Catholicism about as long as Morant shared your bed."

"It wasn't like that."

"Then tell me how it was. Start with the beginning."

Dunham lowered himself back into his chair by the computer. "Like I told you, we met when I went to a Dignity mass at St. Mary's in the Village. Michael and I hit it off right away. He was different then, kind of a crusader for change. And frankly, really hot. We fell in love." Dunham looked up at Orlando and gave him a wistful smile. "Or maybe I should say, I fell in love with him. He was so warm and compassionate. Now I know a great love for mankind in general can sometimes preclude the ability to love an individual. Who can say if someone as tormented and conflicted as Michael could ever have loved another person?" Memories darkened his face. "At least he told me he loved me. It was tough."

"I'm listening."

"We had to keep things quiet. It was okay for a priest back in those days, and we're talking pre-October '86, to play around supporting gay rights and maybe saying birth control is okay, and even that the church should change its stance on divorce. But for a Catholic priest to come out and state that he's gay, no way. You'd be out on your ass, and being a priest meant everything to Michael. This may be hard for you to understand, but there are priests who felt comfortable giving mass to Dignity and supporting gay rights while at the same time being wracked with guilt over their own homosexuality. We had to keep our relationship secret, even from other gays in Dignity. I think only a few people knew about us. There was a friend of his, a nun, who he told because he knew she'd be understanding. But we would never be seen in public together unless we were in a group. But the time we spent here in this apartment, when Michael could sneak away from his duties, it was really beautiful. Michael was the one relationship I've ever had that went beyond the tricking stage; he was the one man I let really become a part of me."

"Maybe you let your guard down for once because you knew it was impossible."

Dunham's voice went brittle. "You can be really cruel, you know it?"

"Sorry, I try to blame the job. My mother warned me it would make me mean."

Nodding grudgingly, Dunham continued, "In October of '86, the Ratzinger letter came out, cracking down on homosexuality in the Church. Bishops around the country began kicking Dignity out onto the street. It was a very painful time for a lot of gay Catholics. Michael and I had been seeing each other for a year then. They transferred him over to a parish in Brooklyn when he made the mistake of criticizing the new policy." Dunham stared at the desk, but he seemed to be seeing the past. "I assumed things would continue as they had. There was only a subway ride between us."

"But it didn't. Shea got to him, right?"

"His spiritual adviser," Dunham said contemptuously, looking up at the detective. "The exploiter of his self-loathing and guilt. The little voice prying into the back of Michael's head telling him it's a mortal sin to be queer, worse even than sticking gum under the pews during Sunday mass. Shea is the kind of priest who brags that if you give him a kid till he's seven, he'll give you a Catholic for life. Meaning, the guilt is enough to wrack a person's guts for a lifetime."

"Go on."

"Michael wrote me a long letter after that." Dunham gave a mirthless chuckle. "I've never been dumped nicer in all my life. He said he loved me, but he just couldn't live the double life." He stuffed papers into another manila file and went to the cabinet again. "I didn't see him for a long time. He wouldn't return my calls or answer my letters. I went over to St. Agatha once for Sunday mass." He found the place where he wanted the file and slipped it into the drawer, then gazed dolefully at Orlando. "He pretended he didn't know me." Dunham's lip quivered. "You can't imagine how much that hurt."

Orlando adjusted his stance against the fireplace, and a stack of forms came cascading down to the floor. When he bent to scoop them up, Dunham joined him, rounding up papers that had scattered under the desk.

"Sorry about that," Orlando said, handing what he had collected over to Dunham.

"No problem. Someday I'll probably have enough file space to hold all this stuff. Why don't you go ahead and take a seat?" He indicated Jonathan's chair and settled the stack of forms back on the mantel.

Orlando leaned back in the chair, the swivel

mechanism squeaking. "When did you see him again?"

"I didn't, not for a long time. I heard things about him through the grapevine over the years, though. Father Shea had got him to join that tacky organization the Church has to pressure gay men to be celibate." He grimaced. "It doesn't work. They hold it in until they freak out and fuck anything in sight." Dunham came around and seated himself at the desk.

"Then you saw him again, in the last few weeks."

Dunham took a long time to answer. For a minute the only sound was the hum of the computer. "I got a call from Jonathan's school late at night. He'd skipped out and they wondered if he'd come to my place. He hadn't, but I knew where he was. Out visiting those street kids he used to run with who peddle their buns on corners. I drove around checking the spots where they congregate. I didn't find Jonathan; instead I found Michael. Very drunk. I mean totally wasted. Trying to buy some kid. I had gotten out of my car to ask some of the hustlers standing in a doorway if they'd seen Jonathan, and Michael rolls up in his car and tries to pick some boy up on the corner. Then he sees me, and it's like, this terribly anguished expression comes over his face. I don't think I'd ever seen such a look of pure shame before. It was more than just that he was caught red-handed picking up a prostitute. It wasn't just that the kid was underage. It was that *I* had seen him. He had told me he had to give up our loving relationship because it was a sin, and here he was paying to fuck children."

"What did you do?"

Dunham's face softened. "I went over to him and slipped into the passenger side of his car. He looked so scared because he didn't know how I was going to react. I hugged him and told him it was okay, and he started crying in my arms. Just crying and crying, big heaving sobs." Dunham shook his head remembering. "He was in no condition to drive. Even his pores exuded alcohol. I had never known Michael to drink like that." He shrugged. "So I brought him home with me."

"And he told you why he was so distraught. Someone had confessed a murder to him."

"Not right away. We sat and talked. I just wanted to make sure he was going to be okay. I told him he had to watch out because there were rumors being spread over the gay bulletin board that some gay guy had been murdered in this really sick way. I told him he had to be careful. It's people who get drunk and make bad decisions that get in trouble like that. Suddenly he's crying again, his face in his hands, and blurts out that he knows who it is. Once he said it, the rest just came out. It wasn't just the others who might die, Michael was afraid this crazy was going to come after him. I wrapped my arms around him and tried to comfort him, to tell him it would be okay."

Orlando recalled the anguish Morant had gone through in explaining why he couldn't break the sanctity of the confessional, as if Orlando didn't know from a childhood in the Church. But he also understood why Rick Dunham was the one person the priest would have told. Drunk, frightened, filled with guilt for abandoning his lover, and then being caught with a hustler, he had been treated with unconditional forgiveness by Dunham. Who better to share his frustrations and fears with?

"He confessed that this wasn't the first time he had gone out cruising. All these sexual frustrations just built up inside him and he'd sneak out nights. One night he went to this sleaze bar. Apparently Michael had gone out to pick up some young flesh when his conscience got hold of him and he went to drink off his desire at this bar. Anyway, this guy comes up to talk to him. Word got around that he was a priest because some of Michael's former pickups were there. So this guy comes up to talk to him, and finds out where Michael's church is."

Orlando leaned forward. "This guy was the No Exit Killer?"

Dunham nodded. "Next day the guy comes to confession. Michael recognized his voice immediately. But the guy even tells him his name. Everything. Why he's committing the murders."

Orlando remembered with growing excitement Phillip Michaels saying once the detective knew *why*, it would lead to the killer. "You never told me that on the phone. What did he say?"

"Michael didn't get into that. What he did describe was the terrible way the victims were being killed. The guy went into it in excruciating detail in the confessional. All about how he chloroformed them, then shot that drug into them, then pierced them with needles." He shuddered. "Michael said he'd had nut cases confess to him before, people who admitted to crimes they didn't commit. But this was different. There wasn't a doubt in his mind this man was telling the truth. And it terrified him because he realized this guy took the confessional about as seriously as Michael took the headlines in *The Enquirer*. The only reason this nut confessed to Michael was because he knew Michael was gay. It was like, he mutilated some gays physically, and now he had the chance to torment a gay man psychologically with complete impunity." Dunham wearily set his chin in a fist, his elbow on the desk. "Everything else Michael told me I already reported to you on the phone."

"But you didn't tell the whole story. What happened with you and Morant?"

"We talked through the night. He told me how lonely he'd been without me, how much I meant to him. He was going to leave the priesthood and come back to me. The years we'd been apart were killing him. You see, he'd found out that he couldn't live without a sex life, and trying to was making him a monster."

"Weren't you suspicious about trusting him, considering his past record?"

Dunham drew himself back in his chair, as if he'd been slapped hard. Color came to his cheeks, and his tone was defensive. "The next morning he called Father Shea and told him he was leaving. We spent a beautiful day together, just talking. It was just like it used to be. I'd forgotten how long it had been since I'd really shared my feelings with someone. That evening Father Shea called. I guess he knew my name from conversations with Michael and looked my number up in the book. At first Michael wouldn't even take the call, but when he finally did, he just told Shea to go to hell and slammed down the phone. That night we went out to dinner together, alone. He wasn't hiding it anymore." Dunham looked triumphant, but only briefly.

"When did Shea come for him?"

Dunham looked away, then studied his hands. "After a few days. He arrived at my door and asked Michael to go for a little walk. He said he wasn't there to change Michael's mind, just to understand. He said it was the least Michael could do after their years together, to make him understand." Looking up at Orlando, Dunham's face had taken on a harsh aspect. "Michael went with him. I listened to Shea as they went down the stairs, and I can guess the rest. Always playing on Michael's weak points, his guilt, his love of being a priest." His voice mimicked the smooth flow of a priest confident he has God's will behind him: "You know this is immoral, you know what you're doing is wrong. I can understand your difficulty with celibacy; your doubts are part of what every priest must deal with. You do such good work as a priest, think of how much would be lost if you left the Church. Truthfully, is there anything else you could ever be? Becoming a priest wasn't a choice for you, it was a calling from God."

Dunham stared despondently for a moment,

then continued dully, "Michael came back half an hour later. I could see in his eyes what was going to happen. He said that he loved me, that he would always love me, but above everything else, he was a priest, and he would always be a priest."

"You wrote to him."

Dunham smiled unpleasantly. "Yes, and we know how much he treasured my correspondence. I told him he was crazy if he thought he could ever change himself and stop being gay. I told him I would always love him. I began thinking about how he knew the identity of that killer, and I knew I had to call the police to tell them what Michael knew. It was my civic duty."

"Did your civic duty include alerting Queer Nation?"

His mouth twitched. "Only after I thought about how much time I'd wasted on trying to make Michael Morant love me." He stared at the desk, ashamed. "I called Anthony Carrara, who I've known for years. I knew he was back in town and causing a stir at the Queer Nation meetings. When I explained my relationship to Michael, he believed what I told him. I made him promise not to reveal my identity to anyone."

"Anthony wouldn't need much to believe anything you told him about the Church."

Dunham studied Orlando's face for a moment. "I guess you're right when you say I left the Church when Michael left me, but it's not the way you think. There comes a time when you just get tired of constantly being abused by those you want to embrace you. You can't be gay and have any real self-respect and belong to that church in its present condition; Michael proved that. Being gay and being Catholic are mutually exclusive as far as I'm concerned. The people who stay with Dignity are only fooling themselves. But let me tell you, the day they start treating their children with a little human dignity, I'll be back."

Orlando pushed up from his chair. He wanted to escape that wounded look in Dunham's eyes.

Dunham rose and led him to the front door. He stood holding the knob as Orlando stepped onto the landing. "I tried to destroy the one person I ever really loved," he said suddenly. "I guess you think I'm about the most terrible person in the world."

Orlando shook his head. "Don't be so hard on yourself. I just went to church this morning for the first time in twenty years. I'm trying not to make judgments. If it will make you feel any better, that nun friend of Morant's, Serra Pritchard, said he was crazy in love with you. He told her so."

Dunham nodded sadly. "Obviously it wasn't enough."

CHAPTER 18

Stewart stood at the far end of the hall as a lookout. He nodded and Orlando pushed the key into the lock. It wasn't a perfect fit, but it would have to do. He jiggled the key while twisting the knob. No go. It was an art, even with this ring of keys that were supposed to go anywhere. The door held, then gave way after another jerk of the key. Stewart tiptoed down the hall and they slipped into Briggs's office and shut the door behind them.

It was dark. The only light came from street lamps glowing through the Venetian blinds, falling in angled slats on the wall behind the desk. They couldn't risk turning on the light because of the frosted window in the door, but they'd brought flashlights. Orlando flicked one on and went to the file cabinet first. Locked. He found a likely key in the light beam and played with the lock until the drawer rolled open. Stewart borrowed the key ring and went to the desk.

Orlando riffled through files. He wasn't sure what they were looking for, anything that would connect Briggs with the Aryan Brotherhood. He had no idea whether the group was stupid enough to take minutes of their meetings. It didn't seem likely with a paranoid hate organization. He didn't even hope for a list of members. All he found was documentation on the current cases Briggs was investigating. The Morant case was at the front of the drawer. Orlando flashed the light over it, leafing through its pages. He'd seen it all before from the copy Mrs. Burdict had pilfered Friday morning. Returning the file to the drawer, he scanned the other files but found nothing pertinent. He shut the drawer and looked back at his lover.

Stewart had worked open the lock on the desk drawer and ran his hands through its contents. His flashlight glowed on a blotter heaped with papers. A thick vase made by a child's hands held pencils and pens and seemed ghoulish in the harsh light. A photo of Mrs. Briggs, a pained expression on her face, sat in a gold frame. Orlando had met her occasionally over the years, and he'd never seen her smile.

"My, my, look what we have here," Stewart whispered. "Our friend has been stepping out on the dour lady." He held up a condom in a plastic wrapper and cringed. "Can you imagine having that creep grunting on top of you? At least he's doing it safely. Well, I don't see anything else in here except pencils, erasers, and paper clips."

Stewart searched the papers on the desk while Orlando went through the rest of the file drawers. When they failed to come up with anything tying Briggs to the neo-Nazi organization, Orlando and Stewart locked up the office again and slipped down the hall.

"What next?" Stewart asked.

Orlando didn't know. If Briggs had any record of his involvement in the group, it was in his home.

Orlando and Stewart had settled in front of the television to watch a video, a big bowl of popcorn glistening with butter between them, when the phone rang. Orlando ran to the bedroom to get his notepad on the bureau, then picked up in the kitchen on the fourth ring. He figured it would be police business, and it was. Ronnie was on the other end of the line.

"I did your autopsy, babe," she said. Her voice sounded tired.

"I owe you," Orlando said, and immediately wondered how Ronnie would demand payment. He cleared his throat. "What did you find out?" He didn't necessarily expect anything different from the other two serial murders, but the ransacking of Peter's apartment had showed a disturbing change in the killer's methods, and he wanted to know if it had spilled over to the murder itself.

"Well," Ronnie began slowly, "he died in the same way as the others. Organ failure caused by multiple needle punctures. To put it bluntly, one of the needles punctured his pulmonary artery, filling his lung with blood, and he literally drowned in it." She paused and he could hear Sally and Amy singing, "Daisy, Daisy, give me your answer, do . . ." in the background.

Orlando didn't like when Ronnie paused like that. It meant a medical examiner hardened to the realities of murder had been taken aback by the brutality of a specific crime. "What else, Ronnie?" Orlando prodded.

He heard her swallow as if in discomfort, then she continued. "There was no Ketamine in his system, and I found no chloroform residue around his mouth to indicate he'd been knocked unconscious in the same manner as the other victims."

Orlando tried to picture it. "No drugs? What are you saying, that Peter patiently laid there while the killer poked needles into him?"

"I wouldn't say patiently," Ronnie answered. "He couldn't help just lying there. And drugs weren't needed to incapacitate him while that maniac stuck the needles in. You see, the killer broke his neck first."

Orlando punched out the number of Dr. Michaels's home phone, and counted the rings. At seven he was about to hang up, but decided to hold on. He had a very bad feeling, and he needed to have it confirmed.

Finally, a gruff-voiced Phillip Michaels answered with "Yeah?"

"Dr. Michaels, Doug Orlando here. Did I catch you at a bad time?"

"Oh, no, no. Just a sec."

The phone clunked down, then a moment later Michaels came back on the line. "Sorry, I was in the shower. I'm okay now."

Orlando explained the latest development in the case, describing the new m.o. as well as the pillaging of Peter's apartment. Michaels was silent for a long moment after he'd finished.

"He's getting scared, and that's bad," Michaels said. "Our killer is not just out for more victims, he's looking back now trying to cover his past trail. He knows you're close and he knows he's made bad mistakes. He's losing confidence and that makes him all the more dangerous. His original intent with the killings is becoming more and more obscure in his mind, but at the same time he's becoming all the more savage. If pushed far enough, he may strike against people other than the narrow profile we've seen so far. Once the carnage really starts, he's not going to be able to stop."

Orlando thought about Trevor. "There's a boy," he said. "He won't talk, but I think he may have seen the killer at the confessional. And I think the killer may have seen him. There's been no attempt on the kid's life so far, but should I be worried?"

"He doesn't fit in the gay tattoo and piercing scene, right?"

"Well, he does have an earring ..." Orlando broke off and thought about his suspicions. What evidence did he have that Trevor was gay? That his stepfather said he didn't like baseball. C'mon. Even so, his intuition told him the boy was, and he made up his mind he'd better report all his suppositions to Michaels, even if they were based only on conjecture. "Hell, I don't know, the kid could be gay."

"Just hope he's not. Before, I would have said that if the killer suspects the boy knows something, he might be reluctant to go after him if he doesn't fit the narrow profile. What you say makes it more likely that the young man fits the focus of the killer's rage. Add to that the additional pressure our killer is under from your scrutiny, and I'd say a time could be coming when he decides to wipe the slate clean of every threat he sees coming his way, real or imagined." Michaels hesitated, then said quietly, "I'm not just talking about the young man. I want you to understand that includes you too."

Orlando wasn't worried about that; he could take care of himself. He wasn't so sure about the boy, though. After signing off with Michaels, Orlando flipped through his notepad and found the Barneses' number and dialed.

"What?" Zachary Barnes said heatedly when he picked up the phone.

Clearly, Orlando had called in the middle of something. "This is Detective Orlando," he said. "If Trevor is there, I'd like to speak to him."

A hand-muffled conversation, then Zachary was back, his voice still severe. "He can't come to the phone right now. He's being punished. What is this all about?"

Before he could answer, Orlando heard Adrianne Barnes wrestle the phone from her husband and attempt a courteous voice. But the strain showed like an old cord pulled taut. "Yes, Detective Orlando, how can I help you?"

"Mrs. Barnes, I'm concerned about Trevor. Is he okay?" The image of her grasping Father Shea's sleeve at church that morning came to him again, and once more he puzzled over what her apprehension had been all about.

Zachary cursed in the background and yelled, "Not in my family, Adrianne, never! I don't want it here, I just don't want it. Not in my house." Adrianne covered the phone for a moment, and Orlando could hear the angry pitch of her voice but none of the words. When she came back to the line, everything was quiet and her voice had returned to normal. "Trevor has been sent to bed early, Detective Orlando. He's being punished for acting up. If you need him I can get him, but maybe it would be better if you spoke with him tomorrow. He'll be working at the church as usual."

The tension in the Barnes house made him uneasy. What the hell was going on? "It's important I see him. Can I come over?"

"It's late and you would disturb my family. You should talk to him tomorrow." Then she hung up the phone.

As he set the receiver in its cradle, Orlando pondered whether he should have a watch put on the Barnes house, but he knew he didn't have any evidence to back up his hunch that the boy was in danger. The No Exit Killer only struck when the victim was alone, so the boy should be safe as long as he was with his family.

Then he thought of the anger in Zachary Barnes's voice, and he wasn't so sure.

When Stewart curled up in bed with Orlando that evening, he admitted he had a secret.

"Ronnie and Sally were not pleased you cut

out early at brunch. They had planned to ask us a certain question before you so rudely excused yourself. Not to worry, we've been invited for dinner next Saturday night."

"Why me? Why not you, or the sperm bank?"

"Well, I'm not supposed to say, but they confided in me as soon as you were out the door. They thought this time around it would be nice to have a father in the picture, and you're the one who makes their hearts go pitter-patter."

Orlando liked kids, but he had never really thought seriously about having any. He liked Ronnie and Sally, too, but this would be treading on new territory for him and Stewart. "Well," he said tentatively, "what do you think? I mean, how do you feel about it?"

"I dunno. I really like Ronnie and Sally. But it would be a big decision." He thought for a moment and grinned. "I guess I might be willing for you to have a kid with Ronnie, but only after you give up trying with me first."

Orlando woke in the middle of the night from a bad dream, his pillow wet with sweat, the sheets damp. He was unable to remember the specifics of the dream, only the disturbing images of faces in anguish. He turned the pillow over and tried to doze off, but he couldn't help mulling over who was going to be next.

CHAPTER 19

Orlando settled himself into a chair at the kitchen table Monday morning and scanned the front page of the *New York Times*. Nothing grabbed him—just the usual political scandals and unsolvable worldwide crises. He bit into a bagel smeared with cream cheese, looked across the table through curls of steam rising from coffee mugs, and watched Stewart reading a daily tabloid. He occasionally bought them from the newsstand on Court Street during his morning walks with Poindexter. Orlando didn't like having the trashy papers in the house, with their gruesome tales of human misery, but Stewart argued the tacky headlines alone were worth the paper's cost in camp value. And Stewart liked to read the movie reviews in all the dailies, always flipping to them first. Orlando recognized it as the paper that had displayed the photograph of the second No Exit victim on Friday's front page, and registered deeper disapproval. He stroked Stewart's leg with his toe.

"Hey, Stewart, let me look through that for a sec." He wanted to see if there were any leaks or pictures of the latest murder. He felt suddenly uneasy and Stewart looked up curiously, sliding the paper across the tablecloth.

Stewart picked up his mug, blew at the steamy surface, and took a sip. "Peter's murder has been relegated to page five," he said matter-of-factly, then grimaced. "Obviously because they have no picture to shock the public this time."

Orlando turned to the page. The article was lurid but short on facts. It focused on the m.o. of the previous killings, breathlessly exposed the kinky dangers of the S&M life-style, and ended with insipid character references from neighbors who obviously had hardly known Peter. Casually flipping through the rest of the paper, Orlando suddenly froze at a black-and-white photograph showing the latest arrests of male prostitutes. He recognized Trevor's blurred face in the group of young men arrested Saturday night.

So that was what the tension had been all about the night before in the Barnes household. The boy had been arrested in a gay prostitution bust. He remembered Zachary Barnes bellowing that he didn't want it in his house. Now it all fit: Trevor's late hours, his chain and diamond earring, Orlando's questions about his sexuality. Then the psychiatrist's theory came back to him: the killer would be very reluctant to attack anyone who wasn't gay. Was the No Exit Killer reading the same paper and deciding Trevor was fair game?

"Oh, my God," he said under his breath. "The kid—he may be next." Orlando jumped up from the table. "I think the boy saw the killer, and now there's nothing stopping that maniac from

going after him. I'm going to need your help,
Stewart. I'll be right back." Orlando's mind was
clicking. Mrs. Barnes had said Trevor would be
at the church as usual Monday morning. If the
boy wasn't still at home, Orlando would find him
at work in the church yard.

Orlando strapped on his Smith & Wesson in
the bedroom, found his notepad next to the
Ruger on the bureau, and brought it to Stewart.
"Find the phone number of the Barnes family in
my notes. They may still be at home. Explain
that you're calling for me and that they are to
get the hell out of the house immediately. The
No Exit Killer is falling apart—he may go after
the family in order to get at Trevor. Tell them
to get in the car and just drive. Not a second to
lose. Their lives may depend on it."

Stewart took the notebook, flipping pages.
"Where are you going?" he called as Orlando
hurried to the front door.

"To the church. In case Trevor is already
there."

The morning was sunny and cool. The chirp
of birds and the rustle of leaves in trees shading
the street were nearly drowned out by the
huffing engines and occasional horn blowing of
cars lined up at the stoplight at the end of the
block. Orlando crossed the street to his Chevy,
then decided he could make it just as fast on
foot. He started out at a jog, then increased his
pace as an urgent sense of foreboding descended
over him. Maybe this was all for nothing, but he
wouldn't feel comfortable until he saw the boy
safe. He couldn't help but believe that Trevor

had seen the killer, who now had an excuse to strike. When he saw the gray stone tower of St. Agatha at the end of the next block jutting against the hard blue sky, his lungs were already complaining. Orlando made it to the end of the block, and spotted Father Shea sprawled on the sidewalk in front of the double door of the church, waving his hands frantically. Where was the boy? He wasn't to be seen anywhere. Orlando's heart sank. Maybe he was already too late and the killer had come for Trevor. As he crossed the street and approached the priest, Orlando saw blood oozing from the old man's nostrils.

"Dear God," Shea cried, gasping for breath. "Help him! That maniac is after the boy! He's going to kill him." He pointed a shaking veined hand up the street.

Orlando turned and squinted his eyes in the bright morning light, only to see Briggs disappear around a corner. Orlando sprinted after him, his footfalls echoing up the deserted residential street. He heard something behind him and glanced back without slowing his gait. Stewart pounded the pavement halfway down the block, the Ruger clutched in his hand. *Dammit.* This wasn't a game. Why hadn't Stewart done as he was told? Seeing Stewart with that pistol twisted a knot in the pit of his stomach. He had committed a sin unforgivable for a police officer: he'd forgotten to reload after shooting at the firing range. His mind scrambled to recall how many bullets the Ruger had left.

He turned the corner, dodged a frightened

woman with a baby carriage, and vaulted over
bursting plastic trash bags squatting on the sidewalk. He spied Briggs disappear down a subway
entrance. He ran past small shops that nobody
seemed to patronize, owned by unsmiling people
with olive skin and thick Spanish accents. A
stocky old man cranked up the rusted metal
guard door of a liquor store, staring as Orlando
dashed by.

Sweat beaded his forehead and his breath was
a low rasp. Orlando felt the rush and smell of
stale heat rising from the subway grating beneath his feet, and the rumble of the approaching
train. His shirt was soaked by the time he
reached the subway entrance, and his gasping
breath pounded in his ears. He caught a glimpse
of Stewart panting behind him, and warned him
away angrily with a wave of his hand, then
leaped down the stairs to the subway platform.
Briggs trotted toward the train standing in the
station. Orlando drew in a deep breath, cata-
pulted himself over the turnstile, and tackled
Briggs with the force of all his weight. The two
men went down, grappling on the gum-scarred
cement.

"You're not killing that boy," Orlando shouted,
landing a fist in Briggs's jaw. He heard a satis-
fying crack.

Briggs snatched the gun from Orlando's holster and rammed it in his face while Orlando
went for his throat. "Are you fucking crazy?"
Briggs growled. "I'm trying to save the kid. That
psycho, he's in *there*." Then Orlando remembered on Saturday night Briggs had said he

planned to drop by the church this morning. He must have come by moments before Orlando. Looking up, Orlando saw Trevor diving into the second train car. Then his eye caught on a familiar face in the front car of the train. Orlando released his hands from Briggs's throat and sat back aghast, the face in the train window burning into his consciousness. He would never forget that expression of frenzied hate, the furious rage that warped the features and turned the skin beet red.

It was Salamander.

Just that moment the train doors began to glide closed. Suddenly Orlando was aware that Stewart was there, spurting toward a door in the second car, flinging himself into the doorway. The double doors bounced against his body, then slid back open. Orlando and Briggs sprang to their feet and hurtled themselves through the door of the first car just as the doors closed again.

The train lurched to a start as the cops threaded their way through the throng of rush-hour commuters standing in the aisle, gripping handrails where they could. Those who had seen their scuffle on the platform avoided Orlando and Briggs, warily leaning away as the men passed. Those who saw the pistol in Briggs's hand stepped back in fear. Toward the front of the car, Salamander shoved people aside and made his way to the door at the head of the train. Exclamations and curses followed him. He wrestled with the latch on the front door, but it was locked. Orlando and Briggs pushed on, nearly

half a car length from their prey. They didn't
know if Salamander was armed, and they didn't
want to take any chances of a shoot-out in the
crowded car. Salamander stared at them, eyes
afire. He had no place to escape to. Orlando
touched his holster, then remembered Briggs
was holding his gun. In the back of Orlando's
mind, he worried about where Stewart was.
Somewhere in the second car, with the boy, safe,
he assured himself.

The door to the conductor's box flew open, and
a middle-aged conductor in uniform stepped out,
oblivious to the drama being played out in front
of him. Salamander snatched the keys hanging
from the man's belt and began ramming key after
key into the front door's lock. Orlando and
Briggs moved in, but they were still more than
a dozen feet from their destination, with passengers obstructing their path. When the conductor
made a grab for the keys, Salamander whipped
a pistol from his leather jacket and blew a hole
in his chest. As the conductor collapsed to the
floor, screams erupted in the car and commuters
dived for cover. Some pounded the side doors.
Others pushed toward the back end of the car,
scratching, kicking, wailing. The detectives
couldn't get a clear shot at Salamander, not with
all these people. It was hard to keep solid footing
as the car jostled and shook on the tracks. Briggs
and Orlando scrambled over bodies flung on the
floor while Salamander found the key he wanted
and threw the door open.

"Briggs," Orlando shouted, "Give me my gun!"
He grabbed at Briggs's shoulder.

Briggs shook him off and forged ahead, pushing hysterical bystanders aside. "Fuck you! This collar's mine!"

The door slammed closed and Salamander disappeared into darkness. But where? There was nowhere to go but the tracks, racing underneath the train at sixty miles an hour.

"The roof!" Briggs shouted. "That motherfucker climbed on the roof." He made his way over cowering bodies to the door and threw it open, Orlando just behind him. A burst of hot air rushed toward them. Headlights illuminated the tracks. There was nothing ahead but blue and orange lights along the rails and blackened ties. Murky puddles reflected the grimy tunnel. Briggs peered upward.

The rest happened in slow motion in Orlando's mind.

First, the aching realization that no way could Salamander fit atop the train—the ceiling of the tunnel allowed only inches. He jerked his head to the side. Salamander clung like a spider to a ladder aside the door. Thrusting his pistol in Briggs's face, he fired. An explosion of crimson and bone sent a shower of blood streaming over Orlando as he tried to grasp Briggs's slumping body. He saw his gun fly and clatter to the track, disappearing under the train. Then Briggs's bulk, spouting blood, slipped from his hands and fell under the rumbling car. Orlando stared madly at the track as a stale wind hit his face. Brightness ahead said they were entering another station.

The barrel of a gun prodded Orlando's face. "You're next," Salamander shouted.

Suddenly steel shrieked against steel and Orlando felt the floor quaking beneath him. Someone had pulled the emergency brake, and the train shuddered to a grinding stop, pitching everyone forward. Orlando gripped the door latch as his body was thrown out of the car and into the rubber tubes guarding the door. He saw the blur of Salamander's pistol clattering to the track and the burly tattoo artist hanging precariously from the ladder.

Salamander retained his hold on the ladder and pulled a six-inch blade from a sheath in his boots. The train had stopped at the far end of the station, deserted of people, with only an exit turnstile implanted in the green-and-white tile walls. Commuters down the subway platform stared at the blood-spattered car and stepped backward in fear. People in the car began to stagger to their feet, a wail rising from a woman hunched over her baby. Orlando had to divert this maniac away from these people, and quick. Drawing him out the platform exit was the best bet. Salamander might do anything now, and the blade in his hand could do a lot of damage. *Once the carnage really starts, he's not going to be able to stop.* Orlando got to his feet, stepped over the rubber guard tubes, and jumped to the grimy platform.

"C'mon," Orlando said teasingly, "I'm one of those faggots, too. Let's see what you're going to do about it." The pieces had finally come together in his mind, and he'd figured out the *why* of the murders. And he was going to use it to get Salamander away from all these people. "You sure it wasn't me or one of my tricks that gave it to you?" He took a few backward steps toward the exit.

Salamander, still on the ladder, looked down at his gun on the track with flaming eyes, then back at Orlando. He knew enough not to venture onto the tracks. A few times a year someone made that mistake and fried like bacon. Salamander seemed to decide his knife was enough to handle the detective. He climbed off the ladder to the brim of the doorway, then jumped to the platform. The knife glistened meanly under the hard hum of fluorescent lights about to go bad.

Orlando turned on his heel and sprang toward the exit turnstile, a revolving door made up of three leaves of iron bars. His plan was working perfectly. If he could just get Salamander up to the street, where the reinforcements would be arriving any moment. He threw himself into the exit, pushing the bars, revolving with the spinning door. Then, suddenly, all motion ceased. Orlando collided with the door of bars in front of him, his head ringing in pain. Orlando contorted to see Salamander's monstrous hands clamped to one of the bars, squelching the door's movement.

And with horror Orlando understood. It was not a revolving door; it was a coffin. He was caught in limbo between the platform and the stairs to the street, metal bars in front of him and in back, to his side the curved metal plate of the door jamb.

Orlando turned to face his predator. Salamander's expression was a twist of hatred.

"I'm going to give all you disease carriers exactly what you deserve," he screamed, and the blade shot through one of the spaces between the bars, jabbing the air accusingly. Orlando sucked in his stomach, pressing himself against the far door of bars. He had lost his momentum and it was impossible to compete with Salamander, holding the revolving door motionless with his considerable weight. The knife slipped away momentarily, then protruded angrily again into the triangular crawlspace Orlando inhabited. Salamander brandished the blade wildly, ripping Orlando's shirt and scratching the flesh underneath.

Orlando knew he had to do something, and quick. With no options, he just had to chance it. He lunged for the flailing arm, grasping it in both hands and wrenching it downward. He felt his flesh rip and his shirtsleeve blossomed red. Salamander's elbow, forced backward against the metal bar, made a sick crunching sound, and the tattoo artist grunted in pain. Orlando bounced the forearm downward in a brutal attempt to snap the elbow joint in two. The joint held, but Salamander screamed out loud, and he yanked his arm from between the bars.

"Hold it right there!" Stewart yelled. He stood shakily in firing stance, the Ruger grasped in both hands, his face radiating fear.

Salamander growled, raised the bloodstained knife, and staggered toward him.

Stewart stepped back till he bumped into a wall of sticky tile. "I'll shoot, you hear me? I will, I'll shoot." His voice held all the conviction of someone who has never held a gun before.

Orlando struggled with the door, but it held fast. It only revolved one way—out to the stairway to the street. He couldn't get back onto the platform without going up the stairs of the exit and re-entering down the block by the token booth. Memories of his father flashed in his head. *It's just a .22, but you could kill a raging bear with this if you shot it between the eyes.* And he remembered Bill Shaw's words at the firing range, *That's five for five, right in the heart.* That meant Stewart had one bullet left to down this monster. And he was powerless to do anything but warn his lover.

"*Stewart,*" Orlando yelled, grasping the bars like a prisoner, "*for God's sakes, go for between the eyes! Shoot him between the eyes!*"

"Don't come any closer," Stewart shouted, pointing the pistol at Salamander's face. Knife raised, Salamander kept coming. Stewart quivered, then faltered and shot him in the knee. The impact hardly fazed the big man. "Next time I'll kill you!" Stewart warned.

But Orlando knew there wasn't going to be a next time. And he was impotent to do anything but watch.

Stewart raised the pistol and fired again, but the only sound was a dead click. He slumped against the wall behind him as Salamander lunged and planted the knife in his chest. Orlando screamed in anguish as Stewart's knees caved in from under him, and he crumpled to the ground.

Tears blurred his eyes as Orlando pushed through the turnstile and shot up the exit stairs. The street was almost empty. Sirens hooped in the distance; a squad car, lights flashing, was already pulled up to the subway entrance. Orlando didn't see any cops as he ran up to the car; they were probably already down in the subway. He tried the car door. Locked.

Clasping his hands together like a club, he smashed the passenger window. Nuggets of glass spat in his face, and small shards cut his hands. He opened the door from the inside and wrenched a riot gun from its holder at the dashboard. It wasn't what he wanted, but it was the best the car offered.

It was a semi-automatic twelve-gauge short-barreled shotgun with a pistol grip attached for easier handling. It was an ugly weapon, killing with massive wounds, puncturing vital organs. But it was a lousy rifle for his requirements. Pellets packed the casing and had a scattering effect; it did a tremendous amount of damage, but he would have to be close or others could be killed by the spread of the pellets.

He raced down the stairs of the subway entrance, passing the uniforms in blue, who stared first in shock, then recognized who he was. No time to explain. Orlando jumped the turnstile and ran down the platform. Stewart lay still on the ground.

Salamander tottered toward Orlando along the edge of the platform, a dazed look on his face. The red spot on his knee had grown bigger. The detective had to get closer to the tattoo artist to make a clean hit; otherwise the scatter of pellets might strike the stalled train car still filled with people. Salamander stopped and leaned against one of the metal girders, the knife dripping in his hand, staring blankly as Orlando approached. Then he glanced over at Stewart's body and smiled in triumph at Orlando.

And for one brief moment Orlando knew the rage he felt welling up inside was no different from that of any killer. As Salamander raised the knife and plunged toward him, Orlando lifted the rifle, aimed for the chest, and pulled the trigger. A tremendous blast reverberated in his ears, and flame burst from the barrel. Kickback jerked the barrel up and sent the gun stock into Orlando's shoulder. A mass of pellets pulverized a red circle a foot wide in Salamander's chest, impact throwing his body back. He stumbled and toppled over the edge of the platform and onto the tracks. If the gun blast didn't kill him, the electrified tracks would.

Orlando set the rifle on the ground and rushed to Stewart, bending down beside him and pressing both hands firmly on the gash in his chest spilling blood. It had turned his shirt red and created a small pool on the concrete. He looked frantically down at his lover, tears burning his eyes, crimson oozing through his fingers, and strained to see a pulse. Stewart was so still, deathly pale, his eyelids half closed. Orlando quelled a gut-wrenching hysteria bubbling up inside him and forced serenity in his voice. "Stewart, I'm here," he said hoarsely. "It's going to be okay. Just hold on. You're going to be all right." Then he saw Stewart's chest rise slightly, and he felt hope. Stewart hadn't bled enough to cause serious problems, and Orlando's pressure was slowing the flow outside the body, but cold fear racked the detective that he might be bleeding internally. If only the ambulance would arrive in time.

A phalanx of beat cops stormed into the subway entrance, trotting down the platform, till they came a few feet from where Stewart lay, and slowed to a stop. A few looked over the edge of the platform at the bloodied body on the tracks. One officer spoke into a walkie-talkie that barked static noise, ordering more ambulances and reinforcements to evacuate the train.

Then the cry of sirens echoed overhead, announcing the arrival of ambulances, and tears of relief rolled down Orlando's cheeks.

CHAPTER 20

The bearded internist, a short man with thick glasses and thinning hair, stood next to Orlando in the hospital corridor, explaining Stewart's status. He spoke reassuringly, but couldn't seem to make eye contact, planting his sights instead on Orlando's bandaged hands. It probably took a lot out of the guy to see the pain in family members' eyes. Orlando knew the feeling.

"He was lucky. It's awfully hard to kill someone from a stab wound," the doctor was saying.

Orlando knew that from his police work, but it hadn't made him feel any better in the terrible moments before the arrival of the ambulance.

"The knife hit him between the ribs and punctured the left lung," the doctor continued. "His shallow breathing was caused by the collapse of the lung. We've put in a chest tube to suck out the air pocket between the lung and the ribs, and he should be out of the hospital in a couple of days."

"Can I see him now?"

"Sure." He moved in a little closer to Orlando and said, "But watch out for Nurse Sloan, who's in there with him now. I strongly advise you not to wrangle with that woman." Only a trace of irony shaded his voice.

Orlando knew whom he meant: a big, blustery woman with a sharp wit, often in the AIDS ward when Orlando and Stewart visited friends. She had rapidly become a legend in the hospital. He stepped into the room and found Stewart lying in bed, wearing a hospital nightgown, an oxygen tube coming out of his nose. Nurse Sloan was tucking in the covers around him.

"Hey, babe," Orlando said, bringing a chair up to the bedside. "How's my hero?" He took Stewart's hand in his. It felt warm and weak.

His voice came out little. "Somebody has to save your neck now and then, the way you throw yourself in harm's way."

"You can be my partner any time. But in the future, I'll try providing a fully loaded gun for a change."

Stewart pinched his hand. "Yeah," he whispered slyly. "In twelve years of marriage, that's the first time I can think of that you haven't had a loaded gun."

Nurse Sloan was over playing with the cord for the drapes. "Hold it," she said. "I learned a long time ago when you guys start attempting double entendres, it's either time for me to leave the room, or it's time for the patient to go home. You're not ready for home, so I better get out of here." She took out a thermometer. "But let me take your temperature first. Do you prefer it . . ." She threw up and hands and said, "Oh, hell, I'm doing it too," and fled to the door. She turned and warned, "Now, remember, he needs his rest. I don't want you staying too long, you hear?"

Orlando stayed until Stewart dozed off, still holding his hand.

Mrs. Burdict had compiled a list of Los Angeles tattoo parlors, and Orlando found the right one on the third call. He leaned back in his chair, phone receiver nestled between his shoulder and his ear, and explained who he was and what he wanted to know.

"Yeah," a deep voice said. "He used to work here, but we had to give him the sack. Salamander did beautiful work, but the guy was plumb fuckin' crazy. I mean, like, dangerous crazy, not funny crazy. To give you an idea, two days after we let him go, we have an arson fire in the shop, lost almost everything. We told the cops our suspicions, but Salamander'd blown town by then."

"How long did he work there?"

"Over five years, but he only went nuts toward the end. His girlfriend made him get the test, you know, HIV, the AIDS thing, and it comes back positive. Well, he loses it, I mean, a total basket case. He starts raging that his life is over, that he's some kind of pariah. He starts talking about how the faggots gave it to him, and he starts remembering all the times he stuck himself with needles while giving gay men tattoos. It was utter bullshit. This was a guy who had been a biker since the sixties and had probably shot up every drug known to man, woman, and beast. But no, it was the faggots that gave it to him." The voice sighed. "We just couldn't keep him. He had a following, did some big names, but, like, we're right on Sunset in West Hollywood, you know? First he starts refusing service to anyone he thinks is gay, then he starts getting belligerent, you know, kind of scary-like. We had to tell him to shove off 'cause it was hurting business. He end up causing trouble over your way?"

"You could say that," Orlando answered wearily.

The detective spoke to Phillip Michaels, and they pieced the psychological puzzle together. It all made sense, but only in a sick and distorted way, as if looking at logic in a funhouse mirror. Salamander was killing the people he held responsible for what he considered his own death sentence, and he chose the means of death for his victims he believed led to his own health status. The needles symbolized Salamander taking control of the event and getting revenge on the group he blamed.

Tisha came by his office and stood tentatively in the doorway. She was wearing a leather biker's jacket and pink leotards. Her eyes and cheeks were red from crying. Orlando ushered her in and gave her his chair. He leaned on the desk and waited for her to speak.

She wiped her nose on the back of her hand and said glumly, "I guess I really screwed things up this time, didn't I?"

"None of this is your fault." He set his hand on her shoulder.

She looked up at him pleadingly. "I'm the one who told Peter we should expand, that there was room for a tattoo parlor in the back. He'd be alive today if I hadn't . . ."

"There's been enough suffering already. Stop kicking yourself. You couldn't have known."

She unzipped one of her jacket pockets, pulled out a small metal box, and placed it on his desk. "You were right. I found this in Salamander's locker in the little dressing room."

"Thanks for bringing it." Orlando remembered the room where Salamander had thrown the detective's jacket the day he got his tattoo. Orlando lifted the cap off the box and peered at the soft wax inside. When clients wanted tattoos on the lower part of their body, Salamander would direct them to take off their jeans in the dressing room. In the middle of the tattooing procedure, he would excuse himself and go into the little room, ostensibly to get some needed supply from his locker. While out of view, he'd take a wax impression of the potential victim's house key, and copy the client's address from identification cards in his wallet.

That was how he got into the victims' homes. Stoker and Carter had both gone home alone; Orlando's pickup theory was all wrong. Salamander went to the bar to spot the men he'd tattooed and whose homes he had keys for. When he saw them leave alone, he'd drive to their apartment and arrive before them because his victims took the subway home. He'd wait inside, pounce when they entered, and knock them out with the drugs he had waiting.

Red Demon, not No Exit, had been the real

connection between the murderer and the victims all along.

Tisha's eyes welled up. "But why Peter?"

"Before you and Salamander left Red Demon Friday afternoon, Peter had said he'd hand over his receipts to me by Monday. Only after you two had walked out the door did he agree to let me have them at No Exit that night. Salamander thought if he killed Peter Friday night, he could steal the receipts before I got a chance to look at them. He was afraid I would learn that all the victims had gone to the tattoo parlor, and I would begin to suspect him. Remember, I had thought No Exit was the only connection between the killer and his victims." Orlando handed her a Kleenex. "I'm sorry, Peter just got in his way."

The garage had been a carriage house in earlier days. Two wooden doors, each hardly wide enough for an American luxury car, faced a cobblestone alley that ran along the east end of the St. Agatha grounds. The quaint pitched shingle roof studded with dormers, and the garage's brick face, coarse and crumbly from merciless weather, seemed to clash with the ponderous stone of the church and rectory.

One of the doors was open, and Orlando stepped inside. Two older-model cars, a Ford and an Oldsmobile, fitted snugly in the space, but there was room for junk along the walls: old tires, empty wooden crates, brooms. A coiled hose hung on the wall of exposed two-by-fours above them. The windows were heavy with dust and spun with cobwebs.

Orlando wasn't sure which car he was looking for. He decided to try the Ford first. It wasn't dirty, but of all its tinted windows, only the glass of the driver's side shined. He reached into his jacket, taking out a ring of keys, and heard the search warrant rattle in his pocket. Putting his briefcase aside, he discovered the key that fit the car lock and pulled the door open. Squatting, Orlando slid his fingers across the vinyl seat. In the feeble light he could spot no blood stains. That didn't surprise him. It would have been scrubbed away. He went to his briefcase and got an aerosol can labeled Luminal. He shook it vigorously, then sprayed all over the seat.

In a moment a dull stain appeared on the blue fabric, and Orlando knew his suppositions had been right. The pieces were finally fitting together. He had found the scene of the murder.

CHAPTER 21

The front door had been left ajar. If Trevor wasn't gone already, he was preparing to leave in a hurry. He'd probably burst in the door and in his haste hadn't even bothered to shut it. The house was quiet; Mr. and Mrs. Barnes would be working at the D.A.'s office at this hour, and the girls were, who knows, probably at a day-care center or with family. Veska barked cheerfully from deep in the house. Orlando made his way through the living room and past the avocado kitchen appliances to the hall leading to bedrooms.

Trevor was so busy frantically stuffing clothes into a small backpack, he didn't notice Orlando standing in the bedroom doorway. Veska sat attentively on the rug, his leash attached to the choker chain, tail wagging but calmer than on Orlando's last visit. Obviously Trevor was taking the dog with him. The boy's bank book and a thick roll of bills lay on the rumpled bedspread. So did a small pistol.

"Leaving town?"

Trevor looked up and froze, his eyes fearful. Then the sulky veil descended and his body relaxed. "Wouldn't you? There's a fucking maniac trying to kill me."

"That's old news. He's dead. Blown away, then fried on the subway tracks. You must have known that. You also must have seen him at the church in the last few weeks, or he wouldn't have been after you."

Nodding, Trevor answered, "Yeah, but I never could have identified him. I bumped right into him as he was walking out of the church one day. I spilled a load of dirt out of the wheelbarrow because of him. But he was just one of a zillion people around there. I didn't realize till he showed up this morning that he was the guy."

"You didn't have to remember him. The fact that you saw him at all and might have identified him made you a threat." Orlando leaned on the door frame and read his watch. "It couldn't have taken this long to evacuate passengers from the train. Where have you been?"

Shrugging, Trevor stuffed the bills in his pocket. "Just walking around in a daze. I was afraid to come home. I thought he might be waiting here for me."

"You knew Salamander was dead. You thought I might be waiting here for you. I see you had time to clear out your bank account."

"I'll need money where I'm going."

"That may be true. But the youth correctional facility won't allow you to bring a dog or carry a gun." He pointed to the pistol. "You'd better plan on leaving that behind."

Trevor analyzed Orlando's face. The detective had seen that expression many times in his twenty years in police work: a suspect trying to figure how much a cop knows and how much he can get away with. "That's Zack's. For his guard job. He must of forgot it this morning. I figure I need protection."

"That's a .22. He doesn't carry a cheap Saturday night special at the district attorney's office. That's a street gun and you know it." Orlando went over to the bed and snatched up the pistol, slipping it in his pocket. "Just so you won't be tempted."

Trevor stared, and for a moment Orlando thought he was going to cry, but then the young man's face hardened. "What are you going to do with me?"

"I'm going to read you your rights, then I'm going to bring you down to headquarters and book you for the murder of Father Morant."

Trevor collapsed in an upholstered chair by the bed, shoulders slumped. "I couldn't help it," he said finally, looking up. "It just happened."

"Murder doesn't just happen."

Trevor was silent for a long moment; he petted the dog in vigorous strokes, concentrating his focus on Veska's fur, as if it was the most important thing in the world. He chuckled caustically. "I guess I know now why he was always so friendly, always so concerned. Putting his arm over my shoulder and counseling me to be good. Acting like a dad to me 'cause he knew how much I hate Zack."

"Maybe he was concerned about you. Maybe he knew how difficult it is to be a gay teen."

"I'm not a faggot," Trevor snapped. He stared despairingly at the carpet.

"I saw the paper, Trevor, I know you've been hustling."

"That's for money. I don't suck dick, I only let these faggots suck me off."

Orlando had heard this line countless times in his work. I'm not one of *them,* I just do it for the cash. A way of getting sex, yet still setting oneself apart. In a way he felt sorry for the boy: What kind of positive reinforcement had he ever gotten for his sexuality? Other than his stepfather's diatribes, Trevor had the admonitions of the Catholic Church, and when he stayed with Zachary Barnes's mother, no doubt he heard the censure of the fundamentalist Baptists. Self-hatred must be prodding the boy from all sides. There weren't many safe havens for a gay kid in a society that gets queasy at the mention of youth sexuality, period.

Orlando came over and sat on the bed by Trevor's chair. Veska, tongue hanging, demanded to be petted. As he stroked the dog, the detective said, "Go ahead. You were on the street with the rest of the boys. It was Thursday night. What happened?"

Trevor's mouth puckered. "This car rolls up. It looks kind of familiar, but I don't think, you know? The other guys are a little down the street, so I know it's me he's interested in. The windows were tinted, so I couldn't really see in, and the guy, he doesn't open the window or anything. So I get in the passenger side to talk to him, and it's Father Morant." The look of puzzlement on his face must have been the same in the car that Thursday night.

"What did he say?"

Trevor went back to petting the dog. "He told me it was dangerous to be out at night, that he would bring me home. At first I thought my parents must have told him how I stayed out late nights and the father must have followed me. But then I thought, how could he? I took the subway and here he was in this car. Then I saw something and I remembered what the guys had said." He looked up at Orlando.

"What did you see, Trevor?"

"He had taken his collar off," he said softly. "The guys told me about faggot priests, how they came out to pick up boys. Sometimes they'd be dressed like normal people; other times they'd be so horny, they'd come by on the spur of the moment and just hide their collars when they picked you up." Trevor swallowed hard and his eyes filled with tears.

Orlando could see how good this boy was going to look to a jury, especially after he'd been all cleaned up by a defense attorney. "What did he do?"

"He just started driving, then he turned to me and said maybe we should stop somewhere and have a little talk. There was booze on his breath. I thought maybe I could talk him into not telling my mom. I told him I would never do it again, that I would change." Trevor's face went strange as he continued to remember. "He stopped the car on this side street. There were all these deserted warehouses and nobody around. I started to get scared."

Orlando could see why the possibility of sex

with Morant was so threatening to the boy, despite his experience as a hustler. Morant was someone he knew, someone he would see every day, a constant reminder of what he really was.

"I told him I got to get home, and reached for the door handle, but he pushes this button and all the doors in the car lock. He says to me it's not safe out there, that he'll bring me home in a sec, but first we got to talk. He says he knows I'm gay and that there are places I can go to meet kids my own age, that I shouldn't be on the street." Trevor was talking faster now, his voice vehement. "I told him I'm not no fucking fag, but he keeps saying, 'I know you're gay, I understand, I know you're gay.' " He sat up straight in the chair. "And then he reaches over and starts putting his hands all over me, saying, 'My poor boy, my poor boy.' I told him to get the fuck away from me, don't touch me, you fucking fag, but he keeps trying to touch me, to put his arms all around me. And I remembered why he'd taken his collar off, and why he'd been cruising the streets, and how he'd always been so nice and friendly at the church, putting his arm around me."

Orlando's gut knotted, and he felt a sick ache inside. "And then you took out your gun," Orlando said.

"I had to. There's this fucking faggot on top of me, touching me all over, and I couldn't stand it."

"What happened?"

"I just pulled the trigger. It went through the shoulder of Father Morant's jacket and smashed the window. Then he gets this crazy scared look on his face and grabs for the gun, trying to wrestle me for it like a madman." Tears streamed down his face. "I didn't mean to do it. He made me." Trevor looked away from Orlando, staring blindly at the carpet. "Then I got the fuck out of there," he added dully.

Orlando had heard this story before, with variations, whenever a gay man was murdered. Sometimes the story appeared only after the accused had talked with a clever lawyer. The story was simple and its root was always the same: The faggot came on to me and I had to kill him. Juries liked the story so much, they freed people who told it all the time. He didn't know how much of Trevor's story to believe, what was truth and what was a calculated appeal for sympathy. The killing he wasn't sure about. But what happened after left no room for debate.

"You didn't run, Trevor. You pushed Morant over to the passenger side of the car, and you drove with his bloody corpse back to the church, thinking all the while who you could pin this crime on. Then you remembered. You parked the car, dragged the body into the church, and went to get the baseball bat. You worked there, you probably had keys for everything, or knew where they were. You certainly knew where the garden gloves were so you wouldn't leave any prints on the bat. You've admitted seeing Herb Chiligny threaten Morant; he was the perfect fall guy to take the rap. I guess I should have figured it all along. Other than the Queer Nationals and the boys on the baseball team, you were the only one there to see their altercation. You cold-bloodedly bashed Morant on the head with the bat. It's the one thing no jury will be able to forgive you for, that you would frame an innocent man to hide the truth."

Trevor blinked incredulously. His tone became sharp. "No, man, that's not how it happened. I ran off. I was as surprised as anybody when his body turned up in the church. I didn't do nothing like that." He stood, arms crossed at his chest, looking wildly around the room, as if for a means of escape. "You can't pin none of that shit on me 'cause I didn't do it. I shot him, yeah, but that was in self-defense, the pervert was trying to touch me. I didn't do nothin' else."

Orlando fished handcuffs from his pocket and mechanically began telling Trevor his rights. He had said the words so many times before they sounded like a litany. But Orlando didn't feel quite right. The pieces didn't all fit together yet. He believed the boy, at least about dumping the body in the church.

The story was still only half told.

CHAPTER 22

He was drunk this time, no question. Weepy drunk. Even a tolerance to liquor built up over a lifetime couldn't hide this binge. An empty wine bottle in the waste basket and another half full on the bureau told the story. He staggered to the bed, his sunken face wet with tears, setting clothes in large cardboard boxes. The tank swinging from his hip didn't help keep his balance. He stopped and looked up, hands propped on the box corners for support, when Orlando stepped into the doorway. For a moment the swollen red eyes held no recognition.

"Oh," Shea slurred, his eyebrows raised quizzically, "it's you." That settled, he stumbled back to the bureau and found a stack of underwear in a drawer. "You seem to show up too late for everything. You always come after people are already dead or already beaten up." He gave an alcoholic grin. "And now you're too late to help me pack Father Morant's things. I'm almost done." He laid the underwear in a box and flipped the lids closed. "Too late."

"Not too late to figure out the truth."

Shea wasn't listening. "Have you seen the tape?"

"It's in front of you, on the bedspread."

"Oh," he said vaguely, picking up a roll of wide yellow tape. "It's all going to the Guatemalan refugees. Father Morant would have wanted it that way. They need clothes desperately." He pronounced the word "despritly."

Orlando came into the room and took the priest's elbow. "We'd better get you in the shower to wake you up. You'll want to wash the stench of booze off you before I take you down to headquarters, anyway."

"Yes," Shea said with resignation, wiping the tears from his face. "Headquarters."

Orlando steered him down the hall and into the bathroom, where he cranked on the cold water. Margarita appeared in the doorway, and she silently assisted Shea in stripping down; evidently, this wasn't the first time she had dealt with the pastor's alcoholism. Orlando asked him if he could do without the oxygen for a while, and when Shea nodded, helped him into the shower, closed the frosted glass door, and leaned against it. The priest cried out.

"Stay in there," Orlando ordered, "until you can think coherently again."

It was a long while before Shea knocked on the glass door and asked to be let out.

"The boy has already confessed," Orlando said. "But he doesn't know the whole story. You do."

Shea leaned back in the upholstered chair in Morant's bedroom, holding Edgar in his lap. The cat had calmed down from Thursday night and laid purring contentedly. Although Shea periodically stroked the cat, he didn't seem to have the energy anymore to sit up. The oxygen tank sat on the armrest. His clothes were clean, black, and starched; he looked very proper, like a corpse ready to be laid out. Margarita had gone to attend a baby crying in the recesses of the rectory. "Yes," he said weakly, "the whole story. I suppose it's time to tell the truth."

"Thursday night would have been a better time, but I'm listening." Orlando lounged against the bureau. The Tennyson still lay open, face-down, next to a Bible.

Shea sucked in a feeble breath, as if the tank could no longer offer him sustenance, then began. "Father Morant was a tormented man, Detective Orlando. He needed constant guidance to choose the proper path. Before he came to St. Agatha, he involved himself in all the things that are wrong with the Church. Supporting abortion, accepting sexuality in teenagers as if it's a given, homosexuality. They say homosexuality is not a sickness anymore, the psychiatrists. Well, maybe it isn't a mental one, I don't know. But it is an intrinsic moral evil, and you could see it destroying him. Eating away at his insides. Filling him with doubt about God and the scriptures. It was like a demon inside him, surfacing periodically, never to be defeated." He shook his head with what strength he had. "It's a compulsion, nothing but a vile compulsion."

"If I need a sermon I'll attend mass next Sunday. Get to Thursday night. I already know about Father Morant's relationship with Rick

Dunham and how you talked him into coming back."

Shea winced. "That relationship was his destruction. He couldn't get it out of his head in all those years. It was Rick Dunham who betrayed him, informed you about the killer, then called that group Queer Nation." He snorted in disgust. "When I think of that awful person with the stringy beard and high heels, the one who spoke blasphemy during the disruption of Sunday mass, pure, unadulterated blasphemy, it just makes me sick."

Orlando could believe Anthony spoke blasphemy, no doubt fluently. He waited for the pastor to continue.

"Father Morant was despondent Thursday evening. He came to me and I knew he'd been crying, and I could smell the liquor on his breath. He was brokenhearted Dunham had betrayed him in such a cruel way. I told him he must forget that man, forget all about it and move on with his life. He sat across from me in the library, staring at me, and the strangest expression came across his face. He suddenly blurted out that my advice had ruined the one love he ever had, and now it was too late for him. He raged against me and the Church, blaming me for all the mistakes of his life." He managed a grim smile. "It was *my* fault that that woman had died at the hands of her husband, because I had counseled him to deny Sister Serra's house for battered housewives any more support. In a torrent of invective he admitted picking up male prostitutes in frustration because the Church denied him a healthy monogamous relationship. I begged him to calm down, to pray with me for guidance. He told me he was through with praying, and stormed out of the room."

"Then you heard him go out the front door."

Shea nodded. "I assumed he was going back to that man, to forgive him for what he had done, and I had to stop him. I got the keys to the other car and followed him. But he didn't go to Rick Dunham's house." The pastor swallowed distastefully. "Instead, he went to another part of town, an area where degenerates find prostitutes. When he picked up Trevor, I didn't know what to think. I was shocked to see the boy in that environment, and for a moment I thought Father Morant might be bringing him home. When he turned off onto a deserted street, I knew I was wrong. I stopped my car down the street, not knowing what to do. I had to stop him from hurting the boy." Shea frowned. "A moment later I heard two shots, and I knew the boy had protected himself."

"And after the boy ran off, you got into Morant's car and drove him home, your mind clicking all the while. You saw Herb Chiligny threaten Morant with that baseball bat. The window of your library looks right out onto the ball field. You could avoid the scandal and quiet a vociferous critic of the Church all in one blow."

"I did it to protect the boy. He's just a child."

"He hasn't been a child for a long time. Thanks to the way people like you have been twisting his mind. You did it to protect the Church," Orlando charged. "But you couldn't have done it alone."

Shea stared at him.

"You needed help to drag the body from the garage to the church. You don't have that kind of strength. You enlisted the aid of Margarita, someone who owed her life to the Church, to help you frame Herb Chiligny."

Shea shook his head, agitated. "No, she had nothing to do with this. I acted alone. I'll confess to whatever you want, but it was me alone."

"Bullshit. She dragged the body and she swung the bat."

"I did it all."

Orlando picked up the Bible from the bureau and slapped it on an armrest. Edgar jumped up and scurried under the bed. "Swear to it." Orlando plopped down on the edge of the bed.

Shea watched him evenly. He placed his right hand on the Bible. "It was I who swung the bat. Margarita wasn't even there." He looked down.

"Then you told her to go back to the rectory after she brought the body into the church. She had to be involved. Your car was still back in Manhattan where you had left it. Margarita drove you back there in Morant's car to pick it up."

"I took the subway."

"In your condition? Not likely."

Shea leaned forward, and his hand clutched Orlando's sleeve. "I want you to understand," he said, "Margarita is not a citizen of this country, she is a refugee with a baby granddaughter to

take care of. You know what could happen to her
if she is implicated in this? She could be de-
ported, and face death, or go to jail." His eyes
moistened. "She has a baby to take care of, for
God's sake, let's keep her out of it. She knows
nothing, she only moved the body for me, and I
swore her to secrecy."

Orlando pondered for a minute. He thought
about those haunted eyes, and the kind of options Margarita had. And he thought about the
baby. He said, "Okay. You dragged the body
yourself and you took the subway to pick up your
car."

Shea nodded in relief. "Yes, that is what happened. I'll sign anything you want."

"The window repairman, who came on Friday. He was here to fix the window in Morant's
car that had been shattered by a bullet. That's
why he was complaining he usually didn't
make house calls. He does car windows. The
windows in your garage are dirty with cobwebs. You forgot one thing, though, you should
have checked Morant's pockets. He had a condom in one."

Shea sat up straight. "Who found it?"

"Don't worry about it. Briggs did, and hid it
in his office desk. Probably because he didn't
want facts complicating his case against Herb
Chiligny. You had help from all sides keeping
Morant's secret."

"The Church is a fragile institution, Detective
Orlando."

Where had he heard that before? It was at his
visit with Herb Chiligny, when the journalist

had told him the story of Anthony's childhood. His parents had been told by their pastor, *the Church is a fragile institution,* and to forget about the molestation. A knot tightened in Orlando's stomach as he recalled Shea's statement that Anthony seemed to be attacking him personally at the Sunday mass demonstration. No wonder Anthony festered with such rage toward the pastor. "It was you," he said softly.

Shea's eyes narrowed. "I don't know what you mean."

"Roll back, say, about thirty years. A priest in your parish molests a boy. You whisk him off to another country. You go to the boy's parents, quiet them down, tell them to gut their conscience for the good of the Church."

Shea swallowed hard. "I don't know what you're talking about, really, Detective Orlando."

"Yeah, you do, it can't happen so often that you could have forgotten. You're not that dead inside. That boy was Anthony Carrara, the guy in heels who gave you such a hard time at mass last Sunday. He hasn't spoken to his parents in two decades." Orlando's lip twisted in contempt. "You once asked me what made people that way. So bitter against the Church." He got up and stepped across the room, leaning against the bureau again. He didn't want to be close to Shea right at this moment. "Now you know. You'd better get up, I'm taking you in."

Shea struggled to his feet, and Orlando glanced down on the bureau top. He picked up the book of Tennyson, and reread aloud the words Morant had underlined. "There lives more faith in honest doubt, Believe me, than in half the creeds."

"I read that," Shea said wearily, tying the oxygen tank to his belt. "I wonder why he underlined it. What did he mean?"

Orlando shrugged and closed the volume. "I don't know, it's something for you to think about." He looked down at the book glumly. "Why don't you take it along? You'll need something to keep you busy in jail." He handed the book to Shea. "Who knows, maybe you could say it was Father Morant's legacy."

Orlando wasn't looking forward to this. He could see the family gathered around the living room as the front door swung open. Most were dressed in mourning, swathed in black against the cream patterned Early American couches and chairs. Some grandchildren sat on the floor at their parents' feet. Untouched food, laid out on the dining table, meant visiting neighbors had come by to show their respects and share grief. In a rocker placed in the far corner, away from the rest of the family, a frail old man in loose clothes sat miserably hunched, as if the world could no longer offer him comfort. A younger version of Briggs stood in the doorway staring at Orlando. He was about thirty, had short dark wavy hair, and a similar budding paunch that promised to grow with the years. But the fleshy lips of his father were toned down from the contribution of his mother's harsh, narrow mouth.

"If you're a reporter, we're not interested," he said warningly.

"It's him," a woman of about fifty said, severe lines etching her lusterless lips. She wore black and her graying hair looked hard from spray. She set knitting needles aside and rose from a couch when she saw the detective. Orlando recognized Mrs. Briggs from the handful of times he'd seen her over the years and from the picture in Briggs's office. Age and mourning had only made her rigid countenance even more unyielding. A finger pointed unsteadily. "You're the one who let my husband die."

"I did what I could to save him, Mrs. Briggs."

The young man's face contorted and he gripped the oak door. "You expect us to believe that? After you did everything you could to destroy his career and hurt our family?" He thrust his chest boldly forward. "We're going to sue. We're not going to rest until the truth is out and you're behind bars for letting my father die."

Orlando ignored him and spoke directly to Mrs. Briggs. "I've got to talk to you, alone."

She stood in the center of the room on a braided oval carpet, fingers laced and tight at her breast. "Anything you have to say to me can be said in front of my family. They are the ones who will never see their father—and their grandfather—again."

Orlando hesitated, glancing at the kids. They watched him curiously, mouths agape. Finally he said, "I've got to know who your husband was having meetings with. Tell me the names of the other cops." His request was coded enough that it wouldn't mean anything to the children.

"I don't have the faintest idea what you're talking about," she said sharply, indicating to her son to close the door. "I think you'd better go."

As the door began to shut in his face, Orlando set his foot firmly into the living room and glared at the young man. "Not so fast." He looked to the gaunt black figure in the middle of the room. "They were neo-Nazis, Mrs. Briggs. Do you want to help people like that get away with hurting people? If I can keep your husband's name out of it, I will. But I've got to know the names of the others."

The old man in the rocking chair stood shakily and went down a hallway, unnoticed by the rest of the family. But he cocked his head strangely at Orlando as he went.

Mrs. Briggs gave a mirthless laugh. "That's funny, you expecting help from me. If you spread any lies about my husband's memory, Detective Orlando, I'll make trouble for you. A policeman's widow has a lot of respect from the men in the department. Now get out."

Orlando shrugged. "I tried to appeal to your decency, Mrs. Briggs. I can see now I judged you wrong. You're as bad as he was." He lowered his head. "My sympathies to you and your family." As he turned around and descended the stairs, the door slammed behind him. Crossing the small cement yard, orange-hued in the late afternoon sun, he remembered his scuffle with Briggs just days before. The scab on his nose felt tight. He had hated and feared his nemesis for many years, but he felt nothing now. No joy, no happiness. Not even relief. Things were not going to be so tough around the station house now that Briggs was gone. He had been the ringleader of all the harassment, the lightning rod that had attracted hatred toward Orlando. But all Orlando felt now was a vague sense of sadness, not at Briggs's death, but at the meaninglessness of all the suffering he'd experienced over the last few years and the pain it had brought to his family. It was over, but he felt too battered and weary to enjoy it.

Heading down the block to his car, Orlando heard the click of a gate behind him and the strained patter of hurried feet. He turned to find the old man approaching. Only it wasn't an old man. It was a terribly sick young man. He had the walk of the very elderly, though: stiff, stooped, his head not so much resting on top of his shoulders as bobbing parallel to them. His face had lost its musculature, and the pallid skin sagged liked melted wax. Up close, Orlando recognized the thinning hair resulting from chemotherapy treatment. Clothes hung loose because of a rapid loss of weight. The feebleness of the old in someone so young was heart-wrenching. In this young man's face he saw the deaths of so many other young men. He didn't resemble the members of the Briggs family, and Orlando remembered the food on the dining table. Perhaps a visiting neighbor.

"Wait," the man called, his voice hardly more than a whisper. "I can help you." He was breathing hard. He looked back quickly to the house, then began. "They met in the backyard. I overheard them once on one of my rare visits. It was terrible, the things they said. It was all hate. Against blacks, Latinos, Jews, and especially gays. Especially you. They talked about you a lot. How they were going to screw up your career, embarrass you to the press, make you seem inept by confusing you. They wanted that serial killer to murder as many gay men as possible. Messing up your case not only made you look bad, it allowed that maniac to keep on killing."

Orlando recalled Briggs's games with needles, designed to throw him off the track and waste time on false leads. "How many were there?"

"Just a handful. But they were trying to recruit, very quietly. They said there were already a number of them with the Los Angeles Sheriff's Department, and in other places around the country."

Orlando leaned closer. "You have any idea of their names?"

The man shook his head. "No, but I went for a little stroll when they came." He attempted a grin, but it came out too faint. "I wrote down the license plates of their cars." He reached around and a frail hand pulled a scrap of paper from a wallet.

Taking the paper, Orlando thanked him. "You may have saved some lives. I may need you to testify to all this. Will you do it?"

He nodded. "Whatever you want. My phone number's there. I'd better get back or they'll notice I'm missing."

The man languidly turned to go, and Orlando touched his sleeve. "Just a sec. Are you a neighbor? How are you connected to the Briggs family? How did you know Briggs?"

The young man looked at him for a long moment with old man's eyes. "I'm his son," he said.

CHAPTER 23

Word had spread throughout the day and by evening, friends were calling and dropping by the hospital. Marie Orlando sat in the waiting room, worrying her rosary beads. Sensing a guilty look on her wrinkled face, and the fierceness with which she clutched the beads and silently mouthed Hail Marys, Orlando sat on the armrest of her chair and put his arm around her.

"It's going to be okay, Ma."

When he was a child, she had taught him there was a saint for everything, telling him which one to pray to if he'd lost a mitten, who to ask for help on tough homework. All questions had pat answers, and that had been comforting. Only when the neat order of their lives was broken did the answers seem inadequate. The Lord's mysterious ways of working didn't seem a satisfactory response to his grandfather's heart attack, taking a good man from his wife and family. And searching for answers, Orlando had looked to himself. What bad thoughts on his part had brought about this loss? What sins of his, too foul to mention at the confessional, had caused his grandfather's death? Only adulthood and skepticism had weaned him from such self-accusation. He knew what his mother was thinking now.

"Ma, it wasn't your fault because you didn't put money in the plate yesterday. Trust me. Now, why don't you go home and I'll call you in the morning and let you know how he's doing?"

She still looked doubtful when he coaxed her to put away the beads, make one last short visit with Stewart, and head on home.

Ronnie and Sally spent an hour with him in the waiting room. He appreciated their concern, and Stewart had lit up during their brief visit. They reminded Orlando that if Stewart was well enough, they all had a dinner date Saturday night.

Bill Shaw had dropped by earlier, saying Chief Sorensen had agreed to meet with him the next morning to discuss the information Orlando had received from Briggs's son. The license plates had been traced, and they now had a list of names. Several were rookies, and the others had been on the force for as long as thirty years. Orlando didn't know any of them personally. Whether Sorensen did anything about it or not, the detective decided to give the story to Herb Chiligny. The public should know.

Chiligny had come by, too, thanking him for all he'd done. Charges against him in the murder of Father Morant had been dropped that afternoon. As they spoke, Orlando noticed to his surprise that Anthony was down the corridor, lingering by the elevators.

"Herb," Orlando began, "don't tell me . . ."

Chiligny shrugged and grinned. "Like you said, hearing the guy out over a cup of coffee certainly can't hurt."

It was late. Their friends had all gone home, and Stewart was sleeping peacefully. His breathing was shallow, but the color had come back to his face and the doctor had said he might be home by Thursday. The doctor had winked, adding wryly that his most worrisome problem was a strange delusion, shared by numerous patients, of being poisoned by the hospital food. Orlando turned off the lamp above the bed, and the only light in the room spilled onto the linoleum floor from outside the open door. He settled in the chair and put his hand in Stewart's, whose moist fingers tightened around his.

Nurse Sloan came in an hour later to check on things, and when she saw that Orlando was still there, she set her hands on her hips. "Look," she whispered. "Do you think we're not going to take good care of your hubby? Other than the toxic food, we're treating Stewart right. Go home and get some rest, honey, you hear? You keep it up and you're going to have to check in here yourself."

"I will," he promised. "In a little while."

She looked at him skeptically, crossing her arms and shaking her head, and left the room mumbling something about gay men. Orlando knew he couldn't pull the wool over her eyes; she'd figured out his plan.

He would be sitting up with Stewart through the night, holding his hand, and he would be there to sneak him breakfast from Feldstein's in the morning.